A SUDDEN DEA'

A SUDDEN DEATH

By Diana J Febry

COVER DESIGN DIANA J FEBRY
PROOFREAD - HTTPS://TWITTER.COM/PROOFERSJ

CHAPTER ONE

Ian Marsh bolted for home as his mother scooped up his sister and sped after him. He pumped his arms and gulped in air, running faster and faster as he blanked her frantic calls. He hated her, him and everyone else. His eyes stung, and his heart pounded as he skidded around the corner onto their road and speeded up. At the front door, he bent double, his hands on his knees, catching his breath. He felt sick. Sick of all of them and their lies. Breathing heavily, his mother reached over him to unlock the door. He shot through in front of her without looking back, raced up the stairs and slammed his bedroom door shut.

He scrunched the painting he had spent so much time perfecting into a ball and shoved it under the bed before flinging himself face down onto the covers. He heard the hum of the television in the living room and his mother's steps on the stairs.

"Ian, I'm so sorry."

"I hate you."

"Can I come in?"

Ian sat up on the bed and wiped his hot tears with his sleeve as the door was pushed open. He closed his eyes tight, wishing it would all go away as his mother wrapped herself around him. She smelled of flowers, and was soft and yielding as he curled his hands into fists and held himself rigid, erecting barriers no one could breach. He wouldn't let himself be hurt again.

His mother's hands, so soft and gentle, carefully wiped away his tears. "I'm so sorry. I should have known he would let you down."

"I hate him. I hate him."

"I'll never let him harm you again," his mother soothed. "If he contacts us again, I'll send him away. I'll call the police if he won't go."

There was a sliver of hope in Ian's voice as he asked, "Would he be arrested and go to jail forever? And only have cold toast and porridge to eat and no nice things?"

"Maybe. Hey, how about we raid the rainy-day fund and go out for pizza?"

Ian nodded his head.

His mother released her hold, leaving him instantly chilled. "There's my big boy. Go and wash your face while I get your sister ready."

Hugh Dolan's afternoon nap was disturbed by the doorbell. He sat up on the sofa, rubbed his face and quickly pulled up a monthly sales page on his laptop screen. He liked his neighbours to think that his wealth was the product of his creative mind, not the money he inherited from his parents. Whoever it was at this time of day, they probably wouldn't come in, but it was best to be prepared just in case. Appearances were everything. The brilliant, mysterious recluse working on his new masterpiece was much more fascinating than the ageing dullard napping to fill his day. They probably wanted him to buy some raffle tickets for the church fund, or they would ask him if they could use his garden for a local event again. Swanning around as the host of the local drama group's play had given him a buzz last summer. As long as they didn't ask him to give a speech. He had nothing to say.

Trying to look bright-eyed and awake, he opened the front door. He didn't recognise the intense man on his doorstep, shifting his weight from side to side. Maybe he was a newcomer to the village, wanting to introduce himself. How quaint. He was about the same age as him, and he recognised the shirt he was wearing was from John Lewis, as he had one hanging in his wardrobe. Somebody with such good taste didn't pose a threat.

"Hello. Can I help you?"

"Hello, Hugh. Don't you recognise me?"

Hugh examined the man's face again. He was handsome and well-groomed, but he was older than he first thought, and his eyes were unnerving. Too close together, maybe. Or were they giving a fleeting insight into the man's madness? A warning he should heed. A sliver of fear ran along his spine, and he cursed himself for being too welcoming. Living in a small, affluent community had made him far too trusting. He started to close the door. "No, sorry, I think you must be mistaken."

"Alex. Alex Woodchester."

Hugh looked again at the man's strong jawbone and was instantly transported back to the night when his innocence was shattered. The one time in his life when he had felt part of a group. A gang. But that was when he didn't distort who he was, a time when he believed he could be himself without fear of rejection or ridicule. They had been a mismatched group of misfits, born out of geography and attending the same school rather than shared interests or personalities. But a group with all the layers of silent rules and commitments, just the same. The stifling pressure to act in unison.

After that night, he had avoided becoming closely entangled with anyone. The fitting in was too difficult, and the cost of belonging was too high. He swallowed his regrets, painted on a smile, and opened the door wider. "Alex! What a lovely surprise. It's been too long. Come in."

Hugh drank himself reckless on the shared bottle of malt whisky as he listened to Alex's intentions with horror. "I understand where you're coming from, Alex. We've all been there. I know I have. But these feelings will pass. You'll get through this, and in time, you'll think back and realise what a bad plan this is."

"But I feel I have to for my state of mind. I want to be at peace with myself."

"It's not just about you, Alex. Think about how it will affect all of us," Hugh reasoned, as a swirling pit of dread churned his stomach. He couldn't deal with being pushed out into the limelight. It would only last a few days, but for him, it would linger. People would point their finger at him, and his meagre sales of books would dry up. "We've already been damaged inside. Think about how much more hurt this will cause us."

"But the family."

"Won't thank you for dragging it all up again. You can't change the past, and everyone has moved on. We have careers and families to think about."

"So, you won't come with me?"

"Definitely not," Hugh replied, shocked to his core at the prospect. "And I beg you not to go ahead with this crazy stunt to make yourself feel better. Even if you receive some temporary relief, it will be short-lived. It won't help you in the long term."

"Sorry to have taken up so much of your time," Alex said, draining his glass. "I'm going to speak to the others."

Hugh followed him to the front door, trying not to beg. "I think they will feel the same as me. Will you promise to come back and talk to me again before you do anything?"

"If you wish."

"It's been great to see you again, but I wish it had been in different circumstances. Let's agree to keep in touch, yeah?" Hugh closed the door, feeling woozy. He didn't usually start drinking until later. He told himself not to worry. One of the others would make Alex see reason.

Chloe Trace put down her guitar and prepared to sing her last song. She shielded her eyes from the spotlight Dan always insisted on using. "Where's Tom Barker?" The birthday boy was pointed out, and she looked in the general direction of where he sat and started to sing Happy Birthday. She knew Dan was out there somewhere working the room, being perfectly charming and attentive to the diners, sharing a joke with the men and flirting with the women. Thank God this afternoon would be the last time she would have to push herself up against the van door to avoid his wandering hands on the way home. How many times could his hand accidentally slip from the gear stick to her knee? Four times in one short trip was his current record.

She thought it a strange coincidence that her first and final performances were singing for the elderly group who met every month in the Carpenters Arms. The pub wasn't somewhere she would choose for a night out, but the staff were welcoming and always gave her a free drink. The group of friends seemed an odd bunch, but they were friendly enough. She couldn't imagine what they had in common. Old work friends may be from a distant time when you had a job for life and zero-hours contracts had not been invented. Over the months, she had gotten to know some of them and liked performing for them, although she could do it on autopilot with her eyes closed. They were easy to please. And if they weren't happy with her performance, what would they do about it? Rush the stage on their Zimmer frames?

She caught sight of Dan at the back of the room, sharing a joke with one of the bar staff. Dan's personality was perfect for the little niche market he had carved out for himself. Who knew providing entertainment for the more mature audiences could be so lucrative? His tired chat-up lines and slightly cheeky but safe humour, which wouldn't be tolerated anywhere else, seemed to be lapped up by them. He prided himself on the range of entertainment he could provide. As well as singers, he had a few comedians and budding actors on his list, but as of today, he would be down one female singer.

Chloe occasionally performed in nursing homes, but usually, it was in large, private houses to celebrate birthdays or wedding anniversaries. It was easy work, and it annoyed her she was quitting because Dan was such a jerk. It paid well, and it left her plenty of free time. But someone else could put up with his lewd comments and unwanted advances in the van. She was done.

Learning the old songs from the 1950s to the early 1980s had been fun. She had never heard of some of the singers before, and she liked the simplicity and innocence of the songs.

One of the ladies who regularly attended these lunches always requested she sing at least one David Cassidy song. She had seen a photograph of him as a young man and understood why he had been so popular and particularly liked singing his songs. When she googled him and discovered he had been an alcoholic, she wondered if that was why she had felt so drawn to him.

She finished her song and walked over to congratulate the birthday boy, and he insisted she give him a peck on the cheek. Dan rushed over to encourage her to sit on his lap and give him a cuddle, but she politely declined and went to pack up her guitar and music stand. Dan constantly nagged her to mingle with the guests once she had finished. Sometimes, their faces came alive, and they grew younger before her eyes as they told daring tales of their past. Other times, they pushed a note or two into her hand as they raved about her performance and how they wished she could meet their sons. Chloe was no mathematician, but they seemed oblivious that their sons would be old enough to be her father. Once her precious guitar was safely put away, she had a change of heart. As it was her last day, she would make the effort to go mingling. Dan could pack up the backing machine and stupid spotlight himself. She hoped he wouldn't take too long about it, as she needed to get home in time to talk to her father again about making an appointment to see a doctor before she drove him to his AA meeting.

CHAPTER TWO

DI Fiona Williams stood at the kitchen counter drinking the cup of weak tea her mother had made while she read through her notes.

"You look very smart this morning, but you should sit at the table. Now, what would you like to eat?"

"Thanks, Mum, I'm giving evidence at a trial this morning," Fiona looked up from her notes to remind her mother. She flicked through a few pages, trying to focus on the facts rather than her mother noisily moving around the kitchen, opening and closing cupboard doors. "You don't need to get up so early just because I need to."

"I always did for your father. I made sure he had a good breakfast before leaving for work. What shall I make you?"

Checking the time, Fiona took another sip of tea and started to pack her notes away. "Sorry, I need to go, or I'll be late."

"You're going to get indigestion."

"See you tonight," Fiona said as she hurried out the door. It was sweet of her mother to get up early on her behalf, but she wished she wouldn't, if it stemmed from an outdated sense of duty rather than a genuine wish to see more of her. Her father's release from temporary respite care had been delayed again, and she had the sneaking suspicion he wouldn't ever be returning. Her mother wouldn't accept the situation easily, but that was a discussion for another day.

After giving evidence at the trial of Duncan Thomas and Angela Olive, Fiona didn't reach the station until early afternoon. The trial had taken an interesting turn when Duncan claimed he was a victim of domestic abuse. Recent bruising to his body had been noted by an officer early in the case but quickly dismissed as irrelevant. At the time, Duncan claimed he had been knocked over by one of his wife's horses, and nobody had questioned his explanation. He had given the same explanation to the hospital when they treated him. Now, he was saying his wife had frequently attacked him. His claim that he was too embarrassed to speak out about the abuse he received was understandable, and Fiona wished she had more time to follow the case.

She quickly updated DS Humphries, who was highly sceptical of Duncan's defence, before she walked to her desk to check for any new messages. As expected, several new files had been added to the growing pile on her desk. She pulled out the files on the most recent burglaries of older people in their area and moved them back to the top of the stack. "Have you had a chance to look at these two new ones? Were the occupants in?"

Humphries said, "One was in, one wasn't. The man who was in has confirmed the intruders wore balaclavas, but the general description of size and build matches the others. Abbie is taking a full statement from him. Eddie and Andrew have gone out to speak to the neighbours and collect any security footage."

Fiona wandered over to the map with markers of all the recent burglaries pinned to the board. "Other than the ages of the victims, there still doesn't seem to be any pattern emerging. Have the two recent victims been asked about tradespeople visiting their homes in the last few months? Interests, groups and taxi firms they use?"

"Neither of them had any work done this year," Humphries replied. "We are starting to see some overlap due to numbers, but nothing that connects everyone."

"Let's hope the cameras managed to pick up something useful this time."

"I'm still wading through the footage from last week," Humphries said.

"Well, you best get back to it," Fiona said. "We'll have another brainstorming session tomorrow on why pensioners with mobility problems are being targeted this way."

"You mean other than the obvious," Humphries said. "I still think this should be passed back to uniform. They have more local knowledge."

"I'm in daily contact with uniform, but I'm convinced there's something more to these burglaries. They cover too wide an area for there to be any continuity if we leave it to local officers. We're in a better position to take an overview," Fiona said testily, as it wasn't the first time Humphries had shared his opinion. "Why go to the trouble of breaking in and scaring the occupier half to death and leave with next to nothing? Why only take personal mementoes like old photographs and medals? Why cause so much pain with nothing to gain?"

"Do I look like a psychiatrist? Who knows why anybody does anything?" Humphries asked. "But I know who is benefiting. Home security experts, the owners of sheltered housing and estate agents."

Fiona glared at Humphries. "It isn't right that elderly residents should be hounded from their homes. You wouldn't be so glib if it were your parents."

DC Rachael Mann joined them at the map. "I think we might have something worth following up on. One of last night's victims regularly attended a subsidised meal organised for retirees in the Carpenters Inn, where she met one of the earlier victims."

"Interesting," Fiona said. "All the victims need to be asked if they have ever gone along to any of these meals, even if it was only once. And whether they have visited the pub on other occasions. Can I leave that with you and Abbie?"

"Yes," Rachael replied. "Abbie should be back from visiting last night's other victim, Tom Barker, in the hospital any minute now."

"And can you pass the information to Eddie and Andrew, and tell them to ask neighbours if they know anything about these lunches? Especially the elderly ones. If that turns out to be the connection, we might even be able to get ahead of them. I'll visit the pub with Humphries and ask for a list of employees."

"Although they use the pub's function room, the meals are arranged by volunteers," Rachael said, glancing down at her notes. "The group call themselves Golden Mischief and were set up by Rose Bulmer, who still heads it. Here's her contact number."

"Good work, thank you," Fiona said, picking up the phone to call Rose Bulmer.

"Sorry to interrupt, but I thought you would want to know. We've another burglary to add to the list. I was handed this on my way up," DS Abbie Ward said, handing a slim file to Fiona while taking off her jacket.

Fiona abandoned the call to skim-read the file. While reading, she said, "Thanks. How was the hospital visit? Was he able to tell you much?"

"Very little, but what he did say matches with what others have said," Abbie said. "He couldn't remember much, but he's a fighter. He says he's going home as soon as the hospital discharges him, and he won't be intimidated by a couple of idiots. His son was a different matter. He was furious about the attack and gave me a right lecture about police incompetence. At one point, I thought I would have to arrest him for assault."

"Take a break before writing up your report. I'll go out to this one," Fiona said, tapping the file. "Humphries, can you call the Carpenters Arms for a list of employees? I shouldn't be gone long."

When Fiona pulled up outside the small bungalow on the edge of Sapperton, she hurried over to catch up with Tracy Edwards, head of the crime scenes unit, as she was leaving. "Connected to the others?"

"Without a doubt," Tracy said. "Very little was taken, and nothing of value. Family photographs, the house keys, and her father's war medals. Petty cash in a kitchen drawer was left untouched. The living room's a mess, but it's only superficial damage. If it weren't for the complete lack of any forensics, I would say it was teenagers thinking it was a laugh."

Fiona shook her head at the thought anyone could consider terrorising vulnerable people a laughing matter. "Callous teenagers wanting to cause maximum distress to elderly people living alone seems so pointless if they're not taking anything of value. There's some logic and planning here, even if we can't see it," Fiona said. "Targeting mementoes while leaving items of value makes it feel personal. Was the householder unharmed?"

"Her name was Alice Dale," Tracy said.

Fiona nodded her acceptance of the retort for dehumanising the victim.

Tracy continued, "Alice disturbed them and was knocked over. She was very distressed and in some pain. I think there's a suspected broken wrist, and her daughter has taken her to the hospital to be fully assessed."

"Did she confirm whether there were two intruders?" Fiona asked.

"Sorry, I don't know. I'm only passing on what I was told."

Fiona looked up at the neat bungalow with a well-tended garden in bloom. It was a home that had been cherished and cared for. It was upsetting that the owner had been physically injured, but it was the dent in confidence that would leave the lasting damage. It infuriated her that they were no closer to catching the culprits, and Humphries was correct about local estate agents. Many of the victims were reluctant to return to what they had considered their home, their sanctuary. As news of the burglaries spread, others questioned their security and considered selling up and moving into sheltered housing. Their independence was being stolen, and she had failed them by not catching the culprits. "If there's nothing new to see here, I'll go straight to the hospital."

As Fiona approached the hospital bed, Alice's daughter sprang up from the bedside chair and shooed her away. "What do you want? My mother's sleeping. We have nothing to say. Go away."

Fiona showed her card. "I'm with the police, not a reporter."

"What are you doing here? Why aren't you out arresting the little bleeders? If I get my hands on whoever did this, I'll throttle them."

"I understand your frustration. I was hoping to ask your mother some questions."

"Oh, you understand us, do you? Are you sure? Do you have any idea how this will affect her?" Alice's daughter asked as angry tears gathered in her eyes. "The mental trauma as well as the bruising. Weeks, months from now? How it's going to disrupt us as a family? I've been sitting here racking my brains, trying to see how I can juggle things so she can move in with us. My two youngest are already sharing a room. No one is going to help us. And you swan in here to ask your questions, write it all down in your little book and then go home and forget about us."

"I do understand. I have elderly parents living in the area," Fiona said. "There are people I can put you in contact with."

"Oh, yeah. Victim support. More ticking boxes. How's that going to help?"

"They're trained to help and will understand the problems you are facing. I can arrange for them to call."

"Whatever. Anyway, she can't tell you anything as they've given her something to help her to sleep. They were wearing balaclavas and never spoke, so she won't be able to help when she wakes up."

"I'll leave it for now, but I will need to speak to her later. She might remember some details that will help us," Fiona said.

"Another tick in the box, in other words, and nothing will change."

"I can assure you I won't go home and forget about it. There's a whole team working on this. We will catch them. I will be in contact in a couple of days," Fiona said. "Before I go, do you know if your mother was a member of the Golden Mischief group run by Rose Bulmer? Among other things, they host meals at the Carpenters Arms."

"Possibly. Mum was getting herself back on her feet after Dad passed. She did join a group recently, but I can't remember what it was called."

"When your mother wakes up, could you ask her and call me with the details?"

Fiona turned to leave and ran straight into a man entering the room. After apologising profusely, he looked past Fiona and said, "I was downstairs on a routine appointment when I heard about Alice. Please tell her we are thinking of her, and if there's anything at all I can do to help, ask, and it will be done."

"Thank you, Ken. I'll pass on your good wishes."

Ken stepped back towards the door. "Well, I won't keep you, but anything at all. You know our number."

After he left, Fiona said, "That was kind of him. Is he a family friend?"

"I guess. Mum met him earlier this year, I think. He's devoted to his wife, who has dementia. They're only in their fifties."

"Do you know his surname?"

"Marsh. Ken Marsh. Anything else? His shoe size?"

"That will be all for now. Please ask your mother about the Golden Mischief group," Fiona said, withdrawing from the room.

CHAPTER THREE

Back at the station, Fiona dropped onto her chair and started to ring Rose Bulmer when she sensed someone hovering by her desk. She looked up to see Superintendent Ian Dewhurst carrying a slim file.

"Ah, DI Williams. I thought I saw you coming in." He placed the file on her desk. "Can you read through this and tell me what you think? Maybe visit the scene and speak to a couple of witnesses? Mr and Mrs Woodchester are a lovely couple I know vaguely from my golf club."

"What sort of trouble are they in?" Fiona asked suspiciously, reluctant to touch the file. She knew before Dewhurst replied that it wouldn't be at the top of her list of priorities.

"No trouble. Nothing like that," Dewhurst said. "Their son fell from the roof of a vaulted barn, and suicide has been recorded. Terribly sad business. I met the lad several times, and he didn't strike me as the type, and his parents think that there's more to it."

"I'm not sure there is a type," Fiona said, incredulous at Dewhurst's insensitivity, especially considering Peter's recent suicide attempt. Eyeing the file, she asked, "Are you asking me to check another officer's work?"

"No, no. Nothing like that," Dewhurst said. "I'm merely suggesting a fresh pair of eyes might read the situation differently. If you come to the same conclusion, then all is well and good."

"I'm incredibly busy right now. We've received a new lead on the burglaries, and I'm keen to follow up on it, so this might have to wait."

"That's excellent news. I agree these burglaries are a priority issue and the public is closely watching us. An early arrest will be good news for everyone," Dewhurst said. "But I'm sure this other matter won't take up too much of your time, and I value your opinion. I would appreciate it if you could fit it in to your schedule."

Annoyed by the false flattery, but knowing that Dewhurst would pester her until she reported her findings, Fiona asked, "What am I looking for?"

"Something that might have been missed in the initial investigation. The decision to call it suicide was made very quickly. See if there's anything that warrants a closer look. Alex's career was taking off, and his partner is heavily pregnant with their first child. He had everything to live for, so I tend to agree with the parents that suicide doesn't make any sense."

"Any previous mental health issues?"

"Maybe," Dewhurst said, not meeting Fiona's eye. "Have a read-through, speak to a few people, and tell me what you think."

"If his parents aren't accepting the suicide verdict, are they suggesting accidental death or foul play?" Fiona asked.

"I don't think they know what they're suggesting. He came from a good family, and there was nothing to suggest he was depressed. I think it warrants a second look," Dewhurst said. Barely drawing breath, he asked, "Have you given any thought to the role of DCI? I know you have been shouldering some of Peter's duties in his absence."

"Sorry," Fiona said, annoyed that she hadn't anticipated the question. "I haven't had the time to give it any serious thought."

"Well, don't take too long. Have a think about it and let me know your decision when you report back on this. It's a great opportunity for you to take your career forward."

"I wasn't even aware the post had been advertised yet."

"Yes, well, I'm waiting on a few things."

Watching Dewhurst strut back to his lair, Fiona used a pen to flip open the file. It reeked of a pet project, and she wasn't happy about it being foisted on her when she was already busy enough.

Attaching it so casually to a promotion, which she wasn't even sure she wanted, added salt to the wound and she was tempted to throw the file in the bin out of spite.

A quick flick through the Woodchester file told her why suicide was being considered, and she was even more tempted to march into Dewhurst's office and drop the file on his desk. Although no note had been left, Alex Woodchester had been alone, drinking a bottle of whisky on the roof of a double-storey barn in the middle of nowhere, in the early hours of the morning, when he fell. The barn's height and the concrete yard below made the fatality a given.

Knowing the circles Dewhurst mixed in, she had assumed that Alex was in his early twenties and a go-getter, probably working in property or finance. According to the file, he was twenty-eight years old and worked as a transitions manager in a school for children with special needs. She had no idea what a transitions manager was, but working with problem children was never easy and rarely lucrative. Only his parents' address put him in the correct social class for Dewhurst to take an interest.

She pushed the file on Alex Woodchester to the corner of her desk and rang Rose Bulmer to arrange a meeting. After jotting down a few details, she called across the room to Humphries, "Are you free to come with me to view a suicide scene?"

"What a cheery way to finish off the day," Humphries replied, grimacing. "What happened to visiting Bulmer and the Carpenters? I told them we would be popping by later to pick up their list of employees."

"I'll take that as a yes," Fiona said. "Don't disappear anywhere while I finish reading this file that Dewhurst has landed me with. We'll be visiting Mrs Bulmer afterwards and then the pub. Be ready to leave in half an hour."

Fiona tutted and shook her head as she read the rest of the file. Alex died of injuries consistent with a fall, and there were no traces of drugs in his system other than the whiskey and a negligible amount of cannabis. He had been hospitalised in his late teens following a suicide attempt, although there was no mention of recent mental health issues. His pregnant partner had returned to Spain two weeks ago, and when an officer rang to speak to her, her family made it very clear that she had no intention of returning. "Great," she muttered, wondering if Dewhurst had even read the file.

One thing she wouldn't be doing is contacting the parents and giving them false hope. She felt for them and the horrendous way to lose their only child, but the verdict was reasonable given the circumstances. Dewhurst could have the pleasure of explaining her findings.

She was only visiting the barn because it was close to Rose Bulmer's home. She was taking Humphries because he was preoccupied with his forthcoming wedding and wasn't as emotionally invested in the burglaries as she would like. With less than a month to go before his big day, he was doing little more than shift paperwork from one side of his desk to another, and she was concerned he might miss something. If Dewhurst was going to insist on someone wasting their time reinvestigating what looked like an open and shut case to appease his golf partner, then Humphries was the perfect candidate.

Driving towards the tiny hamlet of Oxenwood, Humphries tutted in the front passenger seat as he read Alex's file. Sighing, he closed the half-read file and shook his head. "Why are we wasting our time on this? It's incredibly sad, and I get the parents are struggling to accept the situation, but the most logical conclusion is suicide. Why else would someone climb onto the roof of an isolated building with a bottle of whiskey at night? Stargazing? Even if suicide wasn't his express intention, and he fell accidentally, it was a reckless thing to do. If the medical examiner couldn't say one way or another, no one will ever know the truth. We can't change that."

"I'm not disagreeing with you," Fiona said. "But Dewhurst has asked we look into it, and that's what we're going to do. I'm assuming a verdict of misadventure would be more palatable to the parents."

"We can rule out murder. I can't see how a fit young man could have been coerced onto the roof, can you?" Humphries asked.

"It would seem unlikely, but you never know," Fiona said without any enthusiasm.

Humphries read through the rest of the file. "Did you see he made a suicide attempt in his late teens?"

"I did."

"So why have you agreed to this charade, and why drag me into it? Bereavement counselling would seem more appropriate."

"Because it's a request from a senior officer, and this would seem to be as good a use of your time as anything else," Fiona replied. "It's either this or reviewing the burglary files looking for a new connection. Your shout."

"I thought we had one. The pub." Humphries shrugged and looked out the car window. "Do you know who Peter is bringing with him to my wedding?"

"Yes, his daughter, Amelia," Fiona replied. "She's been brilliant the last few weeks. Really taken him in hand."

"Hey! Is that the parents' house?" Humphries asked, pointing to a gated drive.

"Yes, but we're not troubling the family. Dewhurst can pass on our findings," Fiona said.

"Very nice set-up. I can see why Dewhurst is insisting on preferential treatment for them," Humphries said. "What did they do? Rattle their pearls at him?"

"Very possibly," Fiona said with a sigh. "We're going to take a quick look at the barn, and you can make a few follow-up calls to his friends and work colleagues. If there's nothing to warrant changing the conclusion of suicide, I'll be happy to let Dewhurst know."

"How's Stefan?"

"He's good. He's coming back for a few days."

"That'll be a little awkward, won't it?" Humphries asked. "With you staying at your mother's place."

Fiona shrugged but didn't reply. She didn't need Humphries to remind her of her predicament. As her mother was currently living alone, Fiona had asked her to consider moving in with her until they caught the burglars. Her well-meant offer had been met with an accusation that she wanted her mother to follow her father into residential care so she could take possession of the house. Denying the ridiculous suggestion, she had somehow offered to move in with her mother as a possible alternative, which had been accepted. Now, she was sleeping in a single bed in her old bedroom, which hadn't been redecorated since she left for university years ago, and her boyfriend was coming home for a few days. She hadn't yet broached the subject with her mother that she might be returning to her own home for a few nights.

Fiona turned onto a short, rough track from the lane and parked on a concrete yard in front of the barn. The open-fronted, two-storey barn was nestled against a small collection of trees. Made of honey-coloured stone with an old tile roof and a frontal view of rolling countryside, it was surprising it hadn't been converted into a coveted weekend retreat. Plastic-covered haylage bales were packed neatly inside, filling every available space and blocking access to the upper floor and roof. "These bales were here the night Alex fell, so he couldn't have gained access to the roof from inside. The report mentioned some old stone steps leading to the loft area," Fiona said, walking along the side of the barn.

Squeezing between overgrown brambles and the rear of the barn, they came to a set of steep steps without a guard rail leading to the second floor. The steps ended in a small platform at a rotted wooden door which creaked open on rusty hinges. Inside were rusted pieces of old farm machinery covered in dusty cobwebs. Along the back wall was an old workbench and circular saw. In the corner were the battered remains of an ancient threshing machine. They checked the ceiling, but there was no access to the roof from inside. They returned to the small platform and agreed Alex had probably used the overhanging tree branch to climb onto the roof.

They carefully descended the steep steps and returned to the front of the barn. Any trace of where Alex had landed on the concrete yard was long gone, but they had a rough idea of where he had fallen from the incident report.

Looking up at the pitched roof, Humphries said, "How can the parents think it was anything other than suicide? Even if he were unconscious, it would be difficult for two people to have dragged him up there so they could push him off. There must be easier places to drop a body from. He climbed onto that roof of his own accord."

"I agree that, for whatever reason, it's likely he climbed up there unaided," Fiona said. "According to the report, nothing was found to indicate he had company."

"Any cigarette butts?" Humphries asked.

"No," Fiona said. "As there were only traces in his system, it was assumed he had smoked the cannabis earlier in the evening."

"It's a nice view, but I can think of only one reason he went up there."

"We've seen enough here," Fiona said. "Contact a couple of his friends and check they have nothing new to add to their statements."

Humphries asked, "Do we have to go through the motions of interviewing the friends? It's obvious that his partner was returning to Spain permanently, and with his history, that was probably enough to push him over the edge."

"No, *you* are," Fiona said. "Once you've done that, I'll tell Dewhurst we've found nothing to contradict the initial conclusions."

"I'm wasting my time with an open mind, then," Humphries joked.

"Let's go and see Rose Bulmer."

CHAPTER FOUR

Rose Bulmer lived in a terraced cottage a few miles away in the old part of Oxentown, a short walk from the Carpenters Inn. She opened her front door with a flushed face, wearing jogging trousers and a T-shirt. "Hello, come in, come in," she said, ushering them inside. "I've just returned from the gym and haven't had time to change, so you'll have to excuse my attire. I'm not sure what I'm doing there, but everyone says exercise is doubly important at my age."

Rose led Fiona and Humphries through the cottage to a bright, airy garden room and invited them to sit. "I'll just check in on Mother and then make us all a drink. What would you like?" Pulling a face, she added, "I'll have my post-workout protein shake. It tastes disgusting, but apparently is good for me. A gin and tonic would be much more refreshing."

"Water for me," Fiona said.

"Coffee, please," Humphries said.

Once they were settled with their drinks, Fiona asked, "Did your mother not want to join us?"

"I did ask, but to be honest, we've reached a stage where it's a good day if she remembers who I am. She's the reason I started the Golden Mischief group. That's what you're here to talk about, isn't it?"

"Yes," Fiona said, after sipping her water. "I'm sure you've heard about the recent burglaries."

"Yes, of course, everyone is talking about them. It's a dreadful business. The sooner you get those hooligans off the streets, the safer we'll all feel in our beds at night. I'm so pleased Mother agreed to move in with me. Not that she would be able to cope living alone. Not now. But at least I know she's safe here with me," Rose said. "What is it you want from me? To organise a security awareness programme? I've been thinking about that myself. We need to find a way to protect ourselves."

"An excellent idea, but that's not what we want to talk about today," Fiona said. "Some of the victims regularly attend your lunches…"

"I knew about poor Tom. We only celebrated his eightieth birthday the other day. Who are the others?"

"Jane Foote…"

"Oh, no!" Rose interrupted. "She's a lovely lady who lived her whole life here, like my mother. She used to run the post office with her husband. Is she okay?"

"She was very shaken up and is currently in the hospital," Fiona said. "Along with Alice Dale. Do you know her?"

"The name does ring a bell. I think she joined us a few months ago," Rose said. "Who else?"

"We are asking all the previous victims if they ever attended the lunches, so there could turn out to be more."

The colour drained from Rose's face. "You think my lunches could be the common denominator? Oh, good gracious, no. That makes me feel so responsible. I had the idea when my mother still lived by herself. With one thing and another, her social life had dwindled to virtually nothing. I thought the group would be a lovely way to rekindle old friendships and create new ones. I had tried encouraging her to attend community events arranged for her age group, but she poo-pooed the idea. It was her pride, you see. She thought those events were for older people who never had any friends. Mother had always been active with a wide circle of friends. After the stroke, she lost her driving licence, and living where she did in a small hamlet left her isolated and reliant on others. The idea of mingling in a pub, and the type of events I arranged, were far more acceptable to her. To think somebody could be using my best intentions to target the very people I've tried to help is intolerable. I don't know what the world is coming to. I don't …"

Fiona realised she would have to talk across Rose, or they would be there late into the evening. She opened her bag, and asked, "Could you look at this list of names and tell me if you recognise any of them."

"These are all victims?" Rose asked before taking the list. When Fiona nodded, she looked through the names. "James Casey, he joins us now and again. And Lucy Johnson. Oh, and I'm sure I've seen Rupert Colley. I'm not sure about the others. I don't recognise the names, but that doesn't mean they've not come along in the past."

"Do you keep a membership record?"

"No, sorry. It's more of a fluid arrangement without membership fees. I like to think of it as a general invite. I don't want to exclude anyone. We've always made it clear that everyone is welcome to come along to any of our events."

"Do you have a list of volunteers?" Fiona asked.

"I can't believe one of them could be responsible," Rose replied. "They're the loveliest bunch of people you could hope to meet."

"We don't believe anything at this stage," Fiona said. "Is there a list?"

"Yes, I'll get it for you, but mostly they're friends I've pressurised into helping." When Rose returned with the typed list of volunteers, she added the names of carers who sometimes helped on an ad hoc basis. Handing it over, she asked, "Is it okay if we carry on? It's a lifeline for some of them, as it's the only time they leave their houses. I know how much they look forward to my little soirees."

"When's your next event scheduled?"

"In a couple of days."

"Would you mind if officers attended and spoke to a few people?"

"No, of course not. I'm sure their presence would be a reassurance."

After leaving Rose, they walked along to the Carpenters Inn to discover the pub was shut on a Monday and Tuesday evening. Fiona knocked on the door but received no reply.

"We'll run a check on the volunteers' names tomorrow. Hopefully, by then, we'll also have a list of the pub employees, and we'll take it from there," Fiona said. "Do you want to be dropped off at the station or home?"

CHAPTER FIVE

Humphries ended his call and stood to look around the incident room. "Anyone know where Fiona is?"

"Yes, she's in the custody suite dealing with the people involved in the brawl outside The Riser last night," Abbie said. "She offered to help out as it's so manic down there, and Sykes was pulling his hair out."

"I'm going to find her," Humphries said, leaving his desk.

"That only leaves me here to go through all this footage. I know it's boring, but it has to be done," Abbie moaned. "Can't it wait until later? She'll be back soon."

"I won't be long, and this can't wait," Humphries said. "By the way, you have noticed Sykes is bald?" which resulted in Abbie throwing a pen at him. He picked it up and slipped it into his shirt pocket. "Thanks."

Sykes was equally unimpressed with the urgent need to call Fiona out of an interview room. "I should have finished my shift an hour ago but can't leave until this lot is processed and released. Can't someone else help you?"

"Sorry," Humphries said. "This is something she's going to want to know about."

"Okay. Wait here."

Fiona emerged from one of the interview rooms, frowning. "What is it, Humphries? Have you and Abbie found something on the footage?"

"Not exactly." Humphries indicated he wanted them to move along the corridor. Once satisfied that they couldn't be overheard, he said, "I've just received a call from Ann Guppy."

"Guppy? The name doesn't mean anything to me."

"She's Matthew Guppy's wife. It's about the suicide case Dewhurst asked us to look into last week."

"Alex Woodchester? I thought you were done with that, and it was just a case of writing up your notes."

Humphries nodded. "So did I, until five minutes ago. I spoke to Matthew because his business card was found in Alex's pocket. Alex had recently turned up at his house out of the blue. They had been friends at school but lost contact with one another when they went to university. Matthew told me that it was a pleasant surprise to hear from Alex, and they went to a local pub for a general catch-up. Matthew insisted nothing was said that evening to make him think his old friend was suicidal, but he was quite vague about what they discussed. And to be fair, he pointed out that after such a long time, he wasn't the best person to ask about Alex's state of mind."

"Nothing unusual there," Fiona said. "Alex was probably feeling nostalgic and wanted to speak to an old friend one last time."

"That's what I thought," Humphries said. "Anyway, Matthew must have told his wife that I spoke to him about them meeting up. She rang me this morning to say he died a couple of nights ago. The official line is it was suicide, but she's refusing to accept that conclusion. She wants us to investigate his death as murder."

"Seriously? I haven't formally reported back to Dewhurst on Alex's death yet, but he caught me as I was leaving the station yesterday, and I told him it was looking likely that the suicide verdict was correct. And now you want to reinvestigate another suicide?"

"But don't you think this might change things?" Humphries asked. "Maybe something was going on after all, and we missed it."

"You've changed your tune. We agreed suicide was the correct conclusion, and I need you to be concentrating on the house burglaries," Fiona said, trying to remember the last time Humphries was so keen to follow up on something. "I know ploughing through surveillance tapes and going back over statements is monotonous, but it's our best chance of stopping the house break-ins before someone gets seriously hurt."

"We've interviewed all the staff at the Carpenters Inn and most people connected to Golden Mischief, and found nothing conclusive so far."

"Which is why I've asked you to look at the footage again now we have a list of all their cars," Fiona said. "If one of them was in the area the nights of the burglaries, we'll have them."

"There hasn't been another burglary all week, and surely a double murder would take precedence," Humphries replied.

"Whoa!" Fiona said. "That's rather a leap, isn't it?"

"Possibly," Humphries admitted. "But the fact they were in contact with one another is strange. It should at least be looked at."

"Is this second suicide in our area?"

"Just. Matthew Guppy lived in Swanswick."

"Have you read the initial report?"

"I've requested it and spoken to the case handler."

"And? Did they have any reason to suspect murder?" Fiona asked.

"On the available evidence, suicide does seem to be the correct call," Humphries admitted. "It has been confirmed that he fired the gun, but …"

"But?"

"The officer admitted they were scratching their heads as to why, and like with Alex, there was no note," Humphries said. "Don't you find it odd that two old friends meet up after ten years and both decide to kill themselves shortly after, even though neither of them was showing any signs of depression, let alone suicidal thoughts? Matthew had never suffered with his mental health. His wife said he was annoyingly optimistic about everything. More like a big kid than an adult."

"It's a little strange, but it could be a very sad coincidence," Fiona said. "I need to complete the interviews back there. See what more you can find out, and I'll join you as soon as I'm finished."

"What do I tell Ann Guppy? She's expecting a callback."

"We're looking into it," Fiona said over her shoulder. "If the evidence warrants it, we'll arrange to see her, but don't make her any promises."

Fiona was starting to regret offering to help clear the backlog as it was taking longer than she had anticipated. The last two detainees she had to interview had girlfriends, steady employment and parents waiting to take them home. An excess of alcohol and a drunken jolt at the other end of the bar had started a fight that spiralled out of control, sucking them all in. Their raging hangovers and embarrassment may have been sufficient punishment, had it not been for the thousands of pounds of damage to the pub and several cars parked outside. Somebody had to pay for the repairs and the realms of paperwork their rampage had created. At least they were polite and remorseful, and Fiona hoped the experience of a night in the cells and a charge would lead to improved life decisions.

Fiona completed the interviews and went through the motions of releasing the men under pre-charge bail, pending further investigation, as her mind wandered. Things may have gone quiet recently on the burglaries, but she doubted they were finished. Even if they were, she hated the idea of them getting away with all the upset they had caused. There would be something amongst all the evidence they had gathered. It was just a question of spotting it.

The last thing she needed was Humphries inventing cases that needed investigating, but Humphries generally had good instincts, and she wondered if she had been too hasty to dismiss his concerns. She could let him run with the idea that the deaths were related to whatever they discussed when they met. His input on the burglaries wouldn't be missed, and he might be less of a distraction to the rest of the team if he was preoccupied elsewhere.

She found Humphries slumped over a file, nursing a cold cup of coffee. "Have you found anything?"

Humphries shook his head as he handed over the file on the investigation into Matthew Guppy's death. "The coroner is satisfied beyond any reasonable doubt that he fired the gun himself, so there has been minimal investigation. What was completed at the scene was limited."

Fiona groaned and pulled out the chair next to Humphries. "I agree the two deaths happening so close together seems suspect, but we would be wading into very sensitive territory if we opened a second investigation. Where are our grounds if the medical evidence is so conclusive? All you can do is call Guppy's wife and say you've reviewed the case, but hard as it is to accept, suicide is the correct conclusion."

"Could we at least go out in person to hear what she has to say?"

Fiona sighed and picked up the file to flick through it.

"Nobody has been able to give any explanation as to why he killed himself," Humphries said. "He had a happy family life and a good career. His friends confirmed it was completely out of character. Nobody even knew he had a gun."

"Do we know when he purchased it, or whether he had a licence for it?" Fiona asked.

"That's the other thing. There's no trace of him buying it. No one knows who it belonged to," Humphries said. "It's been assumed he paid cash for it. But there's no record of him asking questions or being in contact with the sort of person to sell it to him."

"How about the gun itself? Has it been connected to previous crimes?"

"No one has bothered to check," Humphries said. "Reading the file, I think his family has been given a raw deal, and it reeks of a cost-cutting exercise. The officer I spoke to said he wanted to spend more time on it but was told to wrap it up."

"You can go to explain our conclusions, but that's it," Fiona finally said. "You can listen to her, but don't encourage her to imagine there might be an alternative explanation. Even if there were grounds to reopen the case, the request for it to be transferred to us because of the connection with Alex, would have to go through Dewhurst. Take Rachael with you. She needs more experience out in the field," Fiona said, handing back the file.

CHAPTER SIX

Humphries and Rachael pulled up outside a modern three-bedroom house in a new housing development on the edge of Swanswick. Ann Guppy, barefoot and dressed in jeans and a sweater, answered the door immediately and led them through a hallway littered with children's toys and a tricycle. "It's probably best we talk in the kitchen."

It was hard to avoid the brightly coloured paintings stuck to the fridge with magnets, and the cereal boxes marketed to children on the counter, as they took their seats. "We are sorry for your loss," Rachael said as they sat, thinking how much the room reminded her of her own kitchen.

"Are you?" Ann asked. "Sorry enough to investigate what's really going on? Our children deserve to know the truth. Matthew did not kill himself. Why would he? He had no reason to. No reason at all. Somebody murdered him. It's not right that his children should grow up thinking they weren't worth living for."

"Where are your children now?" Rachael asked.

"With my mother so we could talk." Ann fought back her tears, and her face hardened. "Have you anything new to tell me?"

"Not really," Rachael said. "We've gone back through the files, and there is nothing to contradict the initial findings."

Ann's eyes darted to Humphries. "But I understand you've reopened the file on Alex Woodchester's suicide. That's why you spoke to Matthew. Why can't you do the same for him?"

"We reviewed the case," Humphries said, wondering how much he could say. "We looked at the evidence and concluded he took his own life. We can't go into details, but there were things going on in his life ..."

"Don't give me that rubbish!" Ann said, jumping from her chair and starting to pace. "Alex didn't kill himself either. Matthew was sure of it. Aren't we important enough to you to launch an enquiry or whatever it is that you do?"

"I wasn't aware that you knew Alex," Humphries said.

"I didn't, but there must be something linking their murders. It's the only thing that makes any sense."

"It's very easy to start creating connections when there doesn't seem to be any logical explanation ..." Rachael started to say.

"I don't want to hear your psychobabble. I'm not making connections that don't exist. Somebody coerced Alex and Matthew into taking their own lives. Of that, I have no doubt," Ann said.

"If there is a connection, we haven't found it," Humphries said. "Matthew went to school with Alex, but we understand they haven't been in contact for years. Did Matthew talk to you about why Alex made contact and what they discussed?"

Ann retook her seat facing Humphries. "I'm sorry, I don't know what they discussed, but I do know Matthew lied to you. I asked him about it after you left, but he said it wasn't important. You didn't need to know."

"Know what?" Humphries asked.

"I don't know," Ann said, curling her hands into tight fists. "Up until the day he knocked on our door, I had never even heard the name Alex Woodchester. All I know is he came around here to speak to Matthew, and a few weeks later, they both ended up dead. And they didn't have a general catch-up like he told you."

"But you have no idea what it was that they discussed?"

"No! All I know is Matthew wasn't happy about it. The meeting rattled him, and he said if Alex came to the house again, I was to tell him that he was out, and he should leave us alone as he had nothing more to say."

"Did Matthew's mood or behaviour change after the meeting?" Rachael asked.

"For a while, yes. He was nervy and on edge all the time. Then we heard about Alex's death, and he seemed to relax. He was back to his old self. We were planning a trip to Disneyland, and he was more excited than the children. He said he couldn't wait to see their faces." Ann's face crumpled as she started to sob. "Now, he never will. He'll never see them growing up."

"We're so sorry," Rachael said.

Tears ran freely down Ann's face, but her expression was resolute. "Then find out who did this. Matthew would never do this to the children. He simply wouldn't."

Rachael looked around the kitchen at the brightly coloured mugs, the children's paintings, family photographs, funny fridge magnets and cookery books, feeling out of her depth. It was the room of a pleasant, happy family, who did everyday things like plan family holidays and didn't blow their brains out with a shotgun. A home very similar to hers.

"The evidence is quite conclusive," Humphries said.

"Damn the evidence," Ann said. "It's wrong."

"Did your husband have any financial worries?" Rachael asked.

"No! He had just been promoted at work and received a healthy bonus. He wasn't expecting it to be so good," Ann said. "We danced around the table, this table, and decided we would take the kids to Disneyland. We're not rolling in it, but we're comfortable. We were happy as a family and a couple. He didn't kill himself."

"Did Matthew keep in contact with any of his other schoolfriends?" Humphries asked.

"Not really, no," Ann said. "He always said the past should stay where it belonged. We did bump into someone a few months back when we were in town. He said they were at school together, but I don't remember much about him except his name was Hugh, and Matthew said afterwards that he was a writer."

"Do you know where they went to school?"

"Yes, a private school in Birstall. I have the details somewhere," Ann said, jumping up to look through a kitchen drawer. "It probably explains why he's found it harder to keep contact with old friends. It's not like when you go to the local comp, and your mates live in the next street. Here we are. It was in Clifton."

Humphries looked at the invite to a recent school reunion., "Did he go?"

"No, like I said, he was all about looking forwards, not backwards."

Humphries knew Matthew was an only child, and his parents had passed away, so contacting the school was the only way they could find out anything about his friendship with Alex. Maybe there was a reason they didn't keep in contact when they left school. "Can I keep this?"

"Of course, if you think it would help."

CHAPTER SEVEN

"Well, what do you think?" Humphries asked as soon as they returned to the car.

"From what his wife said, I agree Matthew's suicide seems surprising, but having not met him, I have no idea if her convictions were correct or wishful thinking. But the house had a happy, optimistic feel and seemed so ordinary. I think the family deserves some answers. Are we going to tell Fiona that the suicide warrants a full investigation? I think we should."

"We can't rely solely on the house's ambience and the wife's comments," Humphries said, disguising how pleased he was with her enthusiasm when he had expected the opposite. As a slightly older team member, Rachael was known for being sensible and level-headed. He suspected that was why Fiona suggested she join him for the visit. He decided to sound Rachael out by playing Devil's Advocate so he would be prepared for Fiona's objections to a further investigation. "There could have been other issues going on in Matthew's life that she knew nothing about or chose to ignore."

"Issues aside," Rachael said dismissively, "funny how she thought his mood changed after Alex's death. Do you think he may have had something to do with it? She described him as stressed by the unexpected visit and whatever they discussed but relaxed after they heard he had died."

"I looked at Alex's file again before we left, and because of the limited access to the barn roof, I'm struggling to see how Alex's death could have been anything other than suicide. In Matthew's case, the evidence confirms he shot himself," Humphries said, acknowledging the stumbling blocks to arguing neither case was suicide. "So, what are you suggesting? Their meeting wasn't amicable, and Matthew made some harsh comments. And what then? After initially feeling relieved, he became so overcome with remorse for driving an old friend to suicide that he took his own life. A little dramatic, don't you think?" Humphries asked. "We only have Ann's word that he lied to me about their meeting. He gave me the impression that they shared a pleasant night down the pub and agreed to meet again."

Rachael slumped her shoulders and looked out the car window. After they had driven a short distance, she turned to face Humphries. "I would love to know why Alex contacted Matthew and what unnerved him so much. As they hadn't been in contact since their school days, it must have been about something that happened back then. We could contact the school."

Although that was exactly what Humphries thought, he said, "It wouldn't change the final verdict, though."

"It would give the families some answers."

"Judging from my previous dealings with private schools, if there were an event in their past they would rather forget, I doubt they'll be very forthcoming. At least it's a mixed school. Not all girls like Langley House School."

"We could contact Alex's parents."

"Which Fiona doesn't want us to do. Something about it being wrong to raise their hopes unless we have something more substantial to tell them about the death of their son," Humphries said. "We need something more to persuade her that Matthew's death is connected to Alex's and needs further investigation. To overcome the medical evidence, we would need to show he was not suicidal and was coerced into killing himself. Possibly, Alex was as well, but it would be harder in his case due to his previous attempt."

"Years ago, when he was a teenager," Rachael said. "Do you want to at least try to show there was more to the deaths? I know I do."

"I do," Humphries admitted, although he felt torn about what to do. He understood why Fiona wanted to concentrate on the burglaries and didn't want the distraction of what appeared to be two suicides. Rachael's enthusiasm boosted his suspicions about the deaths, but all he had was a feeling that something was amiss.

"So?"

"The problem we have is there is nothing to suggest a crime has been committed. Just the coincidence, and that you feel it was a happy house." Humphries turned off the dual carriageway towards Birkbury, and said, "We return to the station and report our findings to Fiona. She can decide whether we should further investigate the two deaths."

◆ ◆ ◆

Fiona listened to their argument for connecting the two deaths and viewing them as suspicious. The last thing she wanted was to create unnecessary angst for the grieving families. But she agreed there didn't appear to be any rational explanation for Matthew's suicide, and Rachael was very persuasive, even though she was more swayed by emotion than facts. Previously, she would have considered talking it over with Peter, but that was no longer an option. Dewhurst would have to be told before they started asking questions at the school or anywhere else for that matter, but he wasn't someone she would ask for advice.

Humphries had said less than Rachael, but she thought he had probably encouraged Rachael to press for a further investigation. He didn't appreciate the corrosive effect the burglaries were having on the community and how elderly people were genuinely afraid. An attitude that had annoyed her from the start. But he was a good officer, and his instincts were often correct. It wasn't as if he would automatically throw himself into the burglary investigation if she turned him down flat. "You can have another day to tie up any loose ends. If something interesting comes up, we can look at it again. But before you do anything, I'll need to clear it with Dewhurst."

Dewhurst's reaction was much as Fiona expected. "Well, that's just brilliant. I told Alex's parents that an experienced officer had carefully considered the evidence and concluded the initial decision was correct. Now, you are telling me you want to investigate further. Which is it? Senior officers should lead by example. You must make clear decisions and stand by them, not keep swapping and changing your mind at the drop of a hat," he ranted. "Maybe it was for the best that you've taken extra time to consider applying for the DCI position. You're not quite ready for the role."

Fiona knew Dewhurst was more annoyed about losing face with a fellow golf player and wasn't sure she wanted the DCI role, but the criticism stung. And it was unfair as it was hardly her fault if he had spoken to the family before they had completed their investigation. "With all due respect ..."

"Which means you have none," Dewhurst said.

Fiona ignored his comment and continued, "A connected out-of-character suicide has changed the situation. The two men were school friends and had recently met up at Alex's request. Evidence suggests that whatever was discussed at that meeting was the catalyst for both men's actions. Finding out what that was will be helpful to both families."

"What evidence?"

"Okay, a suggestion of evidence," Fiona admitted. "And I think it's worth trying to find that evidence."

"Will you be speaking to Mr and Mrs Woodchester?"

"Possibly," Fiona said. "The plan is to allocate two officers to reinvestigate the suicides. They'll start with the school the two men attended and then speak with their work colleagues and friends. Possibly Nicky Perez, Alex's partner. I wouldn't want to trouble his parents unnecessarily."

"Oh, you fancy a trip to Spain," Dewhurst said.

"No, I'm sure a telephone call with Nicky could suffice," Fiona said, determined to remain calm and not bite.

"Do you think it's acceptable for his parents to find out from others that the case has been reopened again? Or were you expecting me to tell them?"

"No, I was thinking I would prefer not to raise their hopes until we complete the initial investigations," Fiona replied. "Matthew Guppy's suicide is harder to explain and more recent, so I was going to concentrate our efforts there."

"Despite your assertion that Alex's visit was the catalyst for the two deaths," Dewhurst said. "I have no objection to more junior officers speaking to the school, but I expect you to give Mr and Mrs Woodchester the courtesy of a personal visit. Is that understood?"

"Of course, sir," Fiona replied through gritted teeth.

"In the circumstances, I would like to see Alex's death being given precedence over this other chap. Keep me advised of developments," Dewhurst said, dismissing Fiona before she had time to object by turning his attention to his computer screen.

"There is one more thing, sir," Fiona said. "Although Matthew Guppy lived within our area, his body was discovered by a neighbouring force. As I currently have no acting DCI, could you request the change of jurisdiction?" Dewhurst didn't look up or acknowledge the request in any way, forcing Fiona to continue, "Having full access will be essential to our investigations."

Without looking away from his screen, Dewhurst said, "Leave your formal request on my desk, and I'll see to it."

The walk back to the incident room did nothing to calm Fiona's temper. She spotted Humphries and Rachael in the corner and plonked herself beside them. "The insufferable little man."

"It went well, then," Humphries said.

"Does that mean we can't follow up on it?" Rachael asked.

"You can contact the school tomorrow, but he wants me to interview Alex's parents. As if I haven't enough here to do. Call me with your report when you leave the school, and I'll arrange the visit. But we can't touch the Guppy case until Dewhurst finds the time to request the transfer."

CHAPTER EIGHT

Leaving the station on time for once, Fiona decided to call in on Peter for a coffee on her way home. As she parked her car, he waved from his front garden and wandered over to greet her at the gate. "This is a lovely surprise. I've just been doing a spot of weeding to tidy up out here. The whole place needs brightening up. Come in and help me choose the paint for the front room."

Following Peter to the front door, Fiona questioned his buoyancy. She couldn't remember him being particularly house-proud, and she had no recollection of him mentioning his garden before. "I'm no expert on house décor, but I'll take a look. It's only a quick stop. Mother has tea on."

"You're still there, then?" Peter asked. "You've not strangled each other yet?"

"It's come close at times," Fiona said, sitting at the kitchen table covered with home design magazines and colour samples. "I love her to bits, but there's a reason why I left home at eighteen and never looked back. How are you keeping?"

"Have you time for a proper coffee, or shall I stick the kettle on for an instant?"

"Thinking of the grey, wishy-washy tea her mother insisted on making, Fiona said, "A proper coffee would be great."

"How's everything going with Stefan?"

"Okay," Fiona replied carefully, not wanting to rub in how deliriously happy he made her feel when Peter's partner had recently returned to France to live. "We're taking it slow. One day at a time. He's been away the last couple of weeks setting up this new project in Exeter, so I've not seen him."

"Do you think you'll follow him down there?"

"We haven't seriously discussed it. He's only renting. If we take things further, we could buy a place in between."

"Giving you both a long commute," Peter said. "I assume this new project is the one I was supposed to lead?"

Flicking through one of the magazines, Fiona wasn't sure how to reply. Peter's dramatic exit from the police still felt too raw for her, and she wanted to avoid discussing the position that he should be taking up. "You didn't say how you were doing?" She looked up when Peter sat opposite her, saying nothing. "Is everything okay?"

"Everything is just fine," Peter said. "But there's one thing that's starting to annoy me. And that's people walking on eggshells around me. I did a stupid thing, but it's done. I won't be doing it again, so please talk to me like a normal person. I'm not a fragile freak that needs to be treated with kid gloves. It makes me think that you don't have any faith in me."

"Sorry, I didn't mean to make you feel like that," Fiona said. "How about I drop the subject if you tell me how you are really doing?"

"The therapist says I'm doing great. And yes, I'm keeping my appointments like a good boy, and I don't regret leaving the force. I'm working on getting the house and garden up together while I have the time before planning where I'm going work-wise. Everyone can now stop worrying about me and my state of mind."

"That sounds great," Fiona said. "But don't forget, people worry because they care about you. If we know you're okay, we'll stop fussing."

Peter planted two hands on the table and stood. "Good. That's that cleared up. The coffee should be ready by now. While I'm making it, tell me how things are really going with Stefan and at work."

"Things with Stefan are good. Really good. He's special," Fiona said, smiling at the thought of his name. "Work is busy, and Dewhurst is a pain. After my reluctance to drop everything to investigate his golf partner's claim, I think I'm off his list for promotion. Today, he played power games, making me wait for a straightforward transfer request."

"You know he can't do that," Peter said, returning to the table with the coffee. "You need to stand up to him."

"It's fine. It's just annoying."

"What about promotion? Have they advertised my old role yet?"

"I'm not sure, but I'm not interested. I don't want the extra pressure," Fiona said, taking a grateful sip of coffee. "I've been an unpaid acting DCI in everything except name for the last few weeks, and I've not enjoyed it. Sometimes, I can't sleep because I'm worrying about a case at night, but at least I generally wake up with new ideas. With the extra duties I'm currently juggling, my mind flits from one thing to another, and I never come up with any solutions. It's exhausting. The sooner he appoints a new DCI and takes the pressure off me, the better. I've decided I'm a doer, not an organiser."

"Don't put yourself down," Peter said. "You can learn to compartmentalise."

"Wow! Who has swallowed the management handbook, and where's Peter?"

"You know what I mean. You're perfectly capable and have a solid team behind you. Humphries can be Humphries, but he's experienced, loyal and genuine, and Rachael has great potential. She's smart."

"I know, I know," Fiona said. "That's enough about me. What are you planning on doing workwise?"

"That's something I wanted to talk to you about. How well do you know Simon Morris?"

"Other than he's my friend's partner, not that well. She's happy being with him."

"I've been speaking with his business partner, Charlie," Peter said. "He says he's honest but a bit of a dreamer and downright lazy at times."

"Oh?" Fiona said. "Kate always says how enthusiastic he is, although she says he is a very private person and doesn't always show others his true feelings."

"According to Charlie, he's very enthusiastic about taking cases on, but when it comes to the leg work, he rapidly loses interest and leaves Charlie to pick up the slack. That's why he sounded me out on whether I would like to work alongside them. I would only do it freelance so I can pick and choose the cases that interest me. What do you think?"

"I've only met Charlie once, but I liked him, and I know Kate completely trusts him," Fiona said. "If you want to give it a go, then go for it."

They were interrupted by a loud banging on the door. "Brace yourself," Peter said. "That's probably Gladys," before going to answer the door.

Gladys bounced into the room with a swirl of her colourful skirt and pounced on Fiona. "Darling! I haven't seen you in ages. Let me see you properly. Are you eating properly? You're looking a little thin."

Standing to leave, Fiona said, "I'm good. It's lovely to see you too, but I must be going."

"Oh, what a shame! I'm taking Peter out for something to eat," Gladys said. "Are you sure you won't join us?"

"Another time," Fiona said, edging towards the door.

"I've been trying to persuade Peter to come ballroom dancing with us. There are never enough men. You should come along, too."

Trying not to laugh at Peter's tortured face behind Gladys, Fiona said, "I'll check my diary and let you know." Looking at Peter, she added, "It might be fun. We could surprise Humphries at his wedding with our dancing skills." Caught off guard, she was engulfed in a flower-scented hug. When she was finally able to extricate herself from Gladys, she quickly said, "Well, I'm off. See you both very soon. Maybe at a dance class," and hurried to the front door.

Fiona smiled at the thought of Peter being press-ganged into ballroom dancing on her drive home. She knew how hard it was to say no to Gladys and her partner Dick. Despite their eccentricities, they were a fun couple, and she was pleased Peter had stayed in contact with them. They would take him under their wings, whether he wanted it or not.

Opening the front door to her mother's house, she was greeted by the smell of a casserole cooking. If she didn't catch the house burglars soon, she would be going up a dress size. "Hi, Mum! I'm home."

"Oh, good," her mother replied, appearing at the end of the hallway. "Supper will be ready in ten minutes. I was worried you were going to be late again."

Fiona followed her mother back into the kitchen, where the heat from the cooker was stifling, despite an open window. "It smells delicious."

"It would taste delicious if I could put real meat in it instead of that awful pretend stuff you insist on."

Sitting at the table, Fiona said, "I could make my meals separately."

"And double my electricity and grocery bill. I'm not made of money, you know."

Not mentioning she insisted on giving her mother enough housekeeping to more than cover any increased costs, Fiona said, "There's something I wanted to tell you before you go shopping again."

"What's that, then? A list of more exotic foods with even more exotic prices?"

"No. Something has come up, and I will have to move home for a couple of nights."

"Oh, something has come up, has it? Would this be a man?"

"Work is going to get incredibly busy the next few days. I probably won't be getting home until very late, and I don't want to disturb you. Would you consider moving in with Richard and Emma while I'm away? I know how much you enjoy spending time with your grandchildren, and they would love to have you stay for a while."

"Oh, not this again. I'm quite capable of fending for myself. I won't be chased out of my house and stay miles away. How would I visit your father? It's only a short bus trip from here."

"I'm sure Emma would be happy to drive you," Fiona said.

"I need to retain my independence. I'm sure Emma would be lovely, but I don't want to burden her or anyone else. I need to be here keeping everything going until your father comes home."

"I know," Fiona said, deciding this wasn't the time to mention the possibility of him never coming home. "You're not a burden to anyone and I worry about you."

"Well, you can stop that right away. And anyway, I've been invited out this weekend."

"Oh? Who by?"

"Nothing like that. An old work colleague is having a birthday bash at his house. I wasn't going to go without your father, but I bumped into Sally today at the newsagents, and she insisted we go together. It's going to be quite fancy, with live entertainment. I'll have to buy a new frock tomorrow."

"I remember Sally. Dark hair and into yoga and mindfulness." Fiona said.

"Yes, she's coping very well on her own. Better than most people expected after her husband passed away. She's joined numerous groups and constantly talks about how she's expanding her social circle. I feel tired just listening to all her new interests."

"Maybe you could stay with Sally for a few nights while I'm away."

"That's enough, young lady. I'm not going to impose myself on others. Now, I'll see if supper is ready. While we're eating, you can tell me about this man coming to stay with you. Is it Stefan?"

CHAPTER NINE

Patrick Burke, headmaster of Berkhampstead School, ended his call and immediately summoned Stuart Dunn to his office. While he waited for him to arrive, he paced his office before looking out the window. He watched a group of students heading towards the tennis courts carrying racquets. Not a sport he had ever enjoyed. He was a rugby man through and through. When he was younger, there was talk that he was good enough to go professional, but a niggling knee injury shattered those dreams. He had hoped to coach someone of the same standard, but the talent had never arrived. Now, he was coasting to retirement, waiting for surgery on his arthritic knee.

"You wanted to see me," Stuart said as he passed through the door. "Is it so urgent? Only I've had to leave my history class unattended."

"Yes, unfortunately, it is. Take a seat," Patrick said. "I'll try not to take up more of your time than necessary, but you'll need to organise cover for your next lesson as well."

"Why? What's happened?" Stuart said, sinking into the chair. "Has there been a complaint?"

Patrick gave him a quizzical look. "Is there something I should know about?"

"No, of course not," Stuart quickly said. "I can't think of anything."

"Well, two police officers are on their way to see us," Patrick said dramatically. "They're investigating the deaths of Alex Woodchester and Matthew Guppy."

"I saw about that on the news. Dreadfully sad business," Stuart replied, earnestly shaking his head. "One always wants to hear good news about ex-pupils. When I hear of their success, I like to think I played a small part in helping them on their way."

"Yes, yes, of course. It's always upsetting to hear such sad news about ex-pupils," Patrick said. "The thing is, the police seem to think their deaths could be related to something that happened here."

"I see," Stuart said, as realisation dawned on his face. "I'm not sure there's much I can say about all of that. I'll have a think about how much I can remember."

"I would never ask any of my staff to lie, but I will remind you that what happened was after the boys' final exams when they were no longer students. I don't want any unnecessary unpleasantness to find its way back to our current parents. It could reflect badly on the school, and enrolments are down enough as it is."

"If they're asking questions, they're bound to find out sooner or later."

"About something that happened after the boys left here," Patrick said. "We can't be responsible for students' actions their entire lives. That would be ludicrous."

"I appreciate that, but shouldn't we be helping the police as much as we can?" Stuart asked.

"How can we help them with something we know nothing about, that happened off school grounds involving an ex-pupil?" Patrick asked, looking over his spectacles. "The police will be asking about events when they were students here. Nothing untoward happened to either boy while they were enrolled at this school that could have any bearing on their later actions."

"Understood," Stuart said, tapping his nose. "Mum's the word."

"There's no need to go all MI5. It will only make them suspicious," Patrick said. "I suggest you conjure up some anecdotal stories about the boys' time here and arrange cover for your class. The police should be here shortly. Thank goodness they are sending plain-clothed officers. It would be best if we kept this between ourselves."

♦ ♦ ♦

Humphries and Rachael drove between a grand set of ornate iron gates and parked in the cramped school car park. From the phone call, Humphries had already decided Patrick Burke was a pompous idiot, horrified at the prospect of them turning up during school hours. He had left it to the end of the conversation to confirm that they wouldn't be in uniform on purpose.

After the grandeur of the gates, the rectangular Victorian school building looked austere and underwhelming. The surrounding acres of parkland, woodland and sports pitches were impressive. Humphries slammed his car door and looked over at two groundsmen on sit-on lawnmowers, cutting the already immaculate grass. He sniffed, and said in a loud voice, "Good to see how well it's maintained while state schools literally crumble and are held up by metal props."

"Terrible, isn't it? Luckily, our local primary isn't affected, and I've always been happy with the education they provide. My girls love going," Rachael said, surprised it had taken Humphries so long to share his views on the unfairness of private education.

Humphries grunted and locked the car, indicating they should head to the school entrance without delay. Through the arched wooden front door, they entered a stone-floored lobby with wood-panelled walls. The dark interior had the musty smell of a museum. A middle-aged woman in a tweed skirt and clunky lace-up shoes stepped out from behind a desk tucked into a dark corner to greet them. When Humphries showed his warrant card, they were quickly escorted up a stone staircase and along a long hall to the headmaster's office. The receptionist opened the door and introduced them before slipping quietly away.

"Thank you for seeing us so promptly," Rachael said as they entered.

After standing to shake hands, Patrick sat behind his desk. "It's my pleasure. I wish it could be in happier circumstances. We are deeply troubled to hear about the deaths of our former students and have added them to our morning prayers. How can we be of assistance?"

"It would be helpful to have the names of their wider circle of friends," Rachael said.

"Of course. I've arranged for you to see their housemaster, Stuart Dunn. He should be able to help you with that."

After staring disapprovingly around the room, Humphries said, "The two boys didn't stay in contact after they left here, but they met up shortly before taking their lives. Did anything happen during their final years here that could explain it? We're talking about ten years ago."

"Goodness! No, I can't think of anything of that magnitude," Patrick said. "I've been the head for the past seven years, and before that, I was the deputy head. After your call, I took the opportunity to look through the relevant yearbooks to jog my memory. At my age, one year very much bleeds into the next. You're very welcome to read through them yourselves," Patrick said, tapping the three annuals on his desk. "Behind all the awards and accolades, you'll see this is a happy school with fantastic pastoral care. We strive to ensure every pupil reaches their full potential."

"We're not here to talk about enrolling a new pupil," Humphries said.

"Could we take the yearbooks away?" Rachael asked. "We will return them afterwards."

"Be my guest," Patrick gestured with a wave of his hand.

"What can you tell us about the two boys?" Humphries asked.

Patrick fixed his eyes at a point somewhere above their heads, and said, "I remember Alex and Matthew as typical young boys, full of life and youthful vigour. They weren't outstanding scholars, but they were both on the rugby team and generally the sporty type. I'm sure Mr Dunn will have more personal recollections of the boys. Would you like me to call for him now?"

"Thank you," Rachael said, reaching over to collect the yearbooks while Patrick picked up his phone.

Patrick interrupted his call to say, "I will make this room available for your chat, and step outside if you have no further use for me. A spot of fresh air will do me the world of good."

Rachael handed over her card when Patrick completed the call. "If you later remember something that might be useful, please don't hesitate to call."

Patrick stood to take the card. "I'll be sure to do that. Please pass on my condolences along with those of the entire school community to the parents." Hearing a knock on the door, he said, "That sounds like my cue to exit stage left. I'll leave you in Mr Dunn's capable hands."

Stuart Dunn shuffled his way into the room and uncomfortably sat in Patrick's vacated chair. "Ah, good. I see you have the relevant yearbooks. I've flicked through them myself. It brought back so many happy memories. That's one thing at least."

"Yes, I'm sure they will be useful," Rachael said.

"What can you tell us about the two boys?" Humphries asked.

"I was shocked when I heard about their deaths. I remember them as boisterous schoolboys, running along these corridors without a care in the world and getting into mischief. Matthew, in particular, could be rather cheeky, but it was all good-humoured fun. Alex was a little more reserved and studious. I believe they both applied themselves well enough to go onto university."

"Have you had any contact with them since they left here?"

"No, sadly, neither of them attended any of the school reunions we have each year."

"Any reason why not?"

"I wouldn't know," Stuart replied. "Some do, some don't."

"Did anything happen during their school years that would have kept them away?" Humphries asked.

"No, I've thought back over the years they were pupils here, and I can't think of anything. I do remember that in their final year, we made it to the inter-school rugby finals. Both boys were on the team. I'm sure their achievement would have left a lasting here when it happened, so I don't understand the desperate need to speak to her. She won't be able to say anything more than I've already said to your colleagues."

"We want to know more about his mental health over the past couple of months, and Nicky should be the one who could tell us the most. All we're asking for is a general chat about how Alex had seemed recently and his reaction to her telling him she was leaving."

"I'll tell you what she's told us. The pregnancy wasn't planned, but she found his reaction difficult to deal with. At first, he seemed pleased, but then he became increasingly moody and erratic. He was obsessed with putting things right so he could be a good father. Nicky wasn't aware there was anything wrong with how they were beforehand. His behaviour started to scare her, and she realised she didn't want to be with him."

"Scared her in what way?" Humphries asked.

"She said he was bad-tempered and unpredictable. He wouldn't talk about whatever was going on in his head or even acknowledge there was a problem. She hadn't previously been aware of any mental health issues. They had been kept from her. He tried to kill himself when he was younger. Did you know that?"

"We did," Humphries said.

"Don't you think that was something he should have discussed with my daughter?"

"It would depend on the circumstances. It would be more helpful to speak to your daughter to hear what she has to say in her own words," Humphries said. "Could you ask her to call us?"

"She's upset enough as it is. Why do you need to speak to her as well? I've told you everything."

"Because I do," Humphries snapped at the father's obstinacy.

"But I can answer all your questions."

Suppressing his annoyance, Humphries asked, "Do you know when your daughter told Alex the relationship was over?"

"She'd been trying to break it to him gently for weeks, but he wouldn't listen. Finally, she packed her bags and flew out here, leaving a note for him. That was weeks ago now."

"Thanks. I hope everything goes well with the birth. I wouldn't ask if it wasn't necessary, but I do need to speak to Nicky directly. I will ring again in a few days. Meanwhile, could you at least tell her I rang?"

"I'll discuss the matter with my wife when she comes home from the hospital."

Calling Fiona's number, Humphries said to Rachael, "At least I tried to get something new for her."

Rachael had been flicking through the yearbooks while Humphries was speaking to Mr Perez. She looked up and said, "Guess who used to train the rugby team."

"Enlighten me."

"Patrick Burke. As in the headmaster who claimed he barely knew the boys."

CHAPTER ELEVEN

Fiona drove to Roger and Eve Woodchester's house, feeling she had been manipulated. She wasn't sure how, only that she was making the visit she absolutely didn't want to make. The only plus she could think of was that it was a beautiful, sunny day to be out in the countryside.

The gates they had driven past before were open, presumably in anticipation of her visit, so she turned from the lane to the gravelled driveway. Meadow Brook House was a rambling red brick house hidden behind a well-stocked front garden. Eve opened the front door and stepped outside to greet Fiona as she was parking the car.

Fiona took her time to gather her thoughts before stepping out of her car, knowing she had nothing new to say to the woman who had been eagerly awaiting her arrival. Eve was tall and willowy, looking elegant and relaxed in her flowing summer dress, with a poise and confidence born of wealth. The practice of upper-class girls walking around with books on their heads might seem funny and frivolous, but in Eve's case, they seemed to have served their purpose. She had a commanding presence without moving a muscle. Framed by her country residence behind her, she greeted Fiona warmly, although her practised smile couldn't deny her red, swollen eyes.

Fiona was graciously ushered into a drawing room overlooking the rear garden. The bay window was dominated by a grand piano, gleaming in the sunlight. On the low table between the sofas, a teapot along with fancy cups and saucers and an array of dainty snacks had been artfully arranged next to a vase of freshly cut flowers.

"Please sit down and help yourself. I'll go and hurry my husband along. I do apologise for his tardiness," Eve said, and with a whoosh of her billowing dress she was gone.

Fiona admired the landscape paintings lining the walls before sitting and pouring herself a cup of tea. She had taken her first sip when the double doors from the hallway opened, and Eve walked in, followed by her husband dressed casually in baggy shorts and a sweatshirt. Roger was shorter and stockier than Eve, with a mop of unruly white hair. Eve sat on the opposing sofa with her ankles and knees together, smoothed out her dress and rested her hands in her lap, while Roger took up a standing position with his back to the fireplace. With his hands clasped behind his back, he asked in a nasal, upper-class voice, "So what do you think?"

"Firstly, can I say how sorry I am about your son's death," Fiona said.

"I knew it! You're all going to stick together with the same story," Eve said, jumping to her feet and standing beside her husband. Staring down her aquiline nose, she clearly enunciated, "Alex did not commit suicide."

Fiona lowered her cup and saucer to the table, and said, "After reading the initial report and visiting the scene, it's easy to see how that conclusion has been made."

Roger rocked up and down on his toes. "The easiest option. That's what it all comes down to these days in public service. Whatever happened to British standards?"

"Why won't people listen to us?" Eve asked. "Ian said new information had come to light, and he was putting his top officers on it. We had hoped you would thoroughly investigate the matter, not do a hatchet job like the others."

Silently cursing Dewhurst, Fiona said, "Why don't you both come and sit down and explain to me why you are so adamant that Alex didn't take his own life?"

After a moment's hesitation, Eve dragged her husband to the sofa, and they sat. "He just wouldn't. Not now. He was settled at work, had a lovely home, and his partner is expecting their first child. It's simply inconceivable. We saw him only the day before, and he was excitedly talking about the future. He planned to build a treehouse in their garden to surprise Nicky when she arrived home. The wood he ordered arrived yesterday."

"We understand his partner, Nicky, is in Spain with her family," Fiona said. "There's some question about whether she intends to return."

"Because of what's happened, she has decided to stay longer with her parents," Eve said. "Quite understandable, of course. At a time like this, everyone wants to be with their family. I expect she'll return for the funeral."

"Although we haven't spoken directly to Nicky, her father has told us she has no intention of returning," Fiona said, failing to think of a tactful way to approach their denial of the failed relationship. "She possibly made that decision before leaving."

"I wouldn't read too much into what her father is saying," Eve said. "Nicky has a fiery, Mediterranean temperament. She was always saying rash things she didn't mean, even before she fell pregnant. Expecting a first child is always an emotional roller coaster ride full of worries and doubts. I remember my mood swings in the weeks leading up to Alex's birth."

"Do you know when the baby is due?" Fiona asked.

"Yes, in a couple of weeks," Eve said. "They had all the scans, so we know it's a little boy. I'm wondering now if her doctors will advise her to stay in Spain until after the birth, so she'll miss the funeral. That would be a terrible shame, but I'm sure we'll see our little grandson soon enough."

Thinking Eve was kidding herself on several fronts and silently cursing Dewhurst, Fiona asked, "Does Nicky have British citizenship?"

"It was something they were looking into," Eve said. "Why? Is it important?"

"Possibly, yes," Fiona said. "Was Nicky in employment here?"

"She used to teach Spanish at the local school, but she gave that up a while back," Eve said. "She wanted to stay home with the new baby."

"Did they discuss marriage?"

"People don't bother with all that these days," Eve said.

"They do when there's a potential problem with nationality," Fiona said, frustrated by their denial of the situation.

"They considered themselves to be married. They lived together and were looking forward to the birth of their first child." Eve stifled a sob. "Our grandchild. There won't be a chance of another, now."

"There, there, now," Roger said, patting Eve's back. "No need to go getting yourself upset again. Maybe we could take a trip to Spain to see Nicky and the baby? Something for you to look forward to."

"Could we?" Eve asked, wiping her tears with a tissue.

"Of course," Roger said. "We could look at flights this evening."

As Eve brightened at the prospect of the trip, Fiona carefully said, "We understand Alex had tried to take his life before. When he was in his late teens."

"That was all dealt with, and it's why I know Alex would never put us through this," Eve said. "He simply wouldn't. And certainly not now. He knew the value of life and understood the devastation a sudden death leaves behind for loved ones."

"Could you explain what you mean by that?"

"Why can't you accept what we say?" Eve asked, dialling her agitation up a notch. "We're his parents, and we knew him best."

"I'm sorry, but we'll need something more than that."

Eve and Roger looked at each other before Roger said, "I know how much the memories hurt you. Perhaps we could have a word outside? As this young lady has come all this way to speak to us, we should consider talking about it." Roger carefully said. "If we tell her everything, maybe then she'll take us seriously."

"That would be helpful," Fiona said.

Eve stood and seemed to take up more space in the centre of the room than her size allowed. Finally, she said, "You tell them, Roger. I'll wait in the lounge."

CHAPTER TWELVE

After escorting Eve from the room, Roger retook his position in front of the fire with his hands clasped behind his back. "I don't think parents ever get over it, you see. The recriminations. The feelings of failure when your child tries to take his life. I have been thinking of reaching out to John as someone who would understand. If he were a stronger man, I think I would. But I think my wife is correct about Alex. He saw what it did to everyone. He wouldn't put us through it."

"Can you backtrack a moment?" Fiona asked. "Who is John?"

"It's the tenth anniversary, you see," Roger said. "We only realised afterwards."

"Anniversary of what?" Fiona asked, wondering if he was trying to confuse her on purpose. Maybe, like his stance in front of the fireplace, it made him feel superior. "If you have evidence that would alter our view of the situation, we need to hear it. Clearly and concisely from the start. No starting in the middle and disappearing off on tangents. Okay?"

"Ten years ago, one of Alex's classmates killed herself by jumping from the same barn. It was a dreadful time. Alex had known her since primary school, and they were in the same group of friends. Alex was devastated. After it happened, he cut himself off from all his friends and barely left his bedroom. Eve was already beside herself with worry and self-blame, when out of understandable teenage angst, he overdosed. It was a cry for help rather than a serious suicide attempt, and we arranged the best counselling available for him. By the end of the summer, he was back to his old self, and he left for university as planned. He never repeated his mistake, and we agreed never to speak about that terrible, dark time ever again."

"I understand what you're saying, but depression is a strange creature. It creeps up when you least expect it and affects how you think and ..."

"Alex wasn't suffering from depression. Not now and not then. He was but a child desperately upset by his friend's death and struggling to come to terms with the complexities of adult life and mortality. As my wife has already pointed out, the experience taught him how precious life is and how devastating it is for those left behind. That's why we are so sure he would never choose to take his own life. Do you see?"

Rather than answer, as she knew the suicide risk was raised in the family and friends of people who had taken their own life, Fiona asked, "Do you know the name of the friend?"

"Of course. It was Jenny Trace. Her sister and father still live locally," Roger said. "John, that's who I was referring to earlier. He's a ghost of the man he once was, but at least he stayed and tried to pick up the pieces for Chloe."

"Chloe?"

"Jenny's younger sister. She was far too young to understand when it happened. She's grown into a pretty, young lady. We see her from time to time helping her father out on the farm."

"And the mother?"

"Her," Roger said as if it was a bad taste in his mouth. "She wasn't our type of person if you know what I mean.

"Not really, but carry on," Fiona said, although she had a good idea what he meant by the comment. "What happened to her?"

"She couldn't cope. When trouble hit, it didn't take her long to find a new cash source," Roger said, wrinkling his nose in disgust. "Not long after her daughter's death, she upped and left with her new man. Last I heard, she's living in London somewhere. Never visits her daughter. One doesn't like to judge, but to abandon your own child is unnatural."

"What was her first name, and how would I contact her?"

"Jade," Roger said. "As to how to contact her, I wouldn't have a clue. My understanding is neither does John."

"Do you have the names of Alex's friends when he was at school?"

"I can give them to you, but after that summer, Alex dropped all contact with them. I think Mathew and Paula still live locally, but I've no idea where or what they do. He was friendly with Hugh for a while, but his parents have moved away. I also remember the names Jamie and Kate, but they could be living anywhere. I'm not sure how much they could help you. We're the ones who cared for Alex. I knew my son, and I agree with my wife. Alex did not kill himself. Of that, I'm absolutely sure. I would stake my life on it."

"You gave the name, Matthew? Do you mean Matthew Guppy?"

"Yes. We saw him in Waitrose a few months ago," Roger said. "He was in a rush to be somewhere, so we never had the chance to chat. That's young people all over nowadays. Rushing about. I suppose we were the same once."

"Did Alex ever talk to you about Matthew?"

"No, and we didn't mention seeing Matthew to him for fear of stirring it all up again."

"What do you mean, stir it all up again?" Fiona asked.

"The young girl's suicide, of course. We all found it very upsetting."

"Would it be fair to say your son never got over his classmate's suicide?"

"Of course, he did," Roger said. "We put that dreadful business behind us years ago, and he moved on."

Roger's stiff demeanour indicated he had been brought up to believe blanking things out and avoiding any reference equated to moving on, so Fiona saw little to be gained by labouring the point. Alex's parents seemed oblivious that much of what they had said supported the verdict of suicide. Keeping a stiff upper lip had worked for generations, so why not now? There again, if current thinking was correct, there should be a tsunami of suicides in the upper classes, yet there wasn't, so who was she to say differently? Instead, she asked, "Did you know Alex visited

Matthew shortly before his death?"

"No, I didn't," Roger replied. "That's another good indicator of his positive state of mind, surely?"

"Why do you think Alex contacted him after ten years? Was there unfinished business to discuss?" Fiona asked.

"I can only think he wanted to rekindle an old friendship. Maybe Matthew recently moved back to the area? I don't know if that's true, but you could check."

"He doesn't live locally, but I believe he's lived in his current address for some time," Fiona said. "What do you think Alex was doing up on the barn roof in the middle of the night?"

"We've no idea, but I don't think he went there willingly," Roger replied.

"Alex was a fit young man who regularly visited the gym. There was no sign of a struggle anywhere near the barn or strong drugs in his system, so we think it unlikely he was forced to go up there," Fiona said. Roger probably already knew these details, but she hoped in time, he would start to accept the situation and start the process of healing. She hadn't wanted to call on the family, but now that she was here, she could at least insert some doubt into their way of thinking.

"The fact remains that he didn't kill himself," Roger said stubbornly.

"Did Alex have any enemies? Someone strong enough to coerce him to climb onto the roof?"

"No, there was no one like that. Our son was a thoughtful, caring young man. A son to be proud of, and everyone liked him. I can only think someone felt jealous of him. You have to find out who took our Alex out there and killed him," Roger said. "If you don't, we will hire someone more capable."

"Do you think it possible that Alex climbed onto the barn roof to remember his old friend and fell accidentally?" Fiona asked.

"No. Alex would drive miles out of his way to avoid driving past that barn. He had sessions with his counsellor, but he couldn't go near the place without having a panic attack," Roger said. "It's the last place on earth he would go. Somebody forced him to go out there. Maybe someone saw who it was and could describe them."

"Nobody has reported seeing anything. It's a very isolated spot," Fiona said, aware that no one had been asked.

"Please find out who murdered our son."

Roger's eyes were pleading, but Fiona wasn't going to give him fresh hope, that wouldn't help in the long term. "I'm sorry, Mr Woodchester, but all the evidence suggests your son took his own life, possibly by misadventure. Either way, there is nothing to suggest anyone else was involved."

"Now you know about Jenny, surely you don't still think it was suicide?"

"Thank you for providing this new information," Fiona said, preparing to leave. "I will make more enquiries, but the official conclusion will likely remain the same. Please don't get your hopes up. I'll see myself out."

CHAPTER THIRTEEN

Fiona pulled over to make a couple of calls before returning to the station. The first was to Humphries to have a rant about the headmaster and form teacher at Berkhampstead School for not mentioning Jenny Trace's suicide. Next, she called Alex's counsellor. After consulting his notes, he confirmed they had made several aborted attempts to visit the barn, and each one had resulted in a panic attack, but the attempts had been ten years ago. No follow-up appointments had been made in recent years.

Humphries came over as soon as Fiona walked towards her desk. "Sorry, the headmaster and form teacher flatly denied anything untoward had happened. We specifically asked them, and they denied it. Do you want me to go back for a revisit?"

"Leave it for now."

"I want to know why they lied," Humphries said. "They could be hiding something."

"It was probably to protect the school's reputation in case it scared away prospective parents," Fiona said. "But more importantly, despite this new evidence, I haven't seen anything that makes me question the original conclusions. I didn't have the heart to point out that the suicide rate of family and close friends of suicide victims is higher than the general population. If anything, everything they said supports the original conclusion."

"So that's it? We drop it?" Humphries asked. "Matthew's wife has been on the phone asking for an update, and Dewhurst has arranged for the case to be transferred."

"For completeness, I've spoken to Alex's psychiatrist and

am about to read through the file on Jenny Trace," Fiona said. "Rather than waste more time on Dewhurst's whim, can you concentrate on the burglaries? Do you know if everyone regularly involved in the Golden Mischief group outings has been seen?"

"I think Eddie and Andrew are contacting the last few volunteers this afternoon," Humphries replied.

"Okay, we'll hear what they have to say when they get back," Fiona said. "I have a favour to ask."

"Go on," Humphries said suspiciously.

"You remember I told Rose Bulmer a couple of officers would attend the next Golden Mischief event? I've promised to take my mother out for a meal. Could you go in my place?"

"If I must," Humphries said without any enthusiasm. "But you owe me one."

"Thanks. Let's go over and speak to Abbie," Fiona said, dragging a reluctant Humphries behind her. Her relationship with Abbie was often tricky, and opportunities to be positive were rare. "Hi, Abbie. Humphries has told me you've nearly interviewed all the Golden Mischief volunteers. That was quick. Anything useful?"

"So far, they have all checked out," Abbie said. "On requestioning, we've discovered three earlier victims attended the lunches organised at the Carpenters. They didn't mention it before because it was some time ago."

"Those lunches are the closest thing we have to a connection," Fiona said. "Can we double-check the pub staff's backgrounds, and their car registration numbers against the street footage we have of some of the burglaries?"

"Rachael is already doing that," Abbie said. "I've been concentrating on the group itself. While only three have attended the lunches, nearly all the victims have had some contact with the group."

"Have any volunteer helpers been especially attentive to the victims?" Fiona asked.

"A few names have come up, but not with any consistency."

"It's still worth re-interviewing them. Humphries could make a start on that."

Humphries pulled a face, saying, "Or I could make a start on tracing Alex's old school friends from the yearbook."

Abbie looked between Humphries and Fiona, before saying, "There's only a couple of names, and taken in context, their actions seem reasonable. I can probably speak to them. Humphries could help Rachael with running car registrations through the system."

Knowing which Humphries would prefer to do, Fiona said, "When I spoke to Rose Bulmer, we agreed to send a couple of officers along to the next Golden Mischief event to advise about home security and give general reassurance. It will be a good opportunity to observe and chat in a more relaxed setting. I'm not able to attend, but Humphries is, so it would be useful for him to have had some previous contact with some of the volunteers."

"What evening is it?" Abbie asked.

"Thursday at the White Horse."

"I'm booked off that evening," Abbie said. "Okay, Humphries, when Eddie and Andrew return, we'll decide which volunteers warrant a closer look."

"I'll leave you to decide who you want to take with you to the meeting," Fiona said to Humphries. "I'm going to read through those files now."

Humphries followed Fiona back to her desk. "I do think these suicides need a thorough investigation."

"Okay, your feelings have been noted," Fiona said. "I'll let you know what I think after I've read the report on Jenny Trace."

CHAPTER FOURTEEN

After dismissing Humphries, Fiona pulled up everything she could find on Jenny's death. She had been discovered missing in the late morning by her parents, and her body was found by the stone barn a few hours later. Her death was recorded as suicide due to disappointment with her A-Level results and a breakup with her boyfriend.

The names of her friends interviewed coincided with the names given by Alex's father. Alex and Matthew had been told of her death and interviewed at the home of Hugh Dolan the following day. The three boys had hangovers following a celebration of their A-Level results. They said they hadn't seen Jenny since they collected their exam results three days earlier. Matthew said he had hugged her to cheer her up as she was disappointed with her grades. Two girls and another boy interviewed separately, had said similar things. Fiona noted Alex had been planning to study politics and economics at university, so she wondered how he had ended up working with troubled children.

She couldn't help but think the investigation into the girl's death was weak. In her opinion, the officers were far too quick to decide she had taken her life while alone. They had taken brief statements from her friends without questioning anything they said. Maybe they had all been telling the truth, but nobody had considered the possibility that Jenny wasn't by herself that evening. It wasn't unreasonable to think the three boys alone in a house full of booze a short distance away wouldn't invite their friends over. Someone should have asked the question.

Fiona put the file aside to think the possibility through. Was it possible that something had happened the evening of Jenny's death that haunted Alex and Matthew so much that they took their own lives ten years later? Could that be what caused the rift in the friendship and what Alex wanted to talk to Matthew about? If they had a hand in Jenny's death, it would explain Alex's reclusive behaviour during that summer.

She recalled how guilty she felt and still did about Peter's attempt. She knew firsthand how devastating it was to think you had failed as a friend. The horrid sense that she could have done something to prevent it was crippling.

Whatever she thought of the investigation into Jenny's death, that wasn't the issue. Her focus was the two recent deaths and whether there was anything to warrant a second investigation. The combination of his pregnant partner leaving him and the anniversary of a school friend's death could easily explain Alex's suicide. But Matthew had no history of poor mental health, had a happy family life and was planning a family trip to Disneyland. He had no financial worries and a promising career.

The timing of Alex's visit suggested the tenth anniversary was a topic of conversation. What could Alex have told Matthew that would trump all the positives in his life and turn his thoughts to suicide? It could only have been something major. Fiona's mind kept circling the same question. Were the boys up on the roof with Jenny ten years ago, and were they responsible for her falling? And if they were, why wait ten years to kill themselves in a fit of remorse?

If they were responsible for Jenny's death and her father found out, how would he react? Would he be determined to avenge his daughter? How could he have persuaded Alex to jump off the same roof and Matthew to shoot himself? The forensic evidence was clear that they had taken their own lives, but little had been done to establish whether they were alone at the time. That was also her complaint about the investigation of Jenny's death. Humphries buzzing around the suicides like an angry hornet might just have a point, but she didn't want to rush her decision.

Humphries decided that moment to stroll over. "Anything

relevant?"

"Possibly, I'm still going through the evidence. Aren't you supposed to be with Abbie speaking to the Golden Mischief volunteers?"

"I was, but Abbie decided to do them with Andrew," Humphries said. "So, come on. What have you found?"

"The tenth anniversary of the school friend's death is coming up." Sighing, Fiona said, "Such a waste when she had years of opportunity ahead of her."

"You must remember your late teens," Humphries said. "It doesn't seem that way then. One mistake and your entire life is ruined. The pressure to do well in exams is ridiculous. What investigations were made at the time?"

"They weren't great."

"Come on. What did they find?"

"Jenny had high levels of alcohol in her system along with traces of cannabis. Alex and Matthew were interviewed at a friend's house the following day. The friend's parents had been away, and they had been celebrating their exam success. Despite the house being within a mile of the barn and Jenny's home, no follow-up investigations were made. The boys said they were alone, but as far as I can see, no one asked the obvious question. Had Jenny been invited to their celebration, and had she been there earlier in the evening?"

"Surely someone put the question to them? Or was there something to suggest there had been an earlier disagreement, and she had been excluded? Otherwise, why wouldn't they invite a neighbour and friend?"

"I agree, but the officers believed the boys' account of how they had spent the evening without question," Fiona said. "They accepted the three boys had been alone, taking advantage of an adult-free house and a fridge full of beer and had never left the house. More importantly, they decided Jenny was alone on the roof."

"Do you think the boys met up with Jenny Trace that evening and were involved in her death?"

"According to the file notes, no one considered that possibility at the time. One person who would know is the third boy, Hugh Dolan," Fiona said.

Humphries looked down at the file. "If they accepted the boys' account without question, what did they investigate?"

"They concentrated on the family and Jenny's state of mind. How upset she was by a recent breakup with her boyfriend, and devastated that she wouldn't be able to go to her first choice of university. Earlier in the evening, her parents had a long talk with her about her options, and she went to bed early to think things over."

"Is there an explanation for the delay in the police talking to the boys?"

"The police weren't even contacted until midday on the day of her death," Fiona said. "Jenny's parents didn't hear her leave the house, and the alarm wasn't raised until late morning when her mother went up to check on her. They called on her friends and neighbours to arrange a search before the police were contacted. It was her father who found her."

"Did they ask Alex and Matthew to join the search party?"

"They rang Hugh's house, but no one answered," Fiona said. "The boys claimed they were there but were too drunk and hungover to hear anything."

"Does Jenny's family still own the barn?" Humphries asked.

"Yes."

"I'm surprised they didn't bulldoze it afterwards rather than continue to use it for storage. He's a farmer, I take it?"

"Sheep farmer, although according to Alex's father, he's become a shadow of a man since his daughter's death. It's more of a hobby to keep him going than a commercial concern."

"Okay," Humphries replied. "We should find out where Jenny's father was on the evenings of the two deaths."

"Whoa," Fiona said. "I need to think this through carefully before making a final decision. I agree there has been an insufficient investigation into whether all three - Jenny, Alex and Matthew - were alone when they died. But, right now, we have no evidence of foul play in the deaths, let alone anything to suggest the involvement of a grieving father in the two recent ones. Until I decide, I want you to focus on the burglaries. I really think we're closing in on the culprits, and I don't want this opportunity missed."

"But ..."

Fiona continued over Humphries, "I know you haven't always considered the matter as important as you could, but it's having a far-reaching effect on the community, and I want to see them stopped."

"Abbie and the others are working on them full-time and getting nowhere. There's nothing new to investigate. All I'll be doing is going over old ground and getting in their way. If I discover something did happen the night of Jenny's death, we could at least give the Woodchester and Guppy families an explanation. If there's another burglary, I'll be right on it with my undivided attention."

"Have you spoken to Rose about attending their next meeting?"

"Yes. Andrew has agreed to come with me, which is why Abbie has given the follow-up interviews to him, which leaves me twiddling my thumbs until later."

"I'm sure there's something more you could be doing. How about helping Rachael?"

"She's nearly finished checking all the car registration numbers and didn't want me messing up her system," Humphries said. "The attitude I'm getting from Abbie is that she has it all in hand, and I'm getting in her way."

"I'll speak to Abbie later about that," Fiona said.

"While I could be investigating two murders. We can't drop the investigation now you've identified the errors."

"I'm not saying we drop the investigation into the *suicides*, only that we tread carefully," Fiona said. "We're potentially reopening old wounds and questioning the thoroughness of fellow officers' work. I'm going to contact the crime scene teams and talk through their findings. They might remember details about the scenes that didn't go into the final reports. Meanwhile, once the car registration number checks have been completed, you can contact Hugh. If he lives locally, you can take Rachael with you. But you report back to me before taking things any further. Okay?"

"Yes," Humphries said. "Will we bring in Jenny's father if we find they didn't die alone?"

"We'll talk about our next steps after you've spoken to Hugh," Fiona said. "And if we don't find anything to suggest the suicides were coerced, I want your full concentration back on the burglaries. Understood?"

"Message received loud and clear," Humphries replied with a mock salute.

CHAPTER FIFTEEN

Humphries returned to his desk feeling pleased with himself. He enjoyed working alongside Fiona, especially needling her with his political views, although he had backed off recently as she was struggling to come to terms with Peter's departure. Or maybe her stressed look was due to the increased pressure Dewhurst was putting on her. He would prefer her as the new DCI rather than some outsider being dumped on them, and he hoped they would hurry up and advertise the position. If Fiona successfully applied, it would allow him to move up to being a DI, which would please Tina no end.

He liked the idea of having Rachael as his junior assistant. She was smart and easy to get along with. Having put her career on hold to start a family, she was several years older than Fiona but was fun and enthusiastic. And unlike some people, Abbie in particular, she respected his experience.

His enthusiasm quickly turned to frustration when his calls to Hugh went unanswered. Seeing that Fiona wasn't at her desk, he looked through the school yearbooks while waiting for Hugh to return his call. He made a list of classmates who shared interests with Alex and Matthew and, after a furtive look around the office, called them. The only one who answered was Paula Davidson.

"Oh, right. Yes, I went to school with Alex and Matthew but haven't spoken to them in years."

"I would like to ask you a few questions. Is now a good time?"

"Umm ... yes, why not? Bear with me while I turn the cooker down and check what my children are up to."

Humphries drummed his fingers on the desk while he listened

to Paula settling a squabble between the complaining children and asking them to stay quiet until she finished her important telephone call. He wished she would hurry up as he was cutting it fine to spend a few hours at home before picking up Andrew to go to the Golden Mischief meeting.

Paula returned to the line. "Sorry about that. I kept them home from school today as they were sick last night, but they seem to have made a miraculous recovery. Who did you say you were?"

"DI Humphries. We're looking into the recent deaths of Alex Woodchester and Matthew Guppy. I understand you knew them."

"I only know them from when we were at school together. We were a tight group for a while as we were the only kids in the area who didn't attend the local comprehensive. We all travelled on the same coach to and from school. I guess we didn't have much else in common other than that. Alex and Matthew became distant as soon as they left for university. I tried to arrange some get-togethers during the holidays, but they never came to anything."

"Have you been in contact with either of them since then?"

"I rang Alex when he moved back to the area a few years ago, but he never returned my call," Paula said. "I saw Matthew a few years ago, but he blanked me. I assumed he was in the area visiting his family."

"How about your other school friends?"

"As far as I know, Alex and Hugh were the only two still living in the area. I always found Hugh difficult to get along with. He was always a bit of a loner with a superiority complex, and we didn't stay in contact."

Humphries checked the open school yearbook, and asked, "How about James and Kate?"

"I'm not sure where they are. I might have telephone numbers for them somewhere, but they could be out of date. If I can find them, would you like me to call them?"

"I would prefer it if you gave me the numbers," Humphries said, before asking, "What can you tell me about the night Jenny Trace died?"

After a long silence, Paula said, "Next to nothing. I hardly knew her."

"But you were part of the same friendship group and travelled on the bus together?"

"No, she didn't catch the bus. Her father used to drive her in and out of school."

"Did he ever give anyone else lifts?"

"Occasionally, Alex and Hugh, as they lived so close and were the same age," Paula said. "I lived a little further away and was never asked."

"You must remember something about the night Jenny died."

"Not really. The police spoke to me afterwards, but I couldn't tell them anything as I was at home in bed that night. All I remember is how sad it was, and it's not something I choose to think about." There was a sound of crashing in the background. "Sorry, I'm going to have to go to sort the children out."

"Okay. Don't forget to send me those telephone numbers. We might have to talk again."

CHAPTER SIXTEEN

After updating Fiona on the Golden Mischief meeting the following morning, Humphries returned to his desk to keep trying Hugh's telephone number. Attending the meeting had been a waste of time, in his opinion. How many criminal minds attended flower-arranging demonstrations? To be fair, most attendees had been more interested in asking him and Andrew about how they could improve their security than deciding where to stick their chrysanthemums. At the end of the meeting, over soggy cheese and onion sandwiches and weak tea, they had talked with all the carers present and couldn't imagine any of them being responsible for the break-ins.

Humphries was annoyed that Hugh still wasn't answering his home or mobile phone. He had a recent address for Hugh, but driving out there would be a waste of time if he wasn't home. Having persuaded Fiona there was something worth investigating, he didn't want to stall things waiting for him to return from wherever he was. Drumming his fingers on the yearbook, Humphries eyed the computer files on Alex and Matthew. He made a split-second decision to open the file on Alex and called his employers to arrange a meeting.

He jumped, feeling guilty when Rachael appeared out of nowhere. Closing his computer screen and sliding the yearbook under a pile of paperwork, he asked, "Anything new on the burglaries?"

"Possibly. A car belonging to the son of one of the volunteers has popped up twice," Rachael said. "Abbie isn't in today. Do you know where Fiona is?"

"No, she's been gone about an hour, but she'll want to know

about that straight away. Ring her with the details, and then we're going out on another matter."

"Which is?"

"We're going to speak to Alex's employers and then track down his old school friend, Hugh Dolan. He's not returning my calls, but I have an address for him."

"When did Fiona give the go-ahead for us to continue investigating the two suicides?" Rachael asked. "You might have told me sooner. I'm committed to working on the burglaries with Abbie."

"Well, you'll have to uncommit yourself. Fiona specifically said you should come with me to interview Hugh."

"And Alex's employers?"

"I'll explain on the way once you've told Fiona about the car," Humphries said. "Whose car was it, anyway?"

"It belongs to Ian Marsh."

"I spoke to his parents with Andrew last night. Well, his father, anyway. He seemed a decent chap. A bit boring if anything, but totally devoted to his wife," Humphries said. "Have you told Andrew? He knows the family background, so should be involved in talking to the son."

"Was his wife not there?"

"She was, but she has advanced dementia."

"Maybe that's why the son is doing it," Rachael said. "Everyone's attention is on his mother, and he feels left out."

"Oh, diddums," Humphries said. "Are we really breeding a generation of kids that are that self-absorbed and entitled?"

CHAPTER SEVENTEEN

Fiona was walking across the station car park with Eddie and Andrew when Rachael rang to tell her about the car registration number. "Good work. Have you an address and a place of work?" she asked, grabbing a pen and notepad from her bag. After thanking Rachael again, she told Eddie and Andrew, "We might have something. Ian Marsh's car was parked in the adjacent street during two of the burglaries. Did either of you interview his father, Ken Marsh?"

"Yes, I did at his home," Eddie said. "A quiet, polite guy. His wife has advanced early-onset dementia. I couldn't imagine him being involved. He was the sort who wouldn't say boo to a goose and has given up everything to care for his wife around the clock."

"I spoke to him last night," Andrew said. "Eddie's assessment is about right."

"And I bumped into him at the hospital visiting one of the victims," Fiona said. "He was very keen to offer his help. Wanting to feel involved and needed could be a warped motive. Have either of you met his son?"

"No," Eddie said, his face creasing into a frown as he recalled his earlier conversation. "I wasn't aware they had one. There was nothing to suggest anyone else lived at the house."

"Do you want to come with me to find out? He's a student at the university, and I have an address in Fishponds."

"Sure," Eddie said. "He doesn't live with his parents, then. They live in Sapperton."

"I'll see what I can discover about the family background and will pass on anything relevant," Andrew said, starting to walk into the station.

"Check whether Ken Marsh has visited other victims to offer his help," Fiona said, before turning towards where she parked her car.

As they negotiated the heavy traffic into Fishponds, Fiona asked Eddie what he remembered about his conversation with Ian's parents.

"His wife, Sheila, couldn't join in the conversation, although Ken seemed to understand what she was mumbling. He came across as a compassionate guy and devoted to her. Several other people have mentioned what a gem he is. Always willing to give a helping hand where needed."

"We've always thought that as nothing of value was ever taken from the houses, there was probably an obscure motive for the burglaries. An overwhelming desire to feel useful would fit the bill. The knight in shiny armour who sweeps in to become indispensable afterwards. It could be warped altruism, or there may be a plan for control and financial gain sometime along the line."

"Using his son's car to stay anonymous isn't the brightest of moves," Eddie said.

"Who says he's bright? Or it could be the son is responsible, and his father is so wrapped up in caring for his wife that he doesn't know what he is up to," Fiona said. "Ken could have been giving his son information about vulnerable people living in the area without realising how he was using it."

"I suppose, but it seems strange that such a lovely, caring man would have such a rotten son."

"Genes don't account for everything," Fiona replied, parallel parking. Looking along the street, she checked her notepad where she had scribbled down the car registration and said, "There's his car, but this street looks more residential than student accommodation."

"I think students grab whatever they can afford," Eddie replied.

"Exactly," Fiona said, looking along the row of neat, terraced houses with tidy front gardens. "This looks like a well-cared-for, settled community."

Before they left the car, Andrew rang to say there was no record of Ian Marsh being in trouble with the police. They walked through a short garden and knocked on a recently painted front door. A sleepy-looking teenager in her school uniform opened the door. When Fiona explained who they were, her eyes shot wide, and she disappeared inside. "Mum. The police are out here wanting to see Ian."

"What on earth?" was followed by hurried footsteps. The door was opened wider by a worried-looking woman dressed smartly in a skirt and blouse. "I've just returned home from work to pick my daughter up from school because she was feeling ill. What else can possibly go wrong today? Why do you want to see Ian? He's not in any trouble, is he?"

"Can we come in, Mrs ...?"

"Sophie Francis. What's this about?"

"Does Ian Marsh live here?"

"Yes, my son. The children kept their father's name."

"Is Ian here now?"

"You'd better come in," Sophie said, stepping back to let them pass. "Lucy! Go and get your brother, and then get yourself to bed. He's probably got his headphones on, so you'll have to go in." As her daughter charged up the stairs, she led Fiona and Eddie through the kitchen to a small dining area overlooking a well-tended back garden.

They had settled around the table when a good-looking young man joined them. Wearing ripped jeans and a t-shirt, with a halo of curly brown hair, he stood at the entrance looking dazed and worried. "Lucy told me to come down."

"Come and sit down," Fiona said, already questioning whether she was looking at someone capable of terrorising elderly and infirm people. But then looks can be deceiving, and children often behave very differently away from the family home.

Ian apologetically slid onto a chair and started to chew on a thumb, receiving an immediate rebuke from his mother. "Sit up straight and don't bite your nails." He pulled himself straighter in the chair but continued to look down at the floor.

"Your car has been spotted close to the scene of two crimes," Fiona said. "Can you tell me where you were on the nights of Friday, May 6th and Thursday, May 12th?"

"Not off the top of my head, but I work behind the bar in the local pub most nights, so I was probably there," Ian replied. "I could ring the manager and ask him to check the roster?"

"What time do you finish your shifts there?"

"By the time we've tidied up, I don't leave much before midnight."

"How about later?"

"Later?" Ian asked, looking surprised. "I'm always knackered and come straight home to bed as I have lectures in the morning. Afternoons are when I study before heading off to work."

"I can confirm he always comes straight home after the pub," Sophie said. "I never drop off to sleep until I know he's safely home."

"Do you ever go back out again?"

"No," Ian said, looking surprised by the suggestion. "Why would I do that?"

"I would hear him if he did," Sophie said.

"Do you drive to the pub?"

"Depends on the weather. If it's not raining, I usually walk to save petrol. It's only around the corner," Ian said.

"Do you lend your car to anyone?"

"No, never."

"And that's your car parked outside the front, now?" Fiona asked.

"The blue one, yes. The white one belongs to Mum."

"How often do you see your dad, Ian?"

Looking confused, Ian said, "Every day."

"Rob should be home in about an hour," Sophie said, looking equally perplexed. "Are you saying Rob is in trouble?"

"We're talking about your biological dad, Ken Marsh," Fiona said.

"Oh, right," Ian said. "Well, that's easy. I never see him."

"We don't even know where he lives," Sophie said. "We lost all contact years ago. He left before Lucy was born."

"Have you seen him since then?" Fiona asked Ian.

Ian looked blank, while Sophie answered. "He contacted me once when Ian was still in primary school, saying he wanted to meet him. It was all arranged for us to meet in the park, but he never turned up. We haven't heard from him since."

"Is that right, Ian?" Fiona asked. "You haven't had any contact with your father recently?"

"I wouldn't recognise him if he walked in here now."

Fiona considered Ian. If what he was saying was true, it didn't make sense when they had his car on camera, yet at the same time, his relaxed body language suggested he was being truthful. "Could we go outside to look at your car? And could I take some photographs of it?"

"Sure, I don't see why not," Ian said, pushing himself away from the table. "I'll go and get my keys."

While he was out of the room, Fiona asked Sophie, "How would you feel if Ian was seeing his father?"

"Totally amazed, to be honest. Ian is a good lad who has been brought up to be truthful. He would tell me if something like that was going on," Sophie said. "Plus, like I said, their father has never shown any interest in getting in contact."

"But it wouldn't bother you?"

"I would be annoyed because of how he treated us," Sophie said. "There again, he is their father. I don't see how I could stop them if they wanted to meet up."

Fiona stood as she heard Ian returning from upstairs. "Is it okay if just the two of us go?"

Sophie looked uncomfortable about the prospect but nodded her agreement. Fiona hoped Eddie would continue the conversation about Ken Marsh while they were gone.

Walking out to the car beside Ian, Fiona asked, "What are you studying?"

"Politics and environmental studies," Ian said. "I'm in my final year."

"Any idea what you want to do when you leave?"

"I've applied for several conservation projects but not heard back yet." Ian stopped by the front door of his car. "Do you want to see inside?"

"Please." Fiona poked her head inside the car. Apart from a couple of empty energy drink cans, it was surprisingly clean and clutter-free for a young person's car. On the windscreen above the passenger seat was a large, white, adhesive sticker showing a bird of prey in flight. "Interesting design."

"Thank you. I designed it myself," Ian said. "It's all legal and doesn't impede my vision."

Fiona walked around to the rear of the car. Along the top of the rear window was another sticker claiming, *'One day I will.'* "Will do what?" Fiona asked.

"I don't know yet. I like the concept."

"I would have gone for, 'today I will,'" Fiona said. "Do you mind if I take some photographs?"

"Carry on," Ian said, moving away from the car.

While taking pictures with her phone, Fiona asked, "When did you contact your dad?"

"I haven't. I was telling the truth back there," Ian said. "I remember that planned trip to the park that Mum mentioned. I painted a picture for him the day before in school. I guess he didn't care enough about us to turn up. Rob's my dad now."

Fiona slipped her phone back into her pocket. "Could we take your car away for some tests?"

"That would leave me really stuck, with no way to get to lectures," Ian said. "Why, when I haven't done anything?"

"Or I could arrange for a mobile team to come out. How about that?"

"That would be better."

"I'll make the arrangements now. They'll probably come out this evening. You weren't planning on going anywhere tonight, were you?"

"Other than to work, no, and I can walk there."

"Do you have any enemies?" Fiona asked. "Someone who would

like to see you get into trouble? Because this car was seen in the early hours of the morning at two crime scenes. Possibly more. We're checking now."

"No more than anyone else," Ian said. "Are you sure about the registration number? I would know if someone was using my car without my permission."

"That's it for now, but we'll check your shifts at the pub and your lecture schedule. And could you come into the station tomorrow so we can take your fingerprints for elimination?"

Driving away from the house, Fiona asked Eddie, "Did you ask Sophie about her first marriage?"

"They were both too young and had no money. Ian wasn't planned, but they tried to make the most of it. When she told Ken she was pregnant the second time, he said he couldn't go through it again and left the same day. Apart from that one time when he said he wanted to see the children and didn't arrive, she's not heard from him. He was never violent or aggressive, just immature and uncommitted. She seemed a genuine lady."

"The son seemed to be a good kid as well," Fiona said. "A team is coming out this evening to give the car a more thorough search and take fingerprints. The car has some distinctive stickers. We'll look again at the footage when we get back, but if it's not his car, then someone is using false plates on the same model of car. Which suggests it is someone who knows him."

CHAPTER EIGHTEEN

To stop Rachael from asking questions in the car about why Fiona had agreed to them approaching Alex's employers, Humphries passed his phone to her. "That's Hugh's number. Can you try him again?"

Receiving no reply, Rachael handed the phone back. "He's still not answering. Maybe he's gone away."

"Most people take their phone with them. Try it again in ten minutes."

Taking the phone back and holding it in her lap, Rachael said, "I don't see what difference ten minutes will make. Did you call any of the other school friends?"

Humphries nodded. "All of them, but I only spoke to Paula. She said Jenny's death left a long shadow, and she didn't want to be reminded of it."

"They were very young at the time," Rachael said. "Why did Fiona change her mind? She said to me that there was probably nothing sinister linking the two deaths. The forthcoming anniversary stirred up unresolved emotions, and they took their own lives. In the case of Alex, it might be that he accidentally fell while reminiscing."

"How about his inability to go anywhere near the barn?"

"Fiona said the counsellor helping him with that hasn't seen him for nine years. Her opinion was that all we know is he avoided driving past the area if he could, but that didn't mean he still had panic attacks. With the anniversary coming up, maybe he went up there to prove he could and slipped," Rachael said. "So why did she change her mind about us continuing the investigation?"

"I told you. After reading through the file on Jenny Trace, she realised all three investigations had one major error. It was assumed that all three died alone, and there were no detailed examinations of the surrounding areas to check that assumption was correct."

"Yes, and I understand why we are going to speak to Hugh about his whereabouts the night Jenny died, but how can talking to Alex's work colleagues help us to discover whether he died alone?"

"Why don't you try Hugh's number again?" Humphries suggested. When Rachael hit redial, he said, "Alex's employers are waiting for us. After we've spoken to them, we'll go straight to the address we have for Hugh."

The school where Alex had worked was on a quiet no-through road on the outskirts of Birstall. Mature trees blocked the sounds of heavy traffic on the main ring road, and the narrow entrance lane and green fields created an oasis of calm away from the city bustle. It was almost possible to forget they were only a short distance away from one of the most deprived suburbs of Birstall. The lingering illusion was shattered by the padlocked metal gates and the metal detector they were ushered through.

Alex's manager greeted them and took them through to her office. "We were all devastated by the news and will give you every assistance we can. It came as quite a shock. Alex was a popular team member and will be sorely missed by colleagues and students. Can I get either of you something to drink?"

"We're fine, thank you," Humphries said. "You say it was a shock. With the benefit of hindsight, had you noticed anything about his recent behaviour?"

"No, nothing at all. This job has its fair share of mental health pressures, and looking out for the signs of any potential problems is something we are very alert to. Alex is the last person I would have expected to be suffering with depression. He was always so positive and driven."

"Could you explain Alex's role?" Humphries asked. "I don't know what a transitions manager is."

"Our role is to place and support statemented special needs children across the region. Although we share the site with the school, we're a separate organisation. Alex would oversee transitions from mainstream education to SEN education and then the transitions into either higher education or social services care. He also was involved in transitions from education to palliative care. A varied role that requires many different hats but always compassion and empathy."

"I imagine that can be very challenging at times," Rachael said.

"For sure. Sometimes, it's like banging our heads against a wall, and the funding provided is always insufficient. And still, they expect us to make cuts every year. We're operating on a shoestring budget as it is. Because we're always up against it, we work as a tight team and provide staff support whenever it's needed."

"Did Alex ever request support services?" Rachael asked.

"No, never, but he has supported other team members numerous times. Everyone was in tears when we first heard and couldn't believe it. He was always so cheery and resilient."

"And that was the case for the last few weeks before …?" Rachael asked.

"As far as I know, yes."

"As Alex went to university to study politics and economics, this seems a strange career choice," Humphries said,

"I understand he changed his course halfway through to psychology and economics, and he more than proved his dedication over the last three years working with us. Whether we like it or not, we all have to work within financial constraints and constantly look at the bottom line. Alex demonstrated the financial benefits of making substantial early interventions in children's education in a way no one else could. The money crunchers were happy, and the children's life choices were transformed. A win-win situation for everyone."

"Can we talk to his colleagues?" Humphries asked.

"Of course. We all want to help. Follow me."

Humphries and Rachael spoke to Alex's colleagues in an open-plan office a short distance along the corridor. Often close to tears, they gushed about the kindest, most generous and competent man you could ever hope to meet. They all insisted there was nothing in his behaviour to suggest he was depressed, and if there had been, they would have been there for him. They also said how excited he was about the upcoming birth of his first child. Only one colleague said she thought he had been a little more short-tempered than usual and thought he might have had problems at home.

Leaving the school, Rachael said, "It seems such a shame, as he did seem to be a genuine guy doing an incredibly tough job."

"Funny how most of his colleagues hadn't noticed a behaviour change, but his wife said there had been a dramatic change in his attitude after she told him that she was pregnant," Humphries said. "They're the ones with all the training."

"Not really. We all put on a front to some extent at work," Rachael said. "Plus, he would have known all the signs and been able to hide them from his colleagues. At home, with personal relationships, it's harder to pretend. He clearly never confided he was having partner issues. Whether he was in denial or an extremely private person, we'll possibly never know."

"Let's see what Hugh Dolan can tell us." When Humphries checked his phone, he saw a missed call from Andrew. "I'll just take this before we leave." After ending the call, he said, "That's another nail in the coffin of the idea that Alex took his life voluntarily."

"What is?" Rachael asked.

"Nicky, his partner, called the station earlier wanting to speak to me or Fiona. It seems her parents kept things from her as they didn't want her to return to England. She admits she flew off the handle after an argument and said some stupid things, but she always intended to return to Alex. She was adamant Alex would have known that."

◆ ◆ ◆

Hugh's home was an imposing, whitewashed house set back and protected from the traffic noise on the main road into Birkbury by a row of tall evergreen trees. Humphries parked in the driveway in front of a triple garage. Looking up at the house, Rachael said, "It has an empty feeling to it. I don't think he's in. Are you sure he works from home?"

"Yes, he's a self-published author. Where else would he work?"

"I didn't realise there was that much money in it," Rachael said.

"His family farmed most of the land around where Jenny lived. He would have received quite a sum when he sold it after his parents died," Humphries said, opening a side door to the garage. "Well, his cars are here. As a writer, he probably likes things to be quiet and switches off his phone when he's working. You know, keep the creative juices flowing and all that. Let's try the door."

After knocking several times, Rachael pushed open the letterbox and peered in. "There's a pile of unopened post on the floor inside. I don't think he's been here the last couple of days."

Humphries looked at the neatly mown lawn that ran alongside the house. "Someone has been here."

"A gardener, perhaps," Rachael said, squeezing herself through bushes to peer in a front window. "It looks like a study area, and it's tidy and undisturbed."

"Let's check around the back."

They followed the driveway around the side of the house. At the rear was a large garden sweeping down to the fields below, a wooden terrace to the side looking out over the countryside and another single-car garage. The garage was unlocked and empty, but the back door to the house was locked. Because of the way the ground sloped away from the house, they couldn't see through the rear windows. Humphries collected some plastic bottle crates from the garage and stacked them beneath the window before climbing up to look in. He quickly jumped down. "We need to call it in. He's hung himself in the kitchen."

CHAPTER NINETEEN

"I'm not sure it's the same car," Fiona said, looking at the blown-up blurred photograph of the car spotted parked in the vicinity of several burglaries. "There's no sticker on the windscreen. I'm not even convinced it's the same model. All I can say with any certainty is that the car is a dark, medium-sized saloon." She called across the room, "Andrew, you have more than a passing interest in cars. Come and have a look at this and tell me what you think."

After closely examining the two pictures, Andrew said, "It's a close match. The picture isn't clear enough to say much more."

"We need to go back through the list of volunteers and check who drives a dark, medium-sized saloon," Fiona said. "Eddie, what does Ken Marsh drive?"

"A dark blue Skoda Octavia," Eddie said.

"Is it relevant if he's using an incorrect address to register his car?" Abbie asked.

"So, one theory is that the burglar keeps his car correctly registered, and he swops the plates for his nighttime activities," Fiona said. "Having a connection to the victims, owning a similar car and being Ian's father makes Ken Marsh a likely culprit, but there could be another explanation. It could be someone who knows Ken and that he has a son, and he's using it to his advantage to divert attention away from himself."

"Or herself," Abbie said. "It all sounds very elaborate to me. And to what purpose? We've yet to establish any financial gain. Not only are the items taken of low value, but none have turned up anywhere for resale."

"Could the aim be to frame Ian?" Eddie suggested.

"I wondered that," Fiona said. "When I asked Ian, he said he had no enemies. Maybe we need him to think harder about who he might have upset recently."

"It could be a Skoda," Andrew said, looking again at the photograph. "But like I said, I wouldn't like to say one way or another."

"While we don't rule out someone with a grudge against Ian or Ken, the Marsh family has to be our starting point. Ken Marsh needs to be spoken with. Discovering his son's address and car registration would be simple," Fiona said. "Can you come with me, Eddie, as you've already interviewed him?"

"Are we going to bring him in?" Eddie asked.

"We'll see how the interview goes," Fiona said. "Would his wife be safe to leave alone in the house?"

"Probably not," Eddie said.

Fiona and Eddie were approaching Ken's house when Humphries rang. Fiona pulled over when Humphries told her how they had found Hugh. The colour drained from her face. Humphries had been right to be so suspicious, and they should have picked up on the possibility of a second person being present sooner. Now, they were on the back foot with at least one death that potentially could have been prevented. "Have you secured the area and called the SOCCO team?"

"Rachael is doing that now."

"New evidence has come in on the burglaries, and I'm on my way to visit Ken Marsh. I wouldn't forgive myself if we delayed things and there was another burglary this evening. Can you handle things there? I'll join you as soon as I can."

"No problem. Who needs a social life? Anything else?"

"Yes," Fiona said. "There were three other friends interviewed after Jenny's death. They all need to be contacted and offered protection until we know what is going on. With three deaths already, hopefully, they'll be far more forthcoming about what really happened the night Jenny died."

Before re-starting the car, Fiona made a second call. Stefan didn't pick up, so she left a brief message. "Hi. I've no idea what time I'm going to finish tonight. Let yourself in, and I'll see you when I see you. Sorry."

Ken Marsh lived in a three-bedroom detached house in the old part of Sapperton. Here, the older homes had large gardens and were far more expensive than the modern housing thrown up in recent years. Ken's Skoda was parked in the driveway. It had a removable disabled sticker on the front windscreen but no other distinctive markings. Not in the best of moods after being forced to change her plans for Stefan's first night home, Fiona pressed hard on the doorbell.

"Okay, keep your hair on. I'm coming." The front door was opened by a slight, balding man in paisley pyjamas, slippers and dressing gown. "What is it, at this time of the night?"

Fiona held up her warrant card. "Can we have a word, Mr Marsh? It's not that late. Early evening, by my reckoning."

"What? No!" Ken said, looking between Fiona and Eddie. "We've just had tea, and we're settling down to watch the television before bed. Whatever this is, can't it wait until the morning?"

"I'm afraid not. It would be best if we went inside," Fiona said. "And you might want to get dressed in case we need to continue the conversation at the station."

"I'm sorry, but I'm not going anywhere. I can't leave my wife unattended. She's not well."

"Is there someone you can call to stay with your wife?" Fiona asked. "Or we could contact social services."

Resigned to having no option other than to speak to them, Ken said, "Come in, by all means, but what's this all about? I'm sure there's been some type of misunderstanding." He shuffled along in his slippers, leading them along the hallway and into a tidy kitchen overlooking a covered patio. Through a closed door, there was a peal of laughter from the television. "I would turn it down, but it's my wife's favourite programme. She enjoys so little these days."

"If you're not going to get dressed, could you sit down," Fiona said. "We want to talk about the recent burglaries."

Ken sat, and said, "I've already said what little I know. It's a dreadful business. What sort of person could terrorise the elderly and vulnerable? You need to catch them before someone is seriously injured. I know several people are too afraid to sleep at night."

"Yes, it has been noticed that you know all the victims, one way or another," Fiona said.

"I'm sure that's not strictly true," Ken blustered. "I know several of them, but to say I know all of them is an exaggeration."

"We can talk about that later," Fiona said. "Is that your car on the driveway, and are you the sole driver?"

"Yes. I'm the only person here who can drive," Ken said, rising from the table. "Would you like to see the car's documents? I have them safe in the cabinet over there."

"That won't be necessary right now," Fiona said. "While we go through some questions, could my colleague take a look around? Would you mind if he started in the garage?"

"I don't know what you're hoping to find, but I've nothing to hide. You can get to the garage through there," Ken said, pointing to the back door. After Eddie left, he remained standing, hovering near the door, trying to see what Eddie was doing. "What's this all about?"

"Sit back down, please," Fiona said. "A car very similar to the one outside has been parked in the vicinity of two of the burglaries."

"Similar, you said? Then, not mine," Ken said. "Do you have the registration number?"

"Here's the strange thing," Fiona said. "The registration number is listed to your son."

"My what? Sorry, you've lost me. It's just me and my wife here. We couldn't have children."

"I'm sure you know who I mean. Your son from your first marriage."

Ken opened his mouth to speak a few times, but no sounds came out. He looked desperately around the room, before saying, "Can you keep your voice down? My wife doesn't know."

"Know what?"

"That I was married before and had a family," Ken whispered. "It would only upset her."

"So, you're comfortable with lying?"

"No, not really. It was more of an oversight," Ken said, blushing and becoming flustered. "I had moved on and was a different person when I met my current wife. I was very young when I married the first time, and I didn't know what I was doing. The girl I was casually dating fell pregnant, and I tried to do the right thing by marrying her. It wasn't a proper marriage. I'm not sure what it was."

"Yet you managed to get her pregnant a second time."

"Only a paternity test would prove that. I was never convinced it was mine," Ken said. "I admit I was young and naïve. I shouldn't have walked out like I did, but it was a mistake from the start. We didn't love one another, and I didn't know what else to do. I put the whole sorry affair behind me, and yes, I'm ashamed to say, I forgot about them as if they never existed. After a few wasted years, I met my current wife and started a new life."

"And yet you arranged to visit them," Fiona said.

"I did not."

"Your wife and son say you did. He was only a child then, but your son still remembers how you stood them up."

Ken paled and turned away. "Oh, you mean back then. I wanted to … I don't know. See him. See how he had turned out and whether he looked like me. I assume you already know I ran away from that encounter, too. I was too embarrassed to try again, and I've since studiously forgotten about them."

"But you know where they live?"

"Not really, no. I know she married again and lives somewhere on the outskirts of Birstall, but that's all."

"So, if I checked the cameras, I wouldn't spot your car anywhere near their house?"

"That would obviously depend on where they live."

"Fair comment," Fiona said. "How often do you drive in the

Fishponds area?"

"Never," Ken said confidently. "If I drive to Birstall, I get on the motorway."

The back door from the garage opened, and Eddie walked in, shaking his head. "Do you mind if I look upstairs?"

Ken twisted in his chair to look at him. "It would help if I knew what you were looking for."

"Is that a yes?"

"Carry on," Ken said wearily.

After Eddie left a second time, Fiona said, "Okay. I'm going to go through some dates with you."

"If they're the dates of the burglaries, that's already been done," Ken said. "My only alibi for the nights in question is that I was here with my wife. She can't be left alone."

"Even late at night when she's sleeping?"

"No, never. If she woke up and I wasn't there, she would panic. It's a risk I would never take. Not for anything. Can I go to check on her? I don't like leaving her for too long."

"We can finish our conversation in the living room if that would be easier," Fiona said, thinking the problem could be easily overcome with sleeping tablets.

Ken started to object, but as Fiona was already standing by the living room door, he passed her and led the way into the room. "It will be best if I go in first."

"When's supper going to be ready?"

"We've already had supper," Ken said, crouching beside his wife's chair. "We had a chicken pie and your favourite ice cream for pudding."

"Did we? I don't remember, and I'm hungry."

"I could make us some cheese and biscuits. Would you like that?"

"Yes, that would be lovely." Her eyes widened in surprise when she caught sight of Fiona. "You didn't say we had visitors. Why didn't you tell me someone was coming over? I should be dressed for visitors. Is that why we haven't eaten yet?"

Ken picked up a blanket from the floor and tucked it around his wife's legs. "This young lady is here to talk about a road safety campaign. She's visiting everyone in the street. Nothing for you to worry about."

Struck by how easily Ken could lie, Fiona tilted her head towards a dining table at the other end of the room. "Shall we sit over there?" Fiona moved a pile of books from a chair and pushed an old laptop to one side to clear a space at the table.

Ken's face lit up as he came over and opened the laptop. "I can prove my car was right here on some of the dates. After the first couple of burglaries, I had a camera fitted to the front door. It will show the car parked up in the driveway at night."

Fiona looked on as Ken tapped on the screen with one finger. The painfully long time the laptop took to come to life and Ken stopping to peer at the screens made it a laborious process, but eventually, grainy pictures showing his car parked on the driveway appeared. She couldn't tell just from looking, but it would be easy to check whether the video had been edited and Ken was faking his poor computer skills. Resisting the urge to suggest she took over the typing, Fiona asked, "Could you send it all to my e-mail address?"

After copying down the address on a piece of paper, Ken asked, "How do I send it to you?"

"Would you like me to do it for you?" When Ken agreed and pushed over the laptop, Fiona was pleased to see three months of footage was retained. As she sent the file to herself, she said, "We'll look at this at the station tomorrow, and we'll be in contact."

"Phew. We managed to sort it all out. I knew we would," Ken said, looking pleased with himself. "Does that mean we're finished here?"

"I have a few more questions," Fiona said, although she was starting to doubt Ken was responsible for the burglaries. If he was innocent, she needed to find out who was trying to frame his son. "Who else knows about your first family?"

"Shh," Ken said, putting his finger to his mouth. Quietly, he added, "It's not something I've ever discussed with people."

"But surely people around here knew you from before? Weren't you worried someone would mention you had been married before to your second wife? One careless comment and your marriage would be destroyed. That's not a risk I would like to take."

Sheepishly, Ken said, "We only moved back here about twelve months ago. It was after my wife became ill. We lived near Leeds before."

"Could you write me a list of all the people you're in contact with now who knew you before?"

"I could. It might take me a while to think of everyone."

"I'll ring you tomorrow for the full list, but can you think of anyone who knew you before who might hold a grudge against you and possibly your son?"

"The only people that come to mind are my first wife's brothers. They weren't happy about how things turned out. In their eyes, their sister was perfect, and I abandoned her with two young children," Ken said. "My friends could see she was only using me, and they supported me every step of the way. They saw how she was carrying on behind my back while I was working two jobs to provide for them. Of course, her brothers never saw it that way."

Eddie poked his head into the room. "I'm all finished."

"Did you find what you were looking for?" Ken asked.

Fiona stood to leave. "Thank you for your time. We'll be in touch tomorrow morning. It would be helpful if you could have the list of people who knew you before completed by then."

Outside, Eddie confirmed he hadn't found anything of interest, and Fiona agreed to drop him back at the station before she drove out to Hugh's house. "You may as well finish up for the night. Ken has sent me home security footage of his car parked outside every night. When you arrive at the station tomorrow, can you send it to be checked for any editing? Also, follow up on the report on Ian's car and find the current addresses for his uncles. And check back a few years to see if there were any similar burglaries targeting elderly people in Leeds." As an afterthought, she added, "Arrange for a thorough examination of Ken's car as well."

CHAPTER TWENTY

Humphries met Fiona outside Hugh's home. Although he sprang forward to greet her, he looked tired and stressed. "Tracey's team have finished their preliminary examination of the kitchen. She hasn't confirmed yet if they've found any traces, but Hugh definitely had some assistance. There are defensive wounds and a blow to the back of his head. Tracey thinks he was pulled upwards rather than jumped off the chair, although it was staged to look like a suicide."

"Pulled? How?"

"The evidence suggests he was hoisted up to the beam by the rope around his neck, possibly when he was unconscious from the blow, rather than kicking the chair away himself. They'll be bringing the body out shortly," Humphries said, stifling a yawn. "Sorry, it's been a long day."

"Where's Rachael?"

"She looked exhausted, and her husband was calling every five minutes, so I sent her home about half an hour ago," Humphries said. "How did your interview go?"

Fiona shrugged. "He says it isn't him, and he has security camera footage of his car parked outside his house on the relevant nights, so it's possibly another red herring."

"Do you think he's lying?"

"If he is, then he's good. We'll see what the tech guys say about the videos tomorrow." Fiona fell silent and stepped back when Hugh's body was wheeled out. After it had passed, she said, "I'll work out a rota tomorrow, but this now has to be our priority. Is Tracey okay if we go inside?"

"There's not much to see, but get kitted up, and I'll walk you through what we know."

♦ ♦ ♦

Fiona could hardly keep her eyes open as she drove home. She parked next to Stefan's car, but as the house was in darkness, she assumed he was already asleep. After dropping her bag in the hallway, she hauled herself upstairs to check. She stood in the bedroom doorway, listening to his rhythmical breathing. She desperately wanted to wake him and have a normal night like other couples, but he was in a deep sleep, and she had too much going on in her mind. She returned to the kitchen and made herself a coffee.

With three deaths, they could no longer tiptoe around the edges of the initial investigations. The most obvious connection was the death of Jenny Trace ten years ago, and speaking to her family was at the top of her list for tomorrow. But was it the only possible connection? Could something else have happened in their final year that tied them together? Nothing had come to light so far, but how hard had they been looking? It was something to be considered.

But where did that leave the investigation into the burglaries? If Ken's security camera showed his car was parked outside his house during the most recent burglaries, it ruled him out, but the registration number matching his son's car couldn't be a coincidence. She was loathe to scale down the investigation, but she would have to move officers over to the murder investigation.

She had to decide quickly what to do about the burglaries. Three connected murders took precedence, but she couldn't simply drop the investigation. Not with all the local interest and when she was convinced that they were tantalisingly close to catching the culprit. It made no sense, but her nagging thought that there was something more to the burglaries persisted. If Ken and Ian Marsh weren't involved, somebody was making it look that way, but why? If someone had infiltrated the Golden

Mischief group to select their victims, it was only a matter of time before they worked out who it was from the narrowed-down field. But she knew that the whittling down of numbers would take time and effort.

She ripped a page from her notebook to jot down how she would split the team. She definitely wanted Humphries and Rachael on the murder team. And Andrew. And possibly Eddie. That left Abbie to continue working on the burglary investigation, with her helping when she could, which wasn't enough. Tomorrow, she would request the assistance of a couple of constables, and in her absence, Abbie would lead them.

"What are you doing down here? Have you seen the time?"

"Sorry, I didn't want to disturb you," Fiona said, lifting her head from the table and putting down her pen. She rubbed her eyes, wondering how long ago she had fallen asleep. She felt her coffee mug. It was cold. "I have a triple murder investigation on my hands as well as the burglaries. I'm trying to work out the best way to approach the two cases tomorrow."

"You mean later today," Stefan said. "You can't work around the clock without any sleep. No one can. Come up to bed."

CHAPTER TWENTY-ONE

Fiona arrived early at the station and went straight to Dewhurst's office. He had many faults, but being a late starter wasn't one of them. He liked to be first in to get a jump start on the day. Probably so he could catch others out. When she walked in, his opening comment was, "I was going to call you at home in the next five minutes if you hadn't arrived. Where are we on this new murder, and how does it relate to Alex and his friend?"

"We're still at the preliminary stage," Fiona said. "If you've read Tracey's report, you know as much as I do. The obvious connection is the death of a mutual school friend ten years ago, which is where I intend to start. Humphries has already spoken to Alex's work colleagues and his partner."

"Good. I like to see some initiative," Dewhurst said.

Fiona narrowed her eyes, but let the false statement go.

"I want you all focussed on this," Dewhurst continued. "Meanwhile, what are you doing about the break-ins? The media have been pestering again for an update. I heard you have a serious suspect, so I was hoping to give them some positive news."

"That's what I wanted to speak to you about," Fiona said. "We have some strong leads, and I don't want to drop the investigation at a crucial point. Could you clear the way for me to draft some additional constables into the team?"

"Yes. There will be a media frenzy over the murders, but they won't forget about the reign of terror being waged on the elderly in our community, or your failure to apprehend the culprits.

How many do you want?"

"Three," Fiona replied calmly, ignoring the personal criticism. When Dewhurst picked up the phone, assuring her it would be no problem, she wished she had asked for four.

When she returned downstairs, everyone was in and they crowded around for an update, keen to get started. Stefan had been correct. Her mind was far sharper after a night's sleep, free of churning the case over in her head. She felt fresher, but that didn't diminish the daunting caseload they had in front of them, and she was pleased she had scribbled down a plan of action before falling asleep at her kitchen table. "Most of you will now be working on the murder enquiry, but I need to have a quick word with Abbie before we start. If he hasn't already, Humphries can summarise where we are with the three deaths and why we believe they are linked."

Fiona and Abbie moved over to Abbie's desk, where Fiona said, "I would like you to take over the day-to-day handling of the burglary enquiry, although I'll remain the senior investigating officer. Dewhurst has promised us three additional constables who will be reporting directly to you in my absence. Have the reports on Ian's and Ken's cars come in?"

"Not yet, no," Abbie said.

"While waiting for assistance to arrive, can you chase up those reports and make a start on tracing Ken's brothers-in-law and anyone else who might have a grudge against him and his son? Last night, I picked up home surveillance tapes that appear to show Ken's car parked outside his house on the nights of the most recent break-ins. If it hasn't been done already, can you send them to be checked for any editing?"

"Will do," Abbie said, making notes. "As it was Ian's registration plate that showed up near the scenes, should I concentrate on people with grudges against him?"

"He needs to be reinterviewed and pressed on the point but keep an open mind until the car reports are in," Fiona said. "I'm going to be heavily involved with the murder enquiry, but we'll have a briefing every evening. If there are any major developments or you're unsure of anything, I'll always be at the end of the phone."

"Sure," Abbie replied. "Well, I've plenty to do, so I'll make a start now."

Pleased that Abbie was happy with her assignment, Fiona returned to the rest of her team to assign roles. Rachael and Andrew would be piecing together Hugh's last days, especially whether Alex had been in contact, while Eddie would track down the remaining members of the friendship group and Jenny Trace's mother, Jade, surname unknown. She was going to take Humphries with her to interview Jenny's father, John Trace, and the school friend Humphries had already contacted, Paula Davidson. When everyone dispersed, she took a moment to catch her breath. It seemed scribbled notes in the early hours of the morning were underrated.

Humphries called across to Fiona, "Paula can meet us after lunch between finishing her part-time job and the children coming home from school."

"Okay, let's head out to Little Tilbrook Farm to see John Trace now. It hasn't rained for a while, but it's probably worth grabbing Wellingtons, just in case. Roger Woodchester referred to him as a shadow of the man he used to be and the farm more of a hobby, so I'm not sure what to expect."

◆ ◆ ◆

The track to the farmhouse was a short distance from the storage barn. "I still don't get why he hasn't pulled it down," Humphries said as they drove by. "Passing it every day can't be good."

"Unless he moved right away like the wife did, he would still pass the spot," Fiona said. "Maybe he feels that leaving a gaping hole would be a worse reminder, and he couldn't bring himself to tear it down."

The track led to a larger building than Fiona expected. The sprawling farmhouse was three storeys of smooth, weathered stone. As only John and his younger daughter lived there, she imagined the upper floor to be a long-abandoned, cobweb-covered labyrinth of empty rooms full of discarded memories. There was an ancient, small tractor caked in mud and one small car parked in the cobbled yard in front of the house. Weeds grew between the cobbles, and a thick covering of mud was flaking in the sunshine. The green door was smeared by drying dirt, and the grime on the door handle bore witness to it having been routinely turned by muddy hands. Fiona banged the heavy door knocker and stood back to wait for a reply. Considering the number of half-chewed sticks and the filthy remains of tennis balls littering the dusty ground, she was surprised not to hear dogs barking before the door opened.

A slim, stunningly attractive young woman opened the door wearing jeans and a brightly coloured shirt. "Oh, hello, can I help you? Are you lost?"

"No," Fiona said, holding up her warrant card. "We want to speak to John Trace. Is he in?"

The girl tightened her grip on the door, her knuckles turning white, and anxiously asked, "Why do you want to see him? He isn't here right now, but I can pass on a message."

"It's Chloe, isn't it?" Fiona asked. Receiving a shy nod in reply, she said, "We really need to speak to him. When are you expecting him back?"

"My father hasn't been well recently. It would be better if you tell me what you're here about and let me speak to him," Chloe said. "It's important that he's not upset, and he doesn't cope well with surprises."

"Could we come in?" Fiona asked.

After a moment's indecision, Chloe opened the door wider before turning to walk along the corridor. "Close the door after yourselves."

The corridor led to a monster of a kitchen. Fiona sat at a table that would seat twelve comfortably, with her back to a metal-framed window overlooking the rear garden. The table was worn and heavily scratched but spotlessly clean, as was the red tiled flooring. The smell of bleach and air freshener lingered in the air.

In the corner beside her stood a guitar zipped in its case. Along the wall between the table and the kitchen appliances were two stuffed armchairs in front of an open fire. Next to them sat a sewing machine and a pile of colourful fabric on a rickety table. The hum of an ancient fridge freezer and the whirl of a washing machine on full spin played a harmonious tune in the background alongside a popular song playing on the radio. The feel was of a bustling family house, not the home of a grieving, single father and his remaining daughter.

"Can I get you a drink?" Chloe asked hesitantly, switching off the radio. "Something to eat?"

"A coffee or tea if you're having one," Fiona replied with what she hoped was a reassuring smile. Despite the veneer of everyday family life, she wondered if the humming of the domestic appliances and the radio was to drown out the silence and isolation, and how frequent visitors to the farmhouse were.

"Three coffees coming up," Chloe said, opening an overhead cabinet.

Glancing again at the sewing machine, Fiona said, "I like your shirt. I've not seen one like it before. Did you make it yourself?"

Chloe blushed. "Yes, thank you. I like making things."

"You have an obvious skill for it."

"Thanks," Chloe said. "I'm just starting out, but I'm trying to set up my own business and sell the clothes I make online. I already have a couple of influencers who like my stuff. I have my fingers crossed that things will take off, and I'll be making some proper money in a year or two. Well, that's the plan, anyway."

"That sounds like a brilliant plan," Fiona said. "I can see why people would like the clothes you're designing. I hope it all works out for you."

Chloe crossed the room and hovered by the table. "Umm...I don't suppose you would model for me?"

"I'm flattered by you asking," Fiona said, taken aback by surprise. "But I don't think I could do that."

"Shame. You have a great figure and an intriguing face."

"Hey, do you do men's clothes?" Humphries asked. "I don't have my colleague's modesty. I could model for you."

Chloe gave a smile that would put the Mona Lisa to shame before withdrawing to the kitchen counters at the end of the room. "I'll bear you in mind if I decide to try my hand at men's clothing."

"Is this your guitar?" Fiona asked. "Do you play?"

"A little. It passes the time, but what do you want to talk to Dad about?"

Fiona looked at Humphries before saying, "The death of your neighbour, Alex Woodchester, to start with. Did you know him?"

Chloe stopped pouring milk into a jug and held onto the countertop, but she didn't reply. She remained silent until she brought over three mugs of coffee on a tray with the milk jug and a bowl of sugar and sat down. Quietly, she said, "I saw Alex from time to time when he visited his parents, but not really to talk to. A policewoman came and spoke to us afterwards, with it being our barn and all. She was kind and respectful, but Dad was terribly upset afterwards. I'm sure you know what memories it stirred up. It would be best all round if you asked me your questions and kept Dad out of it." Looking down and picking at a splinter of wood, Chloe added, "I don't think he can take any more drama. Not so close to the anniversary."

"I'm afraid that won't be possible, but we'll be as sensitive as possible when we speak to him," Fiona said. "When are you expecting him back?"

"He's out with the dogs, checking on the sheep as he does every morning. He might be back any minute, or it could be in half an hour or longer." Chloe stirred sugar into her coffee, adding, "Rather than waste your time, why don't you tell me what it is you want to ask him? You could come back once I've had the chance to prepare him."

"We're happy to wait," Fiona said, before sipping her coffee. Putting the mug down, she tentatively asked, "Do you remember much about your sister and what happened?"

For a while, it seemed that Chloe was not going to reply. She looked up from examining the wood splinter, and said, "I was very young at the time. Sometimes, I think I remember snatches, but I'm not sure if they're memories or just what people have told me. I think everyone tried to protect me from what was going on. I remember there being people here all the time, being sent to my room a lot, and teachers being extra kind to me at school. The one thing I clearly remember is the hushed voices whenever I entered a room, especially after Mum left. That's about it. It's hard when people ask me if I miss her when I'm not sure if I remember her. There's just a vague feeling of missing something that was there before."

Fiona wasn't sure if Chloe was talking about missing her mother or her sister but decided to leave it there, as it was evident that she couldn't provide any details about her sister's state of mind and why she might have chosen to kill herself. "Do you remember what you and your dad were doing the night Alex died?"

"I do, but only because the police officer came to see us the following morning. I can tell you the same as we told her. That evening, Dad was at one of his meetings. The AA. With the anniversary coming up, he's been struggling, and he stayed late with his sponsor. He can't drive, so I went to pick him up. We were back here around half past eleven and went straight to bed. I had been working in the afternoon but got back here in time to drive him to his meeting."

"What time did his meeting start?"

"Seven o'clock in the community hall in Birkbury." Chloe walked over to the counters and returned with a notepad and pen. "Do you want me to write down the details and a contact number for his sponsor?"

"If you could, please," Fiona said. "Where were you working earlier in the day?"

Chloe finished writing the note and shuddered. "I handed in my notice that day after having enough of the little creep, but I was briefly stupid enough to work for a poxy little company grandly calling itself Murden Entertainment. To give me a little cash until my business was up and running, I did a set singing and playing the guitar. He promised me proper gigs, but his only contacts seemed to be retired people. That lunchtime, I was performing in the Carpenters Arms."

Fiona's heart skipped a beat, but she calmly asked, "Could you add the contact number for your old boss to the sponsor's details?"

"Sure," Chloe said, pulling her phone from her back pocket, looking confused by Fiona's interest before copying down the number. "Here you are. The guy's a small bit chancer with wandering hands. I doubt he knew Alex."

Taking the slip of paper, Fiona said, "Do you know what car he drives?"

"He drives a beat-up, white transit van to transport all the gear. I don't know whether he has a car as well."

"And you said when you worked for him, it was mostly entertaining groups of retired people? Did you often perform at the Carpenters?"

"Yeah. The Carpenters was a regular booking," Chloe said. "Sometimes we went to residential care places, but otherwise, it was mostly in private homes. But why are you so interested in him? I can't imagine he was the sort of person Alex would mix with. He's just a little nobody. I don't want to get him into trouble simply because I don't like him. He's probably harmless."

"It relates to another matter," Fiona said, slipping the note into her pocket. "Can you excuse me for a moment? I need to make a call from outside."

"You'll need to walk down to the old stable yard to get a good signal," Chloe said. "Turn right when you go out the front door and follow the path down."

CHAPTER TWENTY-TWO

Turning right outside the farmhouse, Fiona could just make out the cobbled pathway in the overgrown grass. It wound down to a beautiful row of Victorian stables with elegant metal balustrades. Next to the stables, there were large wooden doors to the barn where the family carriage would have been kept in a bygone age. The view across the fields was breathtaking, but she imagined it would look far bleaker on a rainy, mid-winter day. As she walked, she was struck by the similarities between Chloe and Ian Marsh. Despite difficult childhoods, they were both courteous, intelligent and about the same age, and she wondered if they knew each other. Probably not if Chloe had attended a private school like her sister.

She couldn't get a strong enough signal to call Abbie until she reached the far side of the stable block. "Abbie, I've got a name for you to check. Dan Murden. He runs an entertainment company primarily for an older audience, and is regularly booked by the Carpenters pub when the Golden Mischief group eat there. Has his name come up before?"

"No, I don't think so."

"Well, get on to it. He also works with local nursing homes and private householders. He could be our link," Fiona said. "Have the car reports come in yet?"

"Unfortunately, they gave them low priority and put them to one side. I gave them hell about it about half an hour ago," Abbie said. "But my assistants turned up, and we have made some progress tracing Ken's brothers-in-law. They both live in the Birstall area. One isn't known to us, but the older brother is. Mostly in relation to disturbing the peace when under the influence of drink and drugs. He was in here very recently in connection with the fight that broke out in the Riser pub, so you might have spoken to him. I'm on my way out with one of the constables to interview them."

"Great work. Let me know how it goes," Fiona said. "Will you have time to run a check on Murden before you leave?"

"No, we're leaving now." There was a rustle of paper before Abbie said, "I'll ask the other two to take a look at him."

"Okay, brilliant," Fiona said. "A long shot here. Could you find out what school Ian Marsh attended?"

"I can, but why?"

"Just a feeling I have. It could be nothing," Fiona replied vaguely, not knowing why it might be relevant. "I'll send through the contact details I have for Murden now."

Fiona hesitated before making the second call. She should be hurrying back to the farmhouse, not making personal calls. She should do it later, but she didn't have the luxury of time. Deciding family came first, she hit the pre-programmed number. "Hi Mum, it's me. You said there was live entertainment at the party you're going to tomorrow night. Do you know who is providing it?"

"What an odd question. No, I don't."

"Does it say anything on the invite?"

"I could go and look, but is this important right now?"

"Yes, Mum, it is. Can you go and get the invite and check?" Fiona impatiently walked in small circles when her mother put down the receiver.

"The invite just says live entertainment."

"Can you call your friend and ask if he booked through a company and what the name is?" When her mother started to object, Fiona said, "Please, Mum, for me. It's important or I wouldn't be asking. Oh, and if you're asked, don't say I wanted to know. Say you have another friend looking to hire an entertainment company, or something along those lines."

"Honestly, Fiona! Sometimes you are too much."

"Please."

"Okay. I'll call you later after I've spoken to him."

When Fiona returned to the farmhouse kitchen, Chloe was showing Humphries how to play chords on the guitar. Joining them at the table, she said, "It makes more sense than trying to teach him how to use the sewing machine, I suppose."

Humphries handed the guitar back to Chloe with a wink. "Thanks for the lesson."

"I'm sure Tina would be impressed," Fiona said with an arched eyebrow. Casually, she asked Chloe, "Do you know Ian Marsh?"

Bending to zip the guitar back into its covering, Chloe replied, "No, I don't think so. Why?"

"No reason. I just thought you might know each other. What school did you go to?"

"Sapperton comprehensive. It's a big school, so he might have been there, but he wasn't in any of my classes."

Fiona wondered if she should read anything into Chloe automatically assuming Ian was a similar age to her, and whether she felt resentment that her sister had been sent to a private school. "Did you consider going on to university?"

Standing her guitar back in the corner, Chloe laughed and said, "That's for the clever kids. I was never one for studying. I'm more the creative type, and I like having the freedom to work things out for myself rather than being told what to think. Besides, I'm needed here."

The room was suddenly filled by a cacophony of wagging tails and hot breath. Springing to the door, Chloe pushed the dogs out of the way and accused, "You can't have shut the front door properly. I'll warn Dad that you're here."

Fiona asked Humphries, "Enjoy your guitar lesson?"

"Yeah. She's a complex kid. She may not remember much about her sister, but I reckon her death had a profound effect on her."

"Like the complete upheaval of her life and her mother leaving, Sherlock. I think she's perfectly aware of the life she could have had instead of driving her father to AA meetings," Fiona said, wandering over to examine the pile of patterns next to the sewing machine. "She's a talented girl and uses her time constructively." She turned when she heard footsteps in the hallway approaching the kitchen.

She understood why Roger had called John a shadow of a man. Gaunt, grey and painfully thin, it was hard to see what kept him upright. His knobbly hand shook violently as he rubbed his stubbled chin and leaned against the wall. His lifeless, weary eyes stared out of a tired, pallid face, little more than a skull draped in a cape of melancholy. Struggling to catch his breath, he rasped, "Chloe said you're here to talk about Alex Woodchester."

"Yes, we think there may be a connection to the death of your daughter."

John's eyes shot wide as he hunched forward as if he had been stomach-punched. He pulled himself up straight, and said, "Let's talk outside."

When Chloe started to follow them, Fiona said, "We'd like to talk to your father alone."

Chloe reached for her father's hand. "I'll be sitting on the doorstep. Wave if you need me."

In the sunlight, broken veins beneath the surface could be traced in John's ghostly pale face along with areas he missed shaving. Breathless from the short walk, he sat at an aged, moss-covered picnic bench and pulled a battered tobacco tin from his pocket. With shaky hands, he popped a thin cigarette between his lips and waved a lighter around until Fiona leaned forward and held his hand steady enough to light it. He took a deep drag, followed by several chesty coughs, before saying, "Thanks. Chloe always rolls them for me."

"She seems a caring daughter," Humphries said.

"She is. She's the only reason I keep going."

Viewing his nicotine-stained fingers, Fiona sadly wondered how long it would be until Chloe was arranging his funeral. "When was the last time you saw Alex?"

John's watery eyes looked in the direction of Alex's childhood home across the fields. "I remember him as a lad, always up to mischief with our Jenny. They were like two peas in a pod. We used to say they would end up wed one day, but that was never to be. Shame I don't believe in the afterlife, or I could think of them reunited up there. I don't believe in anything. Not anymore."

Realising she would have to work to keep John on track, Fiona asked, "Did Alex come to see you recently?"

John continued to stare vacantly across the fields. "He sat with his pals at the funeral. He came up to me afterwards, shook my hand like a grown man and said how sorry he was for our loss. I could see he had been crying. Blubbering like a baby in private but trying to be a man in public. I guess he learned it's much harder to be a man than people think."

"Did you ever think he might have been with Jenny on the night she died?" Fiona gently asked. "We understand a house party was going on while Hugh Dolan's parents were away."

John turned to face Fiona, his eyes taking their time to refocus. "He was just a boy trying to act like a man."

"That doesn't answer my question."

"They were best friends. Partners in crime," John said. "I wish I could believe they are together again up there."

"Have you ever thought he might have been with Jenny when she fell?" Fiona asked firmly.

"Why would I think that? He was a good lad. He would have told me if that was the case."

"You've never doubted Jenny was alone that night?"

Time seemed to stand still while John contemplated the question. Ash fell from his cigarette. He looked at it and put the cigarette to his mouth, removing it shortly after. "Damn thing's gone out. Can you light it again?" After Fiona helped John relight his cigarette, he asked, "Is that what you're thinking? That Alex was with our Jenny?"

"It's a possibility we're considering, but we have nothing to say he was," Fiona replied. "When was the last time you saw him? Did he come to speak to you recently?"

"I've not seen him in years, not even from a distance. Chloe occasionally says she's seen him visiting his parents, but I never have."

"Not when you're out working your land?" Fiona asked. "They're your closest neighbours."

"I walk the dogs over to check on the sheep in the mornings and occasionally in the evenings. Other than that, I don't get out much. I don't touch the tractor anymore. I employ a lad from the village to make the haylage. Chloe will pull out a bale whenever I need one."

"I just want to be absolutely clear that you didn't speak with Alex recently," Fiona said. "Did Alex or anyone else visit you in the last month?"

"No. The only people I've seen are Chloe and the other members of that AA group she makes me attend."

"How about Matthew Guppy and Hugh Dolan? What can you tell me about them?"

"The name Matthew doesn't ring any bells. Hugh's family used to live around here, but they're long gone. Whether they're dead or sold up and moved on, I couldn't tell you. I just know they aren't about anymore."

"Chloe said you were at an AA meeting the night Alex died. Is that correct?"

"If that's what Chloe said, then yes. I remember a police officer coming around. A kindly lass. I think she grew up around here. Maybe she knew our Jenny. She would have been about the same age. I often wonder what Jenny would be like now. Something amazing, I expect."

"I need to ask where you were on a couple of other nights."

"I would have been here, I expect. If I was at a meeting, Chloe would know. She writes it all down on the calendar."

Fiona looked back at Chloe, still watching them from the back doorstep. Even if John's mind wanted to kill someone, she doubted his body was capable, and arranging the deaths to look like suicides took planning that would be beyond his muddled thinking. Even if the connection was the death of his daughter, the answers didn't lie with him. "Okay. We'll go on inside and have a look at the calendar now."

CHAPTER TWENTY-THREE

Paula Davidson told her boss she felt unwell and left work early. Since her husband had walked out on them, she needed the money, but the recent sleepless nights had left her exhausted, and she needed time to organise her thoughts before the police arrived. She couldn't see a way out and had started to think she was going crazy. It didn't help that she was annoying everyone around her by being so bad-tempered. Even her children were creeping around the house, checking on what mood she was in before saying anything.

She made herself a coffee and tried to relax, but she couldn't settle long enough to drink it. She paced from the kitchen to the living room and back again, trying to get things straight in her head. She needed to decide what, if anything at all, she was going to tell the police, while hiding the cushion that had a ripped cover.

When Alex had visited, she thought she had talked him out of his ridiculous idea. She rightly assumed the others would give him the same short shrift and tell him not to be so stupid. So, how had it come to this?

She threw herself into the armchair in the living room. What on earth made him want to drag it all back up now? It was never going to help anyone, not even Jenny's family. The damage was done, and everyone had lives to protect. You can't turn back time. The best you can do is deal with the consequences. Which was why she had to pull herself together, accept what had already happened and think of a plan to ensure she wasn't dragged any deeper into the mire. If her ex-husband saw the mess she was in, he would apply for custody, and that would kill her.

They had all struggled to work around the impact of Jenny's death. When it happened, they were thrown into shock, and panicked. In the days that followed, they had been near hysterical under the disguise of grief, uncertain about what to do and had discussed alternatives for hours. She had been the one who said that they should tell the truth from the start, but she had been outvoted. From an early age, she had allowed herself to be pushed around. She learned quickly that others were born to lead, and she was destined to follow, with her father looking on disapprovingly. If they had listened to her back then, if she had stood up for what she thought was right, she wouldn't be facing this nightmare now. None of this was her fault.

The flurry of panicked phone calls that followed Alex's announcement had transported her back to her final school days. When the calls became more frantic, Jamie had been the most outspoken. It seemed to her that Jamie had the least to lose. Maybe not quite as little as her, but still.

When she heard about Alex's suicide, she had felt a mixture of relief and guilt. Relief that their secret was safe, but guilt at the fact she had reacted that way. If she had realised the strength of Alex's feelings, she would have been kinder and more understanding. She would have suggested they stay in contact and talk through his emotions. She could have helped him resolve the issues going on in his mind. Hindsight was a wonderful thing. She wanted to think they all would have stepped up and given support had they appreciated how tortured he was about what happened. They all had experienced moments of doubt but had managed to deal with them in their own way. She should have helped. They all should have helped. She wasn't a heartless monster. Before all of this, she believed none of them were.

She walked back to the kitchen and poured away her cold

coffee. The cracked tiles around the sink reminded her she wasn't the best person to give advice when her life was such a disaster. Just keeping a roof over their heads and food on the table was a daily battle. Finding time to support a depressed person she hadn't seen or heard from since school was a big ask with all the other demands on her time. The others were comfortably off with their successful and fulfilling careers. One of them should have offered to help him. It was unreasonable to think it was her responsibility.

But it wasn't theirs either. Matthew had spoken to an adult. He would never say who it was, but he assured them the advice he had been given was to remain silent. And they had until Alex came along with his guilt trip. They should have pushed Matthew harder to reveal the name of the adult. If they were going to keep quiet about Jenny, surely, they should have been trusted with the name.

It briefly crossed her mind that one of the others might have killed Alex to silence him, but she didn't consider it seriously at first. They were an ordinary group of people with a shared childhood trauma trying to get through life the best way possible. They weren't killers. The doubts crept in at night, but she could discount them as nonsense in the cold light of day. The newspapers said he had committed suicide.

When she heard about Matthew, she knew the newspapers were lying when they said it was suicide. Covid had put a stop to her believing anything they said. Fake news was everywhere. She wasn't even sure the police who contacted her were real. What if they were part of some crazy conspiracy? You're not paranoid if people really are out to get you.

Matthew had been closest to Alex. Maybe he had agreed to go along with Alex, and they were killed to stop their plan. The two names on her list of suspects were Hugh and the adult. Hugh had now been removed, so that left the adult and a new disquieting idea that turned her stomach every time she thought about it. Jamie's angry reaction. If Jamie was responsible, then she was safe. During their late-night telephone conversations, she had made it clear that she thought Alex's idea was crazy and she would have no part in it. But what if it was the adult? She needed to know before the police arrived, but Jamie wasn't answering the phone.

She was about to call Jamie's number again when she heard a car pulling up outside. She rinsed her empty mug under the tap, shoved her phone in a kitchen drawer, opened a random magazine and placed it on the kitchen table. She waited until the bell rang twice and casually walked to the front door.

Fiona and Humphries pulled up outside a detached three-bedroom house on a quiet road a stone's throw from the local shops in Brierley. It was a pleasant enough area, but the house looked like it could do with some maintenance. They waited a short while before the door was opened by a plump young woman in a skirt and blouse. They were shown into a well-decorated, if a little jaded and tired, living room and offered a drink, which they declined.

"We spoke on the telephone before," Humphries said. "Did you have any luck contacting your other friends, James and Kate?"

"No, James isn't answering my calls. I expect he's busy. I was about to try his number again when you arrived," Paula replied. "A friend told me that Kate split from her husband a few years back and moved away, but they didn't know where."

"Well, keep trying," Humphries said. "I know I asked you before, but are you quite sure that Alex Woodchester didn't try to contact you recently?"

After a brief hesitation, Paula replied, "No. I haven't spoken to him in years. I may have seen his parents from time to time around the area, but not to speak with, and not recently."

"And how about your other friends from school?" Humphries asked. "Have you seen or heard from any of them in the last few months?"

"No, and they seem to be dropping like flies." Paula blushed. "Sorry, I shouldn't have said that. Hearing about their suicides has made me a little nervous. Ignore me, I'm always saying something stupid. I'm not in any danger, am I?"

"That's what we're here to find out," Fiona said, taking over the conversation. "Why should their deaths make you feel nervous?"

"Nervous was the wrong word. Upset and on edge would be closer to the truth," Paula said. "I've always had an overactive imagination and watch far too many horror films. I have this image in my head of some crazy with a chainsaw hunting down everyone from Berkhampstead School. There isn't, is there?"

"You're right," Humphries said. "You watch far too many horror movies."

"Would you object to us having access to your phone records?" Fiona asked.

"Yes, I would actually," Paula said. "For what reason? I haven't done anything wrong, and it would be an invasion of my privacy."

"Are you aware that it is an offence to withhold information?" Fiona asked, surprised by the strength of Paula's objection. They had no grounds to insist on seeing her phone history, but it made her wonder what Paula was hiding. It could be something irrelevant, like an affair or a debt problem, but the refusal made her suspicious. "I'm going to ask you again. Did Alex contact you recently, and have you been in contact with any of your school friends during the last few weeks?"

"No, I told you, Alex didn't call me. As for my other school friends, I tried unsuccessfully to contact them after speaking to you. My phone records are private, and I don't see why you need to see them when I've volunteered to help you. I'm not under arrest or anything, am I?"

"We'll leave the issue of phone records there for now," Fiona said, not wanting to antagonise Paula to the point she would clam up and not tell them anything. "We believe the recent deaths may be related to the death of another of your school friends, Jenny Trace. What can you tell us about her?"

"Are you sure you don't want a drink?" Paula stood abruptly. "I certainly do. Will you excuse me for a moment?" She returned seconds later with a glass of wine and retook her seat. "Jenny Trace. I had almost forgotten about what happened."

"What did happen?" Fiona asked.

"She threw herself off her parents' barn roof. It was a very upsetting time for everyone."

"Do you know why she did that?"

"Not really. She had messed up some of her exams and had split up with her boyfriend. We knew she was disappointed and a little down, but none of us realised how much. Depression and mental health weren't discussed as openly as they are these days. All I remember is I felt incredibly stunned and numb when I heard."

"Did it ever cross your mind that she didn't intend to kill herself?" Fiona asked.

"You mean, like an accident?" Paula asked. "For a long time, I wanted to believe it hadn't happened at all. That it was a terrible joke or something. So, yes, probably at some point, I tried to wish it was an accident, but then everyone said it wasn't, so I accepted they knew better."

"Beforehand, did you have any reason to think she was having suicidal thoughts?"

Paula sipped her wine and looked away. "I knew she felt slightly down, but I didn't realise how much. If I had known ... I always felt I failed her. That I missed the signs. I suppose that's why I buried everything. I prefer not to think about it, sorry. Death. No one likes to think about it, do they? Silly, really. None of us can avoid it in the end."

"You were young at the time," Fiona said gently. "When were you told about her death?"

"It was the next day, when my mother came to wake me. She came into my room and sat on my bed, so I knew it was something serious. She hadn't done that since reading me bedtime stories."

"Do you remember what time that was?" Fiona asked.

"Sorry, just that I was in bed when I first heard, so I assume it was the morning."

"Only Jenny wasn't found until the early afternoon, and it would have taken time for the news to spread."

Paula gulped a mouthful of wine. "The joy of being a teenager. And it was the school holidays. It may have been later in the day. I've got all that to look forward to with my children."

"Had you been out the night before? Drinking maybe to celebrate your exam results?"

"I don't remember them being that good," Paula tried to joke before registering Fiona's stony expression. "I honestly can't remember. It was one night ten years ago. I might have been out, or more likely, watching television in my room until late. I've always been more of a night owl."

"Strange you can't remember where you were or what you were doing. People are always saying where they were and what they were doing the days Princess Diana and the Queen died or when they heard the Brexit result. But you don't remember the day your school friend killed herself."

"I was devastated when it happened." Paula pushed herself away from the table and started to pace the kitchen. "The only way I could cope was to block everything out. I'm sorry I now can't remember any precise details, but that's how it is. If it happened today, we might have been offered counselling, but we were left to deal with it ourselves in the best way possible. I guess I buried everything, which possibly explains why I feel so on edge without knowing why. Don't they call it unresolved issues?"

"You could speak to somebody about it now," Fiona said, softening her tone. "It might help."

"You know, I might just do that," Paula said. "If it ends up jogging some long-lost memories, I'll be sure to let you know."

"For now, can you give us your most recent numbers for James and Kate?" Fiona asked. "And are your parents around? They might remember something more."

"I'll get you the numbers, and yes, my parents still live locally, although they've moved from the old house." Paula started to rummage in a kitchen drawer and retrieved her phone. "I'll write down their details as well."

While Paula was writing, Fiona asked, "How far from the barn did you live at the time?"

Continuing to look down at her handwriting, Paula said, "I'm not good with distances. A couple of miles, maybe a bit more."

◆ ◆ ◆

In the car, Fiona asked, "Did you do a background check on her?"

"Nothing came up on our registrar. She married young and has always lived in this area. Her divorce was finalised eighteen months ago, and she has custody of the children. Her ex-husband is also from this area and isn't known to us."

"She's clearly lying about the night Jenny died, but why?"

"I think she's frightened," Humphries said.

"That was my impression, but of what or who? And why so defensive about her phone records?"

"I'm guessing we don't have enough to seek a warrant."

"On what grounds? She's an old school friend who says she hasn't been in contact with the victims for years. If we discover different, we'll look at it again. Once we track the two other friends, they might tell a different story. We also need to speak to her parents. They might remember where she was that night. To still be asleep gone midday suggests she was out somewhere." Fiona was interrupted by a call from Abbie.

◆ ◆ ◆

"Most of the burglary victims had recently attended events where Dan Murden provided the entertainment," Abbie said. "We're waiting for the responses from a few of the others. A background check on him has turned up some unsavoury details about him. He previously ran after-school drama clubs for children in Cornwall until complaints against his behaviour towards some students started to snowball. An investigation showed that he and two friends, a schoolteacher and a local Tory councillor, enjoyed sharing indecent images of young people. He did some time inside and moved to this area on his release."

"He needs to be brought in for questioning," Fiona said. He sounded like the type of guy she would like to put away for a long time, although being a pervert didn't necessarily make him a thief. If several victims had a connection to him, it was a good starting point, but they would need something more.

"I thought that was how you would respond. We're all set to bring him in."

"Okay, go ahead. I'm on my way back to the station and would like to sit in on the interview," Fiona said. "He should be on the sex offenders list, and it would be interesting to see what tabs they kept on him. See what you can find out before the interview. Also, check to see whether there were any similar runs of burglaries where he operated clubs in Cornwall, concentrating on single parents rather than the elderly."

"Will do. Anything else?"

"That's it for now. We'll have a chat when I get back," Fiona said. "How did it go with Ken's brothers-in-law?"

"We spoke to them at their place of work. They both work in the same supermarket warehouse. They have provided statements under caution, but we haven't had time yet to check their alibis."

"What was your gut feeling about them?"

"They were angry about how Ken treated their sister, but they claimed that they didn't even know he had returned to the area. I tend to believe them."

"We'll prioritise Murden, but their alibis still need to be checked."

◆ ◆ ◆

As soon as Fiona ended her call with Abbie, Humphries said, "If you're heading back to interview Murden, where does that leave the murder enquiry? Couldn't Abbie deal with it without you holding her hand?"

Fiona heard the annoyance in his voice, and she knew he had a point about her lack of trust in Abbie. It wasn't the first time it had come up. But if Murden was their man, she didn't want any mistakes in the interview. Afterwards, she could leave Abbie to quickly wrap things up while they concentrated on the murders. "While I'm interviewing Murden, take Rachael with you to speak to Paula's parents. And continue trying to track down the other two friends."

CHAPTER TWENTY-FOUR

Fiona hung back when they arrived at the station. While Humphries walked on ahead, she turned towards her car and called her mother. She didn't answer, so Fiona left her a quick message asking her to ring her back. She pocketed her phone and caught up with Humphries, waiting by the door. Holding the door open, he asked, "Who were you ringing?"

"It's not important. They didn't answer anyway," Fiona replied. "I'm going to find Abbie. Let me know how the interview with Paula's parents goes."

Fiona quickly found Abbie, who was in her element organising the three constables. Fiona introduced herself to them, thinking Abbie would make a far better manager than she ever would. After a quick update over a coffee, Fiona and Abbie walked down to the interview rooms.

Fiona took an instant dislike to Dan Murden the second they walked into the interview room. He was a small, weasel-looking man with dark hair and acne-scarred skin. He was the sort who would look grubby five minutes after stepping out of the shower. His bored scowl was full of disdain as he grunted and rolled his eyes to acknowledge their entrance.

Having read through his old charge sheet, Fiona knew it would be a battle to remain unprejudiced. Several more victims had recalled attending events where he provided entertainment, and Eddie was pressing the final few for where they might have crossed paths. Having direct contact with many of the victims was suspicious, but so far, that was all they had. As well as his transit van, he had owned a white Ford Fiesta for the past six years. They had nothing to connect him conclusively, and it was questionable whether they had grounds to search his home, especially if he was able to provide alibis for the nights of the burglaries. They were also scratching around to think of who his partner might be.

After the formalities for the tape were complete, Abbie asked Murden if he knew why he had been brought in.

"Not really, no," Dan replied petulantly. "I was hoping you were going to tell me."

"You're helping us with our enquiries concerning the recent burglaries targeting the elderly in this area," Abbie replied in a businesslike manner.

"I've always thought that was a bunch of kids, that your lot were too useless to catch."

"Any particular reason for thinking that?"

"Not really. Just a feeling after reading between the lines of the odd newspaper article," Dan said. "They're running rings around you, so I suppose you have to make it look like you're doing something, but how you think I can help you is beyond me."

"Well, the thing is, we've discovered many of the victims had recently been entertained by your company and remember talking with you during or after the events," Abbie said, a little too sarcastically for Fiona's liking. Dan was trying to rattle Abbie, and she hoped she wouldn't bite. It wasn't an interview she wanted to take over if she could avoid it.

Dan leaned back in his chair and gave a false laugh. "As my business is providing entertainment for senior citizens, that's hardly surprising. I try to attend as many events as possible, check we provide good value for money, and listen to any feedback. That's hardly a crime. They are lying if anyone suggests I ask for addresses or anything like that."

"It's been noted you tend to home in on the single people," Abbie said.

"To check they're okay and enjoying themselves. What can I say? I'm a friendly guy and don't like to think of anyone being left out. I chat a bit, flirt if they're female, and try to make them laugh. Smile, at least. It's all part of my personal service," Dan said. "I've been physically sickened by the recent assaults. I'm one of the good guys."

"How many cars do you own?" Abbie asked.

"Just the one. A Fiesta, and I have a van for the music gear," Dan said. "Look, I haven't bothered because I didn't think it was necessary, but do I need to go to the expense of a legal guy?"

"That's entirely up to you. At this stage, you're merely helping us with our enquiries," Abbie said.

They all turned at the sound of a knock on the door. A constable came in and hesitated before whispering an update in Fiona's ear. Fiona thanked him while Abbie gave him an angry glare as he slipped out the door.

Leaning back in his chair, Dan said, "Well, come on. Let's hear your questions."

Before Abbie could respond, Fiona said, "I have a few dates I want to run by you."

"Nights of the burglaries, I take it?"

"There's quite a lot of them, so you might want to take some time to think about where you were on these nights," Fiona said, handing over the typed list she pulled from the file. "We'll leave the interview there for now."

"Am I free to leave?"

"For now, but please don't leave the area. We might need to speak to you again," Fiona said. As soon as the tape was switched off, she shot out of the room, leaving Abbie looking furious and as surprised as Dan.

◆ ◆ ◆

Abbie caught up with Fiona on the stairs. Red-faced, she demanded, "What was that all about? Why did you end the interview there? I hadn't even started."

Fiona stopped and turned. "Because they finally got around to sending us the reports on Ian and Ken Marsh's cars, and guess what? Ken's fingerprints are all over the steering wheel of Ian's car. Rather strange since they claim never to have met. Also, a thorough search of Ken's car revealed a ring caught under the carpet in the boot. They are checking whether it matches any of the items reported stolen."

With the wind taken out of her sails, Abbie said, "A shame they didn't complete the reports a little sooner. It would have saved us a lot of time."

"Agreed. That's why I ended the interview," Fiona said. "We need to bring the father and son in. I'll take one of the constables with me to bring the father in. You take another and bring the son in. Assuming he was telling the truth about his schedule, you should be able to pick him up when he leaves his lecture at the university. Keep in contact."

As they carried on up the stairs, Fiona switched her phone back on, which immediately started to ring. She looked at the screen and said to Abbie, "You go on. I'll catch you up in a minute." When Abbie opened the door into the corridor at the top of the stairs, Fiona accepted the call. "Hi, Mum. Thanks for calling back."

"I was visiting your father earlier, but I have the name of the entertainment company you were after. Murden something or other."

"Okay, thanks," Fiona said.

"Is that it? Are you going to tell me why it was so important?"

"Maybe later. Sorry, I've got to go. I'll call you back," Fiona said, ending the call and hurrying to the incident room.

◆ ◆ ◆

Ken Marsh opened the door to Fiona and the uniformed constable with a smile. "Oh, hello again. Is there something else I can help you with?"

Not happy with being lied to and the time that had been wasted, Fiona briskly said, "Yes, Mr Marsh. We would like you to accompany us to the station to answer more questions."

A frown crossed Ken's face. "Not this again. I've already told you that I can't leave my wife."

Fiona pulled out her phone. "I have social services on standby, or you can arrange some care for your wife." Her tone made it clear the matter wasn't negotiable.

"Well, this is highly inconvenient, but I prefer to call our neighbour, who usually pops in if I have to go out for any reason. Can I tell her how long I will be away for?"

"It may be for some time, so professional care might be more appropriate," Fiona said. "Your neighbour could sit with her until they arrive."

"This is ludicrous! I'm sure this is something we can sort out over a cup of tea like before. Why don't you come in and sit down?"

"I'm afraid that's unlikely to be the case. Do you want to call the neighbour now so we can get started?"

"Can you at least tell me what all this fuss is about? I thought we had cleared everything up the other day. My wife needs me."

"You should have thought about that before lying to us," Fiona said. The continued lies were annoying, and she wanted him in an interview room as quickly as possible.

"I did not," Ken said indignantly. "About what?"

"About you having no contact with your son. That was a lie, wasn't it?"

"I don't know what you mean?" Ken whined like an injured dog.

Feeling her temper rise, Fiona said, "Are you going to call your neighbour?"

"Okay. If you would like to wait outside, I'll see if she's available," Ken said, closing the door.

Fiona stepped forward to prevent the door from being fully closed. "We'll come inside to wait while you make the call."

"Follow me." Ken was polite with the neighbour and tenderly told his wife he needed to go out for a few hours, but she shouldn't worry as he would return shortly. Once the neighbour was settled in the living room watching television, he kissed his wife goodbye and obediently followed them into the hall, where

Fiona read him his rights. He sat in the rear car seat, sullenly looking out the window, remaining silent. When they pulled into the station car park, he took a deep breath and said, "Do I need legal representation?"

"That would be advisable," Fiona replied. "Do you need us to appoint someone for you?"

Polite to the last, Ken replied, "If you could be so kind. Thank you."

◆ ◆ ◆

Fiona read through the reports preparing for the interviews with one eye on her phone, waiting for either Humphries or Abbie to call with updates. When her phone buzzed, she didn't recognise the caller. "Hi, DI Fiona Williams."

"Hi, this is DC Jim Menzies. I'm outside Birstall Uni with DS Abbie Ward."

"Hi, Jim. Is there a problem?" Fiona asked, instantly alert once she realised who was calling.

"We had a few problems extricating him from the lecture room, but we're on our way now," Jim replied.

"What happened?"

"To be fair, he didn't put up much resistance," Jim replied. "It was his fellow students who caused all the fuss. Mostly comments about the police state and Big Brother when we interrupted their lecture."

"I can imagine," Fiona said. "Why did you take him out mid-lecture? Once you established that he was there, you could have waited by the door until the lecture was finished and taken him to one side as he left."

"DS Ward thought it best to bring him in as soon as possible."

"Will she never learn? A student riot is all we need. No wonder she didn't call herself," Fiona muttered under her breath. To Jim, she said, "I'll speak to her later. Has he been read his rights and been offered legal representation?"

"He has. He wants us to appoint someone."

"Once he's booked in, arrange representation, and then come up to see me." Fiona put the phone down and rubbed her temples. She couldn't remember if she had explicitly told Abbie to wait until the lecture was finished, but it was common sense. The combination of Ken's feigned innocence and Abbie's reckless action was giving her a headache. If Ken and Ian hadn't wasted their time by lying, she could be concentrating on the murders. At least she fully trusted Humphries to do the right thing, especially when he had the steadying influence of Rachael with him.

CHAPTER TWENTY-FIVE

While Fiona was finalising her notes for her interviews with Ken and Ian Marsh, she received a call from Murden's legal representative. They had worked through the list of dates and had credible alibis for most of them. Abbie was still sulking from her dressing down for not waiting until the lecture had finished before bringing in Ian and had slinked out to speak to Ian's mother, who was kicking up a stink about her son's arrest. Fiona asked one of the constables to check Murden's alibis and invited Jim to sit in on the interviews, starting with Ken.

As soon as they were all seated and the formalities completed, Ken's legal representation said, "My client would like to make some changes to the statement he gave you previously and explain why he was keeping his recent meetings with his son secret."

"That would be a good start," Fiona replied. "Let's hear it then."

"I wasn't trying to deceive you intentionally," Ken said haltingly, looking to Fiona for a reaction. When she raised her eyebrows but remained silent, he continued. "Ian contacted me a few months ago. Of course, I was delighted he had reached out to me, but we both realised his getting in touch could hurt people we care about. He feared his mother would see it as a betrayal, and he didn't want to upset her. With my wife so ill, I wasn't in a position to explain the situation to her. We both decided it would be best if we kept things between the two of us."

"I appreciate your good intentions with regard to your family. That is none of my concern," Fiona said. "But you chose to lie under direct questioning in a police investigation."

"I couldn't see how being in contact with my son could be relevant to these dreadful attacks, so I decided not to mention anything to you."

"Even though you knew a car displaying his registration number was seen in the vicinity of several crimes?" Fiona asked.

"I've not known Ian for long, but he's a good lad. He has a job, a stable home life and is studying for a degree. He's not the sort of lowlife who would steal from elderly people."

"In your opinion," Fiona said, making it clear she was less than impressed. "How and when did Ian make contact with you?"

"I can't give you the exact date, but it was about four months ago. He turned up on my doorstep unannounced one evening, and we've taken things from there."

"Shortly before the burglaries started," Fiona said. She remained silent for a few minutes to let the timing sink in before asking, "Who decided your meetings should remain secret? One of you must have instigated the conversation?"

"We decided together," Ken said. "I honestly can't remember how the question of secrecy came up. It was fairly obvious from how he spoke about his mother that he wouldn't want to upset her, and I've explained my position."

"How often have you been meeting up, and where?"

"Different places. We've been meeting every couple of weeks. We usually go to a café or occasionally a pub and have a chat over a drink."

"Has it always been amicable?"

"Mostly, yes. He had some issues about me abandoning them, but we seemed to have ironed that all out. Come to an understanding. He was more accepting when I pointed out to him that I was only a little older than he is now."

"Does he usually pick you up in his car for these meetings?"

"No, we make our own way to a pre-arranged place," Ken said.

"Have you ever been in his car?"

"No, never."

"And has he ever been in yours?"

"No, I told you," Ken said. "We made our own transport arrangements."

Fiona looked down at her notes. She looked up, and asked, "When did you drive his car?"

"His car? How could I when I've never been in it?" Ken said, sounding tetchy. He took a deep breath to calm himself, and said, "There is probably some mix-up or perfectly innocent explanation for where his car was parked, but it has nothing to do with me. You'll have to discuss that with him."

"You're saying you have never driven your son's car?"

"Yes. That's exactly what I'm saying."

Fiona pulled the fingerprint report from her file and passed a copy to the legal representative, keeping eye contact with Ken. "Then how do you explain your fingerprints inside the car?"

Ken's eyes darted around the room, and he fidgeted in his seat before saying, "Oh, yes. I remember now. There was a time I helped him to carry some textbooks to his car. I would have opened the door and put them on the seat."

"Which seat?"

"Let me try to remember," Ken said, becoming flustered. "It could have been the rear seat or the front passenger seat. It was such a simple thing to do, the details haven't registered in my memory banks. Sorry, is it important?"

Fiona waited to see if it would dawn on him how stupid and futile it was to continue lying. He already knew the car had been spotted near crime scenes, and he had lied about knowing his son and being inside his car. Instead of trying to backtrack, Ken smiled, seemingly oblivious to his situation. She gave him one more chance to volunteer the truth rather than having it dragged out of him when confronted with the evidence. "Are you saying you have never borrowed or driven your son's car?"

"Yes."

Fiona tapped the fingerprint report on the table. "Then how do you explain your fingerprints being on the steering wheel, gear stick and handbrake?"

The legal representative realised his mistake in putting the fingerprint report unread to one side and started to scan the report. "Can we take a break while I digest the contents of this report and have a word with my client?"

"There's no need. I remember now," Ken said. "There was an occasion recently where I did park the car. Ian had injured his back at work lifting a barrel, and it was a tight spot to pull into. He asked me if I could park it for him to save him from having to twist in the seat. Sorry, it was only the one time, and it completely slipped my mind."

"Funny how easily things slip your mind," Fiona said, putting the fingerprint report back into the file and pulling out a series of photographs. "Do you recognise this?"

Ken leaned forward to look at the pictures. "Well, it's obviously a ring. I would guess a man's wedding ring, but I don't recognise it. I'm mean, to the best of my knowledge, I've never seen it before."

"To the best of your knowledge?"

"I guess it could have been worn by somebody I knew. It's a fairly generic wedding ring, so I couldn't say I had never seen it before."

"Interesting," Fiona said. "This ring belonged to Alice Dale's husband. Do you remember popping into the hospital after her break-in to say how sorry you were and to offer her your support? It was stolen from her house along with other items, and we found it in your car. You've explained about the son you denied knowing and the car you denied driving until confronted with evidence to the contrary. Can you explain how the ring got into your car?"

"I'm genuinely shocked. I only met Ian a few months ago, and I didn't see this coming. He seems a very level-headed, intelligent boy working hard to make a future for himself. I said earlier that he couldn't be involved, but I could be wrong."

"I'm a little confused," Fiona said. "Are you saying that you might have passed on details of where several vulnerable people you've met, through groups like the Golden Mischief, lived to your son? And you think he may have dropped the ring in your car?"

"No, that's not what I'm saying at all. I can't imagine what you think we discussed, but it certainly wasn't where other people lived. What sort of person do you think I am?"

"What did you discuss?"

"How he was getting along at university and his future plans. His interests and passions. That sort of thing. Certainly not where people lived."

"You haven't explained the ring being in your car, but perhaps I can help you out there," Fiona said. "My colleague has been talking to Alice's mother. You kindly gave Alice a lift home from a meal in the Carpenters a while back. Do you remember?"

"Oh, yes! That could have been how the ring ended up in the car," Ken said, smiling. "She could have dropped it."

"You're now saying that she dropped her late husband's ring, that she always keeps in a drawer at home, in the boot of your car when you gave her a lift to her front door."

"No. Stop you're confusing me. I gave her a lift in my car, but I don't know anything about a ring. I have no idea how it ended up in my car unless Alice dropped it there. That's the only possible explanation I can give."

"I can think of a few others," Fiona said.

"Could we stop this interview now while I have a talk with my client?"

"Okay, we can stop here. We have a warrant to search your house, Mr Marsh. We'll reconvene once a thorough search has been completed, and we've spoken to your son."

Ken paled and muttered, "You won't find anything."

CHAPTER TWENTY-SIX

Ian Marsh looked terrified when Fiona and Jim entered the interview room. His boyish face and halo of brown curls added to his look of a little boy lost and out of his depth. He tried and failed to contort his pensive look to a smile when they took their seats. A maternal instinct that she didn't know she had, told Fiona she wanted him to be an innocent used by his father. She ignored it. The jury was still out on his involvement. Two people were responsible for the break-ins, and he had already convincingly lied to her about knowing his father.

After the formalities for the tape, Fiona asked, "Do you know why you're here?"

"I guess because my car was parked in the wrong place at the wrong time, which I've already said I can't explain. I gave another officer my shift timetable for the pub, and he said it was fine. I can only think there's been some mix-up or another."

"It's a little bit more than that," Fiona said. "Can you tell me again whether you have been in contact with your father?"

Ian looked at the ceiling before saying, "Mum's going to kill me. She always said he was no good. I just wanted to see for myself. The fact that I'm here and you keep asking about him suggests she was right. I've never been inside a police station before, let alone an interview room."

"So, you have been in contact?"

Ian nodded his head. "I called around his house one evening. Even after I knocked on the door, I was in two minds about whether to tell him who I was. I thought once I had seen him,

I could say I was lost, or sorry, wrong address or something. I wish I had now."

"But you didn't, and he invited you in?"

"No way. He shot out of the door and hustled me away. He didn't want his wife to see me," Ian said, shaking his head. "I should have walked away then. If he was that embarrassed about me, what was the point?"

"What happened next?"

"He walked me to my car. Once we were away from the house, he soon changed his tune. He said how often he thought about me and how he had thought of making contact. He told me he was sorry for being a coward and shutting me out of his life, but he wanted to arrange for us to meet properly. We couldn't talk then because he needed to arrange for someone to care for his wife. Anyway, we arranged to meet in a few days, and everything has gone from there."

"What do you mean by everything?"

"He wanted to make our meeting a regular thing. I wasn't sure, but I mostly went along with it because I didn't know what I wanted. I thought in time things would become clearer once I got to know him a little better."

"And did they?"

Ian shrugged. "I was building up the nerve to tell him I wanted to cool things down and see him less often when this happened."

"For any particular reason?" When Ian shrugged his reply, Fiona said, "We need something for the tape. Was there a reason why you wanted to stop seeing your father?"

"I didn't want to stop all together. It's just that seeing him so regularly, we were running out of things to say. I think he might have money problems. He can't work because of his wife's illness, and it's left him isolated. I don't think he has many friends, and he started being needy and wanting us to spend more time together, not less. My life is pretty busy, and I don't have much spare time. And I didn't want my mum to find out. She was already asking questions about where I was going. A mixture of all of those, I guess." After a pause, Ian added, "He started wanting to borrow things."

"What sort of things?"

"Stupid things to give him an excuse to arrange another meeting. My jacket, some money ... and my car."

"Your car?"

"It was only the once, and it was weeks ago, but I was getting tired of him wanting to borrow things. Apart from anything else, it meant we had to meet again for the things to be returned."

"Did he say why he wanted the car?"

"His had broken down or something, and he needed to take his wife somewhere."

"Do you remember the date he borrowed your car?"

"It was a while after we first met, but I can't remember the exact day." Ian chewed his nails before adding, "Funny thing, I haven't found my spare key since he borrowed it. I thought he had given it back, but maybe he didn't… And there have been a few mornings when my car didn't feel right."

"How do you mean?"

"It would be parked where I left it, but it felt like things had been moved and put back," Ian said. "I can't say for sure it had been used without my permission, but it's possible."

Fiona slid the photographs of the ring from her folder. "Do you recognise this?"

"Only as a ring. It's not mine."

"When you were chatting, did your father ever mention the Golden Mischief group or much about his wife?"

Ian shook his head. "He said his wife was poorly but never said why. I thought it might be cancer or something like that. He didn't want to talk about her, nor did I. It would seem disloyal to my mum. He never offered, but I didn't want to meet her anyway. As for the Golden Mischief, I've never heard of that group. What sort of music do they play?"

"The decision to keep your meetings secret. Was that something you discussed?" Fiona asked.

"I don't think so. It was more of an unspoken understanding.

We never met near where he lived, and I might have said I don't want my mum to know, but that's about it."

Fiona closed her file. "We're nearly done here. There is a team searching your home. When they're finished, we'll talk again."

"What! You mean my mum knows all about this? What do I tell her?"

"I'll leave that up to you," Fiona said. "One more thing. What schools did you go to?"

"Sapperton primary and secondary."

"Do you know Chloe Trace? She would have been in your year."

"You do know how big Sapperton is?" After another shrug, Ian said, "I knew of her. She wasn't in my classes, and I never spoke to her, but everyone knew who she was. Her sister had gone to some private school and killed herself. I guess her parents thought there was something to be said for comprehensives after all."

"Have you seen her since leaving school?"

Ian shook his head. "No. She may not have gone to a private school, but she thought herself a cut above the rest of us."

"How do you know that if you didn't know her?"

"I'm going mostly on what other people said," Ian said. "But you could tell by the way she walked around that she thought a lot of herself. You know the type. I was in the nerdy group. Not someone the cool people spoke to."

CHAPTER TWENTY-SEVEN

Humphries was waiting for Fiona when she returned to her desk. She had hoped to see Abbie first, but she hadn't returned to the station. Depending on the outcome of the searches at Ian and Ken's homes, the investigation could be close to a conclusion. She should be able to leave Abbie to finalise things so she could focus solely on the murders, but she wanted to set a few ground rules first.

Accepting that she couldn't speak to Abbie until later, she asked Humphries for an update.

"We've managed to speak to Paula's parents, and they're on their way here." Humphries pulled a face before adding, "Police turning up on the doorstep would lower the tone of the neighbourhood. Rachael has spoken to another of their friends, Kate. She wasn't too happy about being woken up." When Fiona gave him a quizzical look, he explained, "She emigrated to Australia. I guess she really wanted to put some space between herself and her ex-husband. She couldn't add anything more than we already know about Jenny's suicide. She told Rachael that she had spent the night at home with her parents and was called in as part of the search team. They were driving to Jenny's house when they learned of her death. She hadn't heard about Alex, Matthew or Hugh because she cut all ties when she emigrated, and as her parents retired in Spain, she's not kept up with any local gossip."

When Rachael walked over to join them, Fiona asked, "Did you sense Kate was telling the truth about the night Jenny died?"

"Hard to tell over the phone. She was half-asleep and shocked by the news about her school friends," Rachael said. "I figured she can't be involved in their deaths as she lives on the other side of the world, so it wasn't worth pushing."

"How about the other friend, James?"

"He's proving far more elusive," Humphries said. "Eddie is still working on tracking him down, but he has spoken to his parents. They live locally but haven't seen or heard from him for several years. A year after Jenny's death, he dropped out of university, and his drinking and drug abuse became a problem. He walked out after one argument too many, and no one has heard from him since."

"Was he reported missing?" Fiona asked.

"No. His parents say he left of his own accord."

"Did Eddie ask them about the night Jenny died?"

"He did," Humphries said. "They don't remember much. James was in the year below and was only on the group's periphery. Their memory of the night was vague, but they are generally bitter about what happened."

"Bitter?" Fiona asked.

"They think it was Jenny's death that set him on the path of self-destruction," Rachael said.

"They said he wasn't the same boy afterwards," Humphries said. "He became moody, which they put down to him discovering drugs to help him to deal with the death."

"So, they just shut him out rather than help him deal with his grief," Fiona said.

"He could be full of anger and blaming his old classmates for how his life turned out," Humphries said. "He could be our killer."

"We don't know how he turned out," Rachael said.

"Without family support, dropping out of university and becoming addicted to drugs rarely ends well, but we'll see," Fiona said. "Do you know when Paula's parents are likely to arrive? I would like to speak to them, if possible, but it will depend on where we are with the burglaries and whether I can find Abbie. It's looking possible that Ken Marsh is our man."

They were interrupted by Abbie crashing into the room, holding her phone. "The full report on the search of Ken's house should be with us shortly, but they found a car key that doesn't fit his car and a couple of war medals. As soon as we have photographs, I'll see if they match the ones stolen."

"Where were they found?" Fiona asked.

"In the lining of one of his jacket pockets, found at the back of his wardrobe."

"If the medals match those stolen and the key fits Ian's car, we've enough to charge him," Fiona said. "How about the search of Ian's house? Have they found anything there?"

"Only a furious mother," Abbie said.

"Congratulations," Humphries said. "It seems there was some point to the tedious checking of the security footage in the area."

"Not exciting enough for you, though," Abbie said. "It was so boring you had to go and discover a triple murder to get yourself out of it."

Before Humphries could come back with a sharp reply, his phone rang. "That was the desk sergeant. Paula's parents have arrived."

"Wait for the report and check for matches before you do anything," Fiona told Abbie. "I'm going to be in an interview relating to the murders. Call me if you're unsure about anything, but only if it's urgent."

◆ ◆ ◆

Paula's parents were elderly but were fit and in good health. Fiona thanked them for coming in promptly and asked if they knew what they wanted to discuss.

"Of course, we're old, not demented," Paula's father, Gordon, snapped. "We come from a generation that takes civil responsibilities seriously, so of course, we want to help as much as we can. The only delay was we took some time to reflect on that terrible time, so we could be as accurate as possible with our replies. By good fortune, my wife keeps a daily journal, which we've brought in. Libby, would you like to read your entry for that morning?"

Libby reached down for a hessian bag for life on the floor and produced a thick journal with an elastic band marking the relevant page. She coughed nervously as she carefully opened the diary. "Would you like to read it?"

It wasn't clear who she was asking, but her husband took the journal, coughed to clear his throat, and started to read. "I feel mortified now about my reaction. When Jade rang in the morning about sending out a search party, I decided she was being hysterical and dramatic. I thought Jenny had probably spent the night with a boy. I feel terrible for judging her so harshly now we know the truth. I cringe just thinking about how brusquely I said we had a prior engagement and carried on getting ready. Note to self – I need to practice being kinder. It was only coffee with a couple from the cricket club. I don't even like them that much. They're Gordon's friends. When we returned and heard the sad news, my first thought was Paula. Was that selfish of me? I'm worried about how this will affect her. When I told her, she was stoical and brave. I told her it was okay to cry, but she asked me to leave her room and threw the covers over her head. I feel I failed her. I will encourage her to talk about it tomorrow."

Gordon closed the diary, looked up and said, "A fairly exact account of that morning."

"Did you speak to Paula the following day?" Fiona asked Libby.

Libby shook her head. "I tried for several days, but she didn't want to discuss it. I could see how upset she was, so we thought it best to leave her to get over it in her own way. I wish I had forced the issue. Maybe if I had tried harder, she wouldn't have rushed into a marriage that was clearly going to fail."

Gordon snorted, and said, "She was a grown woman capable of making her own decisions."

Fiona noticed Libby flinched at her husband's words but didn't contradict them. Gaining eye contact with her, she asked, "Did you discuss it at all afterwards?"

"Not really, no. I could see she was hurting, but I couldn't reach her. She rarely came out of her room until she left a few weeks later for university."

"We didn't realise she went to university," Fiona said.

"She fell pregnant and dropped out the first year," Gordon said. "At least he married her. That was something, I suppose."

"Can we go back to the morning Jenny was reported missing? Did you see your daughter before you left the house to meet your friends from the cricket club?" Fiona asked.

"No," Gordon replied. "We called up the stairs to say we were leaving."

"We've racked our brains, but can't remember whether she replied," Libby said apologetically.

"You're not completely sure she was in the house when you left that morning?" Fiona asked.

"Of course, she would have been," Gordon said. "Where else would she have been?"

"Did your daughter know beforehand that you were meeting friends for coffee that morning?"

"Possibly. Probably," Libby said. "We usually let each other know where we would be and when we would return."

"Fiona asked, "Do you remember the time you returned home and went to see your daughter?"

"No," Libby said, stifling a sob. "I think it was early afternoon."

"That was a long chat over a coffee," Fiona said.

"At opening time, we moved onto the pub," Gordon said. "I don't know why my wife is being so coy about it. It's not like we were leaving a child alone in the house. Hardly a crime. We can't be any more accurate about the time we returned home than early afternoon."

"And your daughter was still in bed under the covers. Was it usual for her to lie in so late?"

"Not usual, no," Gordon said. "But there had been sleepless nights waiting for her exam results. You know how young girls can work themselves into a tizz. And, if I recall correctly, she had gone out the night before to celebrate her grades. We thought it had all caught up with her."

"By the night before, do you mean the night Jenny Trace died?"

"No, sorry. It was the night before that," Gordon said. "That evening, we watched television and went up to bed together somewhere around eleven."

"Would you mind if we took a copy of your diary entry for that week?" Fiona asked Libby.

"I don't see why not," Libby replied. "But I didn't write in it every night. The next entry is the day of the funeral."

"Thank you. It could prove very helpful," Fiona said. "How did Paula get along with Jenny? Were they close friends?"

"They were school friends who lived near one another. Jenny stayed with us on sleepovers maybe once or twice, and they occasionally met in a group on the weekends, but I wouldn't say they were close," Libby said. "Back then, Paula's best friend was probably James. I don't think they were boyfriend and girlfriend, but she saw more of him than the others."

"She would have been barking up the wrong tree with that one, in my opinion," Gordon said. "Good job, too, as I heard he's a junkie living in a squat in Birstall these days."

"Do you know where he's living?" Fiona asked.

"No idea, but that's the story that went around the clubhouse a few years back," Gordon said. "His parents say it is all nonsense, but they can't give a clearer picture of what he is doing with his life. They change the subject if anyone dares to ask."

"Is there anything else you can remember about the time of Jenny's death?"

Libby shook her head. "It was a dreadful way to end their schooldays, which we always thought were happy. There was nothing to foretell such an awful tragedy."

"Thank you for coming in to see us. I'll copy the diary entries, and you can be on your way," Fiona said, handing her card to Libby. "If you do happen to remember something else, don't hesitate to get in touch with us."

After seeing Paula's parents out, Fiona said, "There was

nothing in the initial report about a coffee morning. Paula could have been anywhere that morning. She could have been out all night, and then waited for them to go out so she could sneak back into the house."

"Do you want to interview Paula again?" Humphries asked.

"Most definitely, but first, let's concentrate on finding the final member of their group, James."

CHAPTER TWENTY-EIGHT

"I've finally tracked down James Rosefeld," Eddie said. "There's a reason it took a while. He now calls himself Jamie. Miss Jamie Feld. That's probably why his family disowned him."

"I will never understand parents turning their back on their child, whatever the circumstances," Rachael said.

"Reputation is everything in some circles, don't you know," Humphries said. "Some will happily sell their souls for a step up the social ladder."

"We don't know that for sure. There might be more to it," Fiona said. "Let's not pre-judge them until we have all the details."

"I've spoken to them," Eddie said. "They were snobs."

"Imagine being annoyed by a girl committing suicide because it impacted on their perfect life," Rachael said.

Eddie nodded. "I ended the call wondering where their compassion and humanity were."

"Nowhere if it's not bankable," Humphries said.

"Have you got an address?" Fiona asked, cutting across the conversation.

"And a telephone number, but she's not answering," Eddie said. "The address is a flat in Henbury."

"I think I know it," Humphries said, after reading Eddie's note. "It's a long way from the idyllic countryside or the leafy suburbs his parents would be used to. It's not a place you would want to visit alone after dark."

"I need to check in with Abbie, and then Humphries, can you come with me to see if we can find her?" Fiona asked.

"Do you want me to continue looking for background information on her?" Eddie asked.

"Yes, anything you can find will be useful, especially any mental health issues. We're not sure if she's a potential victim or a suspect. The parents blaming Jenny's death for all their ills may have become ingrained. I haven't any evidence, but I wonder if they were all on the barn roof that night and possibly haunted by whatever happened. I think it was guilt rather than grief behind their changed behaviour that summer."

Fiona headed over to Abbie, who was hunched over her desk reading a file. She stopped and looked around the room, "Where are the others?"

"The victims haven't been able to recognise the medals over the phone and were mystified by the prospect of electronic mail. As so few of them have their own transport, I've sent them out to show them the photographs," Abbie said. "I'm going to reinterview Ken once I hear back from them."

"In his initial interview, Ken admitted he had given Alice lifts, but he denied ever driving his son's car. Ask him about that again if the car key they found in his house matches his son's car."

"I heard a short while ago that it's a match," Abbie said. "Why did you complete the initial interviews without me?"

"I didn't know where you were, and things were moving quickly."

"You could have called me. That's what you would have expected me to do."

"Okay, maybe I should have told you I was starting the interviews, but I was angry about the way Ian was brought in."

"That's just an excuse. You simply wanted to do them yourself. Just like you abruptly ended my interview of Murden without any warning, making me look stupid. How am I supposed to progress if you don't allow me to make my own decisions?"

"You were there," Fiona said, thinking it wasn't the right time for this discussion. "That's when I heard about the items found in Ken's home and car."

"It's the way you did it," Abbie said. "You could have shared the information with me first. You didn't even pretend I had any say in the decision, and it made me look stupid."

"I'm sorry you felt that way."

"How did you expect me to feel when you totally excluded me? You just completely ran roughshod over me and took over without any discussion. What happened to teamwork? It never seems to apply to you."

"Are you saying I'm some sort of control freak?"

"If the cap fits."

Swallowing hard to control her anger, Fiona said, "That's simply not true. Right now, I would love to be in a position where I could leave the handling of the case to you, but after your stunt at the university, I can't. Taking Ian out mid-lecture put you and your colleague in danger, and I'm ultimately responsible for your safety."

"In your opinion."

"This is something we'll have to talk out, but not right now," Fiona said. "I'm going out to interview an important witness in the murder cases, but you can reach me by phone."

"What am I supposed to do meanwhile?"

"Re-interview Ken, and if he stays true to form, he'll change his story when he's told we've found Ian's car key and other items in his home. Hear what his excuse is this time for remembering things differently and, if appropriate, charge him for Alice's burglary."

"How about for the others?"

"We can hold him on the one burglary while we build a strong case for the rest. We don't even know who the medals found belong to yet," Fiona said. "When I return, we'll properly discuss our next moves."

"Seems a long-winded way to go about things," Abbie muttered.

"See you later," Fiona said, walking away before she said anything else. It frustrated her that they always seemed at odds. Sometimes, she wondered if Abbie tried to purposely needle and undermine her. She must realise they needed more evidence to link Ken to all the burglaries, and they still didn't know what part Ian played in them. It concerned her that Abbie didn't seem to realise it was a foolish risk to drag a student out of a packed lecture hall. Abbie was a good officer, but she was too bone-headed and impetuous, and one day, it would get her into serious trouble.

Fiona continued to think about her confrontation with Abbie as she headed out with Humphries to find Jamie. She didn't know why Abbie was able to get under her skin the way she did. She thought back to how well Abbie handled the three constables roped in to assist them. Maybe she was partly to blame. Dealing with Abbie caused her to question her ability to lead, give orders and deal with things like discipline. She wanted to concentrate on being a detective, not personnel issues.

"Everything okay?" Humphries asked as they drove towards Henbury. "You seem a little tense. The flats have a bad reputation at night. Kids from outside the area and drugs mostly. But it's still light. Half the residents are elderly or disabled."

"What about the other half?" Fiona had no concerns about entering the flats, but she didn't want to admit she had been ruminating over Abbie. Her hope that her issues with Abbie would resolve themselves if she ignored the hostility was wishful thinking. It would help if she could speak to someone about how best to deal with the problem. Peter, maybe, but not Humphries.

"Single parents, the disabled and elderly and a handful of immigrants," Humphries said. "You know the mix. Pack the vulnerable in and hope for the best. Then wring hands in horror when it all goes wrong."

Fiona didn't want to have a socio-economic debate with Humphries, either. To divert him and give herself some space to think, she asked, "What's your overall feeling on the three deaths?"

"I agree that the connection is buried in their past, but I'm wondering if something else happened around the same time as Jenny's death."

"Are you suggesting it might be something completely different?" Fiona asked.

"It's something we've not considered," Humphries said. "This something else might have been the cause of her death."

"If that was the case, I think we would have heard something about it by now," Fiona said.

"Not necessarily," Humphries said.

Quickly dismissing the idea, Fiona said, "No, I'm convinced the recent deaths are linked to Jenny's death. What isn't so clear, is why now? If someone is seeking revenge, why wait ten years? What changed?"

"If we're talking revenge, is Jenny's father definitely out of the picture?"

"My first thought was that he somehow discovered the three men, boys as they were then, were responsible for Jenny's suicide, but you've met him. He's not even capable of rolling his cigarettes, let alone persuading younger, fitter men to set up their own deaths," Fiona said. "What about the daughter, Chloe? You spent some extra time with her. Is she capable? She's the creative type."

"Hard to say, but I thought she was a sweet kid." Humphries fell silent, thinking the possibility over. "She could barely remember her sister or mother and is devoted to caring for her father. I don't think she would do anything that would put that at risk."

"The same argument could be applied to Ken Marsh and his wife," Fiona pointed out before pushing thoughts about the burglaries from her mind. She needed to focus on one thing at a time.

"Jenny's father could have threatened their loved ones in some way?" Humphries suggested.

"He would still have had to convince them he was physically fit enough to be a threat. Walking his dogs leaves him breathless. I'm also not sure he has the coherence of thought to plan something so devious," Fiona said. "He's a man waiting for his daughter to find happiness so he can crawl away and die. He came across as broken by his daughter's suicide but not revengeful."

"I agree with you there," Humphries said. "Do you think it was only the three of them partying that night?"

"I have my suspicions that they were all up there," Fiona said. "Paula's parents have no idea whether she was in the house that night. She could have easily sneaked out after they all went up to bed. We'll see what Jamie says."

"Do you think that Jamie could be our suspect?"

"It's a very real possibility," Fiona replied, looking up at the tired tower block as it came into sight. "It looks like life hasn't treated her well since her school days. Her parents blaming everything on that night rather than listening to her could have influenced how her mind works. I wasn't overly impressed with Paula's father, but he noticed something effeminate about the boy, possibly from only a few short encounters. Why couldn't her parents see it?"

"Maybe they did, and their reaction was negative."

"Being disowned by her parents, drug addiction and confusion about her sexuality is a heady mix. Anything could be going on in her head."

"Do you think Paula stayed in contact with her?"

"It's something else to discuss when we re-interview her," Fiona said. "They were close as teenagers, and both dropped out of university after a year. It's possible."

Fiona pulled into a semi-deserted parking area in front of the flats. The few cars parked there varied from wholly burnt out to having at least one flat tyre. She turned around and drove straight out to find a space on the road which had a constant traffic stream. She finally found a space about half a mile from the flats. Apart from the traffic fumes, it was a pleasant day for a walk. Having your car stolen when you're a copper is never a good look.

CHAPTER TWENTY-NINE

Jamie's flat was on the third floor of the tower block. They walked past the cardboard out-of-order sign propped outside the lifts and opened the door to the stairway. They powered up the stairs, keen to escape the claustrophobic heat and the cloying smell of urine and vomit. They followed the airless corridor to Jamie's door. Receiving no response, Humphries knocked louder a second time and called Jamie's name.

A disgruntled lady in a faded housecoat opened the door behind them. In a gravelly voice, she said, "She's not in," as she flicked cigarette ash into the corridor.

"Do you know when she'll be back?" Fiona turned and asked.

"She's gone away for a while. Maybe next week, maybe next month. Who knows? But she's not there now. What's she done, anyway?"

"We're not sure she's done anything," Fiona replied.

"Well, if she's not done anything, why don't you give my head a rest and stop banging on her door?"

"We need to speak to her," Humphries said. "Do you know how we could contact her? Otherwise, we're going to keep coming back to bang on her door."

The woman shrugged her skinny shoulders, eyeing them suspiciously. "Who are you, anyway?"

Fiona and Humphries held out their warrant cards for her to squint at. "Do you know where we could find her?" Fiona asked.

"What sort of trouble is she in?"

"We're concerned about her safety," Fiona said. "Could we come in and have a word?"

The lady closely examined them and slipped out through her doorway. After looking both ways along the empty corridor, she opened her door wider, and said, "Hurry up and come on in then. I'm Caron, by the way."

A short hallway with nicotine-stained walls led to an overly warm, cramped living room. Through a haze of cigarette smoke swirling around the room, Fiona saw a collection of cats sprawled on the mismatched furniture. Although the furniture was worn and the carpet threadbare in places, the room was immaculately clean, and there was a faint aroma of polish mixed in with the smell of cigarettes and cats. Framed photographs of happy-looking children covered a large dresser that lined one side of the room.

"Push the cats out of the way and sit yourselves down," Caron said, switching off the television. She stubbed out her cigarette in one of the many ashtrays dotted around the room and sat.

Reluctant to shove the cats out of the way, Fiona hovered by the side cabinet, looking at the photographs. "Are all these your children?"

"Good Lord, no!" Caron shrieked. She gave a throaty laugh, which quickly turned into a cough. "I've always been one for waifs and strays. When my Bob was alive, it was foster kids. Most of them turned out okay. A few even visit me from time to time." Once Humphries and Fiona had perched on the edge of the sagging sofa next to the cats, she asked, "What do you want with Jamie? You said you were worried about her safety. Is she in danger?"

"Possibly," Fiona said, trying to ignore the smell of cat urine wafting up in waves from her seat. "We need to speak to her in connection with something that happened when she was at school."

"Her schooldays, you say. It can't be that urgent, then," Caron grumbled. "Maybe you could leave a note, and I'll pass it on when she returns."

"The matter has since become urgent," Fiona said. "Do you know why she's gone away? Before she left, did she seem worried or scared, maybe?"

"Possibly." Caron was distracted by a tabby cat with ragged ears climbing onto her lap. It purred loudly and arched its back while she rhythmically stroked it.

"What's its name?" Humphries asked.

"I've never been one for ownership, so I don't tie them down with names. They are free to come and go as they wish," Caron replied. "Who has Jamie gotten herself mixed up with? I thought I had boxed some sense into her head."

"Like I said, it relates to something that happened years ago, before she moved here," Fiona said. "We want to make sure she's safe."

"And if she's not, will you protect her?"

"That's our aim, yes."

"She doesn't belong here. Far too classy. I always knew she was running from something. I guess it's finally caught up with her," Caron said. "Naïve as well. But she's always been a good neighbour to me."

"Any idea what she was running from?" Humphries asked.

"People can tell me things if they want, but I never ask questions."

"Do you know where she is?" Fiona asked.

"No, but she left me a number. She asked me to ring her if anyone came looking for her."

"Has anyone? Apart from us?" Humphries asked.

"You're the first."

"Could you give us the number?"

Caron pulled a cigarette packet from the pocket of her housecoat, knocked out a cigarette with a swift tap on the coffee table and lit it. After a while, she said, "I'll ring her and see if she wants to speak to you." She pulled an expensive Samsung Galaxy from her other pocket and stood. "I'll call her from the kitchen."

Humphries looked like he was going to follow her, but Fiona caught his eye and shook her head. When he sat back down, she asked Caron, "Can you tell her how important it is that she speaks with us? We're worried about her and are trying to help."

"I've been worried about her myself." Caron switched the television on and turned up the volume. "She's too gentle and kind for this world. I'll do my best."

Humphries strained to hear the telephone call over the television game show and cast Fiona a quizzical look. Fiona shook her head. It was best to leave Caron alone to make contact. If Jamie didn't agree to speak to them, they would worry about getting the number from her. She sensed that Caron was trustworthy and genuinely cared for Jamie.

Caron appeared in the doorway, puffing on her cigarette. "Do you know the Garden Café on Farleigh Road?"

"No, but we can find it," Humphries said.

"I don't know it, so I can't help you there." Caron walked across the room and stubbed out her cigarette. "She'll meet you there in half an hour. Give her my love."

"Will do. Thank you." Realising they had no idea how Jamie looked as an adult, let alone as a woman, Fiona asked, "Do you have any photographs of Jamie? A simple group snap will do."

Caron scrolled through images on her phone and turned the screen to face them. "That was my birthday bash at the start of the year."

Before they reached the stairwell, Humphries looked up the café's location on his phone. "It looks like it's tucked away in a quiet side street. If traffic isn't bad, we should make it in fifteen minutes. Do you think she'll be there?"

"I think that's what she told Caron," Fiona replied, hurrying down the stairs. "If she knows why the others were killed and is scared for her safety, she might be just as keen to see us. If she's responsible for those deaths, we've given her a half-hour head start. We'll find out soon enough."

"You don't think we should have insisted that Caron hand over the number? This could be a complete waste of time. If we had her number, it would help us track her down," Humphries said. "Why didn't you push for it?"

"I thought Caron was a genuine person and telling the truth."

Humphries scowled and threw up his hands. "What did she say about Jamie being out of place and naïve?"

"Let's just see if she turns up, shall we?" Fiona replied, hoping she had read the relationship between Caron and Jamie correctly. "We can go back for the number later if it turns out that we need it."

"Do you think it will still be listed on Caron's phone?" Humphries said, looking up at the ceiling.

CHAPTER THIRTY

The Garden Café was nestled amongst terraced houses in a street behind a small parade of shops. Inside, it was busier than they expected for a café in a residential area. Customers looked up in surprise, curious about two strangers entering their refuge. Fiona felt their eyes following her as she ordered two coffees, and they took seats at the back of the crowded room. The customers slowly lost interest in them and returned to their private conversations.

The décor and tables were dated and basic, but the coffee was surprisingly good. Fiona had spent far more on inferior coffees in upmarket coffee shops in the past. She savoured a few mouthfuls before saying, "We're a good ten minutes early. I'm going to pop out to call Abbie to find out what's going on with Ken Marsh."

Fiona walked the short distance to her car and sat on the bonnet in the sunshine to make the call. "Hi, Abbie. How's it going?"

"One of the earlier victims has confirmed the medals belonged to her husband, and she has accepted lifts from Ken in the past. We're still working on identifying the others."

"Have you reinterviewed him about it?"

"Would you believe he gave a spiel about how telling the truth is always the best policy? Anyway, he still denies borrowing his son's car. He doesn't know why his son suggests otherwise and can't explain how the key or the medals ended up in his home," Abbie said. "At one point, he accused us of planting them there because we were incapable of finding the real culprit. Can I get on and charge him for the burglaries?"

"Wait until I'm back. He's not going anywhere, so we may as well wait until we have watertight cases," Fiona said. "We also need to discover who his accomplice was so we can charge them together. Have you got anything on the son yet?"

"No, but their builds fit the witness descriptions."

"That's not enough. We need something more," Fiona said.

"How's your interview going?"

"We're waiting for her to arrive. Speaking of which, I had better get back," Fiona said, ending the call.

When she returned to the café, Humphries had somehow found someone to listen to his wedding plans. The big day was less than two weeks away, and overhearing the conversation reminded her that she still hadn't bought herself a dress. She left them chatting and went to the counter to buy another couple of coffees. Humphries was alone by the time she carried them over to the table.

"She's late," Humphries said by way of thanks.

Fiona sat and checked the time. "Only by a couple of minutes. We'll give her a while longer." She hoped she sounded more confident than she felt about Jamie turning up. Without anything to back it up other than a feeling, she had decided that under the harsh exterior, no doubt born by necessity, Caron was a compassionate person and a shrewd judge of character. She wouldn't have befriended Jamie if she thought she was a bad person. But if she were wrong then, pre-warned, Jamie would disappear and be hard to find in the types of places she would likely seek sanctuary.

As soon as Fiona raised the cup to her lips, the café door opened, and Jamie walked in, dressed casually in a t-shirt, jeans and heels. The girl behind the counter started to pour her drink without waiting for an order, and they exchanged a few words before Jamie glanced around the tables. Fiona waved, and Jamie gave a nod of acknowledgement before finishing her conversation and coming over. Fiona and Humphries had already taken the two chairs facing the door. Jamie put down her mug and angled a chair so she shared the view of the entrance.

"Thanks for agreeing to meet us here," Fiona said. "They make excellent coffee."

"Maybe I should ask for a commission." A faint trace of a smile danced around Jamie's lips, but her eyes remained guarded and suspicious. Up close, she had a hounded look about her. Turning her face towards them, she quietly asked, "How was Caron?"

"She seemed okay, other than she's worried about you," Fiona said.

"I hope you told her not to worry," Jamie said. After sipping her drink, she asked. "How much do you know?"

"About Jenny's suicide and the recent deaths of your school friends, very little other than they are connected."

"Is that it? Nothing else?" Jamie asked, her ringed finger nervously turning her mug from side to side.

Fiona gambled with, "The deaths and you going hiding was instigated by Alex Woodchester asking questions."

Jamie looked away towards the door. "In other words, you've put two and two together and come up with five."

"Could you put us back on track?" Fiona asked.

Jamie stirred her frothy coffee and sucked the spoon. "My mate is getting fed up with me on the sofa, my back is killing me, and I want to go home. That's the only reason I agreed to meet you."

"Is that a yes?" Humphries asked.

Jamie eyed him dismissively before turning her attention back to Fiona. "Are you in charge?"

"I'm the senior investigating officer."

"Do you go to a special college that teaches you to speak like that?"

"Are you willing to tell us what happened ten years ago and why you are so frightened?" Humphries asked.

Jamie jutted out her chin. "Who says I know anything about what happened ten years ago, and I'm frightened? I didn't come here to do your job for you."

Despite her bravado, Fiona could sense how anxious Jamie was. She was tense and nervous, and fear seemed to ooze from her. "We came here to help you as much as to seek information from you. Do you want our protection?"

Folding her arms, Jamie said, "I've never thought it was worth much."

Feeling Jamie was wasting time by playing games, Fiona decided to call her bluff. She pushed her coffee mug to the centre of the table and stood to leave. "I guess if you don't want our help, then you're staying on your mate's sofa until you're found. I think we're done here."

"Wait," Jamie said, dropping her spoon in her coffee mug.

Fiona retook her seat. "What happened ten years ago? The night of Jenny's death. Were you all there?"

"I'll tell you what I know if you say you'll find somewhere safe for me to stay for a few days."

"Like a police cell?"

"Is that your best offer?"

"I can't confirm anything until you tell us what you know. The ball's in your court," Fiona said.

"Okay. I'll tell you everything I know, but not here."

"Would you come back to the station with us?"

"Yes."

CHAPTER THIRTY-ONE

At the station, Humphries took Jamie to an interview room while Fiona popped upstairs to ask Abbie for an update on the burglaries.

With a roll of her eyes, Abbie said, "Ken Marsh continues to deny he has ever borrowed his son's car and can't give any explanation for the items found in his possession. Another of the medals found belonged to a victim, and two other victims have confirmed they accepted lifts from him in the weeks before they were broken into, so I've charged him with all four."

"What! I told you only to charge him for the one case until we firmed up on evidence."

"Yes, but new evidence came in, and you weren't here," Abbie replied. "I didn't see the point of holding things up indefinitely just because you weren't around to rubber stamp my decision. It is my case, after all."

"I don't remember telling you that, and I still have some doubts about his guilt," Fiona said.

"You're kidding! We found some of the stolen items in his possession."

"Yes, *some*. Where's the rest?" Fiona asked. "What's his motive, and who was his accomplice?"

"Hopefully, he's going to tell us."

Fiona had never missed Peter's calming influence more. She was certain she didn't want the role of DCI, and the appointment of a new person couldn't come quickly enough for her. Hopefully, it would be someone she could build a good relationship with and discuss operation issues. Right now, she had to clear her mind of her frustration with Abbie to interview Jamie. Within the next hour, she should know the secret that led to the three murders and, hopefully, who was responsible. "I'll deal with this later. I've someone waiting in the interview rooms for me."

Fiona felt a headache coming on as she marched off to interview Jamie. She would deal with Abbie's disobedience when she was calmer and had worked out how best to approach the situation. It had always been clear she was the lead investigator in both cases and had the final say on how they should proceed. There had never been any suggestion Abbie should take over that role. But should there have been? Should she learn to give her team more responsibility, and was her reluctance to hand over control weakness in her leadership? Did she have good reasons for not thinking Abbie was ready and having nagging doubts about Ken Marsh's guilt?

◆ ◆ ◆

Humphries carried a coffee for himself and a cup of tea for Jamie into the interview room. "Here you. I'll apologise now for the quality. The station doesn't provide the best." He placed the plastic cups on the table but remained standing.

"Aren't you going to sit down?" Jamie asked.

"Yes, but first, I need to check the recording equipment is working," Humphries said, fiddling with the dials on the machine.

"You feel uncomfortable around me," Jamie stated.

With a final check on the machine, Humphries sat across the table to Jamie. "Really? What makes you say that? If I thought you were a danger, I wouldn't have given you a hot drink. It would be water."

Jamie pulled a face. "Body language to start with. I don't bite. You're quite safe with me. It's not catching."

Humphries raised both his hands. "Seriously, I don't have a

problem. We are interested in one thing. And one thing only. Discovering who is responsible for the deaths of your school friends. We're not interested in any other aspects of your life. Okay?"

"If you say so," Jamie said. She took a sip of tea and pulled a face. "You were right about the quality. Water may have been preferable. When do we start?"

"When DI Williams returns. We've asked before, but are you sure you don't want legal representation?"

"I've done nothing wrong, so it's not needed. I studied law for a year. If I change my mind, I'll exercise my rights then." Jamie tried another sip of tea, shuddered and set the cup aside. "What made you join the police?"

Humphries was about to reply when Fiona walked in carrying her case file.

"Can we start now?" Jamie asked.

"We'll run through a few formalities first," Fiona said, sitting. "Are you happy for this interview to be taped?" While Humphries fiddled with the recording equipment, she said, "I will be asking you about legal representation again for the tape."

"Can we just get on with it?"

Jamie impatiently answered the required introductory questions and asked, "Can I start now?"

"I have some questions for you," Fiona said.

"Can't I simply tell you what I know, and you can ask questions after? Running through everything might make it clearer in my mind and jog my memory about some things I might have forgotten."

Fiona considered Jamie for a while. Sometimes, people did let unexpected details slip out when given free rein to tell their own story. "Okay, but I may stop you to ask questions along the way."

Jamie cleared her throat and crossed and recrossed her legs, seeking a comfortable position to begin. "It all started when Alex had a crisis of conscience about the death of a mutual friend, Jenny Trace, ten years ago. He was about to become a father, and apparently, that made a difference. Not something I would know about. Anyway, for reasons only he could explain, he felt stirring up old wounds would make him a better father."

"Sorry, can you start with what happened the night Jenny Trace died and explain these old wounds, so we're all clear about what you're saying?" Fiona asked.

There was a flicker of annoyance at being interrupted before Jamie's face broke out into a smile. "It was a dark and stormy night. Sorry. Sorry. Gallows humour. I do realise the seriousness of all this."

"If you could start at the beginning," Fiona said.

"Actually, it was a beautiful clear night. I remember the stars and the smell of recently mown hay."

"Can you just get on with it?" Humphries said.

There were no smiles this time as Jamie launched into her account of the evening. "Like I said, it was a warm summer evening, and Hugh's parents were away for the weekend, so he had the house to himself. Alex and Matthew were staying with him while they were away. I had cycled over to have a few beers with them at lunchtime, and that was when Hugh suggested we have a barbecue. I wish we had left it at that. We all did, but Matthew had the idea of having a late party and watching the sunrise to celebrate our exam results and inviting the girls over."

"Sorry to interrupt again," Fiona said. "Who was he going to invite?"

"Paula, Kate and Jenny," Jamie said. "Kate said straight away that she would be over. Paula was getting grief from her parents about late nights, so she said she would sneak out after they had gone to bed. Jenny wasn't sure. She had some farm chores to complete and didn't think she would be able to get away to buy her booze. Alex fancied her and told her not to worry. He would buy plenty, and she just had to bring herself. She agreed she would come over later.

"Thank you," Fiona said. "So, what happened?"

"First of all, Hugh was happy with the plan as long as we all kept quiet about it. He had promised his parents that he would only have a couple of friends to stay over, and there would be no wild parties while they were away. Then, he tried to call the whole thing off, saying he was worried about drinks being spilled and the damage we would cause. We were angry because we'd just gone out and bought all the booze and stuff. We called the girls to tell them it was all off, but when Alex rang Jenny, being Jenny, she told him to stop having a go at Hugh. She suggested the party go ahead at the barn on her parents' farm. Her dad hadn't started haymaking, so it was empty, it was warm enough, it had an electricity supply, and it was a good distance from the house, so we could blast music without it being heard."

"Did you overhear this telephone conversation, or is it what Alex told you afterwards?" Fiona asked.

After a pause, Jamie said, "Alex told us Jenny had suggested we use the barn." She stopped to sip her tea, although it had gone cold and wiped a tear away from her eye. "It was the sort of thing she would say. Everyone loved Jenny. She was bubbly and outgoing but also kind and generous. She always wanted everyone to be happy. What happened broke all our hearts, but I think it was worse for Alex. He was never quite sure, you see."

"Not really," Fiona said. "Did the party in the barn go ahead?"

Jamie gave a sad smile. "Oh, yes. It was a great evening. We were all drinking and having fun. Jenny made us promise we would meet back at the barn every summer to party. At the time, it sounded a fantastic idea, and we all said we would until we were too old to climb up onto the roof. Of course, we never did."

"Whoa. Go back a bit," Fiona said. "Were you all up on the roof?"

"Not to start with. We were mostly in the barn. It was Alex's idea. He had gone outside for a smoke and noticed the stars. We all piled outside to look. I wish I had the words to describe what a beautiful, clear night it was. Alex said we should climb onto the roof to be as close as possible to the stars. We climbed up using an overhanging branch and carried on the party. We finished the drinks that we had taken with us and started to stand to climb back down." Jamie dropped her head and fell silent.

"We need to know what happened next," Fiona gently urged.

"I didn't see what happened. Matthew said Alex gave Jenny a friendly push, but Kate said it was more of a rough push, as though Jenny had done something to annoy him. We've always wondered if Alex asked her out, and she said no. I guess we will never know the truth."

"Then what happened?" Fiona asked. Although she could picture the scene, she needed Jamie to tell them in her own words.

"I didn't see, but Alex said he saw Jenny miss her footing and reached out to steady her. I turned around just in time to see her fall. The girls were screaming and crying as we scrambled down. I don't think I've ever sobered up so quickly. I remember standing there in a state of shock. I think the girls were still crying. Hugh checked she was dead and started to organise us. We cleared up every scrap of our mess and went home after promising never to breathe a word to anyone about what had happened. We were all to say we were asleep in our beds and act shocked when she was found the following morning."

"You didn't think to call the emergency services, or her parents at least?" Humphries asked.

Jamie shook her head, managing to croak, "We were young, and panicked. If we had been older and if Paula hadn't slipped out without her parents' permission, we would have made a different decision. But we didn't. Nothing we could do or say now would change that."

Fiona reached forward to hand some tissues to Jamie, who was heaving great sobs. "Do you want to take a ten-minute break?" When Jamie nodded, Fiona asked Humphries to pop out for three decent coffees.

CHAPTER THIRTY-TWO

They were halfway through the coffee when Fiona re-started the interview and turned the tapes back on. "Before we move on, can you clarify a couple of things?"

"Okay, but I can't explain why we didn't do the right thing at the time. I was numb with shock and allowed the others to make all the decisions," Jamie said. "I think I just sat there in a heap. I can vaguely remember being shouted at for not helping with the clear-up."

"We can come back to that later," Fiona said. "We understood Jenny was upset with her exam grades, yet the party was a celebration?"

"Her *disappointment* was for her parents' benefit," Jamie said. "They wanted her to go to a top university and become a famous doctor or lawyer, but Jenny had set her heart on nursing. She was such a caring person. She would have been great at it. She denied it, but we wondered if she threw in a few incorrect answers on purpose to lower her grades."

"Okay. And she had recently split with her boyfriend?"

"She wasn't happy about being dumped, but she wasn't exactly heartbroken," Jamie said.

"As far as you're aware, only the six of you knew what happened that night."

"Seven," Jamie said. "The six of us and the adult."

"The adult?" Fiona asked, exchanging a quick look with Humphries.

"After the initial shock, Matthew retook the reins as leader. We talked for days about whether we should tell the truth. We were in a mess. Jenny was our friend. We were devastated and grieving. But the guilt. That was totally crushing. Our conversations went around in circles and always ended in the same place. It wasn't like anything we could say would change anything. Jenny would still be dead, and it was an accident."

"It would have made a massive difference to the family," Humphries said. "Suicide of a child is incredibly difficult to accept."

"And a sudden death isn't?" Jamie shrugged and looked away.

Fiona asked, "Who was the adult?"

"No idea. Matthew never told us." Jamie said. "Although we always came to the same conclusion to say nothing, the guilt gnawed away at all of us. At times, I was physically sick. We agreed that Matthew should ask a trusted adult for some advice. He said he did, but he never named them. I was never convinced he did speak to someone, but he said he had discussed everything and was told that we should keep shtum, and that's what we did."

"You all kept the secret for ten years, but then Alex had a – what did you call it? A crisis of conscience," Humphries said.

"Yes. He visited us all in turn to say he couldn't live with the secret any longer. He was going to tell Jenny's father what happened that night and wanted to know if any of us wanted to go with him. Of course, we all said no and tried to talk him out of it."

"Who do you mean by all of us?"

"Me, Matthew, Hugh, Paula and Kate. Kate hung up on him. She probably thinks she's safe living miles away in Australia."

"The remaining four of you in England were against the idea."

"That's what I believe," Jamie said. "I didn't get directly involved. I've no idea how Alex tracked me down, but I didn't want to speak to any of them. Paula acted as a go-between on my behalf. At one point, she was speaking to everyone several times a day. She told me that they all thought it was a stupid idea and tried to talk Alex out of it."

"And did they?"

Jamie shook his head. "I spoke to Alex the morning he died. He told me he was visiting Jenny's dad that evening. He called to ask one last time if I wanted to go with him."

"You're absolutely sure he was planning to see him that evening?" Fiona asked.

"Yes. He said his mind was made up, and nothing would stop him from finally telling the truth."

"Did Alex say whether he was speaking to the others that day? To give you all one last opportunity to go with him?"

"He didn't say anything, but I assumed he did. There was no reason why he would single me out," Jamie said. "When I heard about his suicide, I assumed his chat with Jenny's father had gone badly. It made sense, as Alex was already disturbed by the possibility that he had pushed Jenny from the roof. We were all drunk, and although we all stood by him back then, we were never sure that he didn't. A few harsh words from Jenny's dad could have pushed him over the edge. Going up to the barn roof seemed fitting. But that was before Matthew and Hugh. Their deaths changed everything."

"In what way?"

"It's obvious, isn't it? Alex told Jenny's father about the roof party, and he is out for revenge."

"It's one possibility," Fiona said, thinking back to the sick man, unable to roll or light his cigarettes and who could hardly breathe following a short walk. Could his ill health have been faked, and how strenuously was he walking before he arrived at the house? "Did Alex know the identity of the adult who advised Matthew to say nothing?"

"I don't think so," Jamie said. "He never said if he did."

"Who do you think it was?"

"We discussed it at length at the time," Jamie said. "I mean the rest of us. Matthew said it didn't concern us. We never came to any conclusions."

"You must have your suspicions."

"No, honestly. We couldn't come up with a single name. Matthew was never good with authority and tended to rub adults up the wrong way. A family member, possibly. His father? Although thinking about it, I don't think they got along when he was younger."

"Can you think of anything else that might help us? Anything that happened around the time of Jenny's death, or something Alex said before his death?"

"No, nothing. Believe me, if I think of something, I'll let you know," Jamie said. "What about me? Can you offer me some protection until you arrest her father? I think I've come to the end of my mate's hospitality."

"Is there anywhere else you could go?"

"If there was, I wouldn't be here talking to you," Jamie said. "You said you would help me."

"I'll see what I can do," Fiona said. "Can you give me your whereabouts for the nights Alex, Matthew and Hugh died?"

"I was in my flat, alone. Sometimes I pop over to Caron's, but mostly I stay in at night."

"You've told us that you didn't want Alex to reveal your secret," Fiona said. "We only have your word that it was Alex who pushed Jenny when you were on the roof that night. Was it you?"

"What? No! I was on the roof but nowhere near her. Ask the others," Jamie said, her voice fading away.

"Only we can't, can we?" Humphries pointed out.

"You can ask Paula and Kate," Jamie said.

"Was Paula fully aware of everything that was going on, every step of the way?" Fiona asked.

"Most of the time, she was at the centre of everything," Jamie said. "She was updating me."

"As you have no alibis for the nights of the murders, we have grounds to hold you while we complete our investigations," Fiona said. "Does that work for you?"

CHAPTER THIRTY-THREE

Fiona and Humphries returned to the incident room, where Fiona updated Rachael, Andrew and Eddie on Jamie's interview. She concluded, "I have two major questions. Why isn't Paula running scared, and who was the adult? Rachael and Andrew, can you find and bring in Paula? Until we have an answer to my first question, she is a suspect and has been lying to us, so take back up with you. Eddie, can you go back through Matthew's phone and electronic messages to see if he was in contact with anyone who could be this adult? Speak to his wife again and ask her if he ever had a mentor or even just someone he looked up to when he was growing up. Also, did we ever make contact with John's ex-wife, Jade?"

"No," Rachael said. "She moved to London shortly after Jenny's death and seems to have disappeared."

"Try to trace her again," Fiona said. "I'm going with Humphries to pick up John Trace for further questioning. If Jamie is telling the truth, I want to know why he denied that Alex had visited him earlier that night."

"What about speaking to Kate again?" Rachael asked. "If Jamie is telling the truth, then she lied to me as well."

"Ring her once you have Paula in custody," Fiona said. "Tell her you know she was on the roof with Jenny and see what she says, especially about where they were all positioned when Jenny fell."

Walking to the car, Humphries asked, "Do you believe Jamie's account of that evening?"

Fiona shrugged. "The only two people alive who could

corroborate or contradict her version of events have already lied to us and the police during the initial investigation. It would be risky to rely on any of their witness evidence. If we can drag it from them, it will be interesting to see where they place themselves and the others on the roof. I have the feeling that they'll all claim they were the furthest away and saw nothing."

"Do you think one of them could have killed the others?"

"If it were only Alex, I would say very possibly, to stop him from telling the truth about that night, but why kill the other two?"

"Because they worked out who had killed Alex?" Humphries suggested.

Fiona stopped in her tracks. She hadn't considered the possibility of two different killers. It could explain why the attempt to make Hugh's death look like a suicide had gone so wrong. She continued to walk to her car. "We need to find out who the adult was."

"Agreed," Humphries said, climbing into the passenger seat. He looked expectantly at Fiona when she didn't start the car.

"I said we would wait in the car for the uniformed officers to join us. They'll follow us in a patrol car."

The sun was low in the sky when the cars pulled up outside Little Tilbrook Farm. There was an inside light on in the kitchen, but Chloe's car wasn't parked outside.

Noticing the absence, Humphries got out of the car and said, "It will be easier if Chloe doesn't see her father being taken in for questioning."

"The light may have been left on for the dogs," Fiona replied. "Aren't John's AA meetings around this time? Neither of them may be in."

"Let's go and see."

Their presence set the dogs barking, but no one came to open the door. After checking around the back, they agreed that other than the barking dogs, no one was in.

Over the continued barking, Humphries asked, "Should I call Chloe?"

"No," Fiona replied. "The AA meetings are in Birkbury village hall. We'll head over there first."

The drive to the hall took them past Rooksbridge Farm and Frank Codrington's home. As Fiona drove past, she couldn't help looking over and wondering how Frank was doing and whether Joyce ever moved in with him. That was the problem with the job. They never got to see the long-term consequences of crime. They barged into lives that were falling apart. When people were emotionally charged, she would cajole and probe until she knew them better than their closest friends. And then walk away, never knowing how they pieced the broken fragments of their life back together and how the story ended. Yet each case left its mark and changed her in some way.

Humphries crashed through her thoughts by asking, "Wasn't your first ever case with Peter a murder on that farm?"

"Yes," Fiona replied. "It seems like a million years ago, now."

"You're not quite that old," Humphries replied, lightening Fiona's mood.

The village hall was housed in a Victorian building that had once been the village primary school. Fiona asked the uniformed officers to wait outside by their car while the two of them went inside.

The front door was open and led into a short, narrow hallway, possibly where children once hung their coats on a row of brightly labelled pegs. From behind an internal door painted an institutional green, they could hear voices. A handwritten sign hung on the doorknob confirmed an AA meeting was in progress. Fiona knocked loudly, waited a few seconds, and pushed the door open to be greeted by a row of annoyed faces.

Fiona quickly located John sitting in the circle and said, "Sorry to interrupt your meeting, but could you come with us, please." To her relief, John obediently stood and walked towards her, hurried even. Under the harsh hall lights, he looked deathly white and gaunter than when she had last seen him.

"What's happened?" John wheezed. "Is it Chloe? Has there been an accident?"

Something caught in Fiona's throat at the look of terror on his face, his deep wrinkles a map of the pain and trauma he had endured. "Chloe is fine as far as we know. We're here about the death of Alex and two other men." Catching sight of the row of inquisitive faces listening in, waiting for the punchline, Fiona said, "It would be best if we talked outside."

Relieved his daughter wasn't harmed, John's body sagged. He meekly nodded his head and followed Fiona out through the hallway. Once outside, he remained silent while Fiona read him his rights and told him they were taking him to the station, where he would be questioned under caution in connection with the murders of the three men. He couldn't even muster the energy to look shocked.

"Do you understand the seriousness of the situation?" Fiona asked.

"As long as Chloe is okay. That's all that matters to me," John said.

Handing him over to the two uniformed officers waiting outside, Fiona said, "You should be more concerned about your own situation. We'll give you plenty of time to talk through your options with your legal representative. If you haven't one in mind, someone will be appointed for you at the station. Do you understand?"

John looked at Fiona with tired, watery eyes. "I understand. I'm not an idiot."

Fiona sat on her car bonnet, watching John being driven away like a lamb to slaughter. She didn't feel proud about taking him in, and she felt in the pit of her stomach that something was wrong. Whatever his other failings, he was a loving father to Chloe. She tried to imagine how he might have reacted when Alex told him the truth about the night Jenny died. His anger, not only about her death but for the years he had believed she had committed suicide and the damage that had done to his marriage, his health and Chloe's childhood. Would he have found the strength to seek revenge for all those years of anguish? Could he have crystallised his anger into such a tight knot that it gave him the clarity to meticulously plan their deaths? No matter how hard she tried, she couldn't see it. She was jolted from her thoughts when the bonnet sank lower as Humphries sat beside her.

"What do you think?" Humphries asked.

"He may have lied to us about Alex visiting, but I don't think he's responsible," Fiona said. "He's utterly broken."

"He could have paid someone," Humphries suggested.

"Within hours of Alex telling him the truth? How would he know who to contact at such short notice ...?" Fiona's voice faded away. She rubbed her temples, trying to make sense of the thought that had occurred to her.

Humphries looked between Fiona and the village hall and twigged what had gone through her mind. "Shall we go back in and get all their names and contact details?"

"Do you think I'm being crazy?"

"No, it makes perfect sense," Humphries said. "According to his daughter, this group is his only contact with the outside world. If Alex confessed just before his meeting, who else would John tell? Isn't that what they do? Sit in a circle and talk about their day?"

Fiona looked back to the village hall entrance and checked her watch. "They're going to be in there another forty minutes, and I want to get back to the station to interview John. I was hoping to leave at a reasonable time today to spend some time with Stefan. Does that make me sound callous?"

"No," Humphries said. "It's probably the sanest thing I've ever heard you say."

"Get Eddie out here to take their details and ask about their meeting the evening Alex was killed."

Humphries pulled out his phone, but before making the call, he asked, "Did you see who else was in there?"

"Not really, I was focussing on John."

"Dan Murden," Humphries said, before putting the phone to his ear.

"Really," Fiona said, trying to think how Murden could be

involved and coming up blank. She could imagine him preying on the vulnerable, older people and youngsters, but she couldn't see him as a killer. After Humphries ended the call, she asked, "Is Eddie coming out?"

"Yes, he's on his way."

"If it wasn't John or one of them in there, that leaves the adult that Matthew contacted for advice. He wouldn't want the truth to come out and possibly had the most to lose."

"That only works if Matthew told Alex and Hugh who he is, and they then made contact with him," Humphries said.

"Maybe Alex did, and they thought they would try a little blackmail." Fiona pulled out her ringing phone and listened to the caller. Ending the call, she said, "That was Rachael. Paula has disappeared with her two children."

"When?"

"This afternoon. When the children came home from school, they were bundled into a taxi with their suitcases, according to a neighbour. The taxi took them to Birstall train station. Rachael and Andrew are trying to discover which train they caught."

"That would have been shortly after we contacted Jamie," Humphries said.

"Call Andrew and ask him to ask Jamie if she contacted Paula after arranging to meet us."

"I can call on the way back. Shouldn't we get going?" Humphries asked, as Fiona continued to sit on the bonnet staring into space. "We need to coordinate the search for Paula and interview John," he reminded her.

"And discover who the adult was," Fiona said, more to herself than Humphries, as she pulled her car keys from her back pocket. "Come on then. I thought you were in a hurry."

CHAPTER THIRTY-FOUR

Fiona was horrified by how dreadful John looked when she entered the interview room. He was slumped over the desk as if he didn't have the energy to hold himself upright, was deathly pale and looked confused and disorientated when he looked up. The deadness in his eyes sent a shiver down her spine. She was pleased to see Linda Wallace was acting as his legal representative. She was experienced, and while she fought hard for her clients, she knew how the system worked and was easy to deal with. Before she sat, Fiona asked, "Are you happy that your client is fit to be interviewed?"

Linda gave her an exasperated look. "I have raised the issue, but my client wants to proceed."

Humphries interrupted. "This needs to be on the tape. Can I run through the formalities and get the tape running?"

Once Humphries had finished, Fiona asked, "Has your client been seen by the nurse?

"Yes. I checked with the custody officer," Linda said. "I share your concern, but he has been confirmed fit, and he wants to proceed."

"Can we get on with it?" John rasped breathlessly.

"I'll start, but tell us if you start to feel unwell, and we'll suspend the interview until you've been fully assessed," Fiona said, looking to Linda for agreement. Linda gave John a concerned look but agreed to the interview starting.

Fiona had never felt so reluctant to question a suspect. She thought about the three victims and where they were found. It occurred to her that they were all found in isolated spots. The barn was on his doorstep, but Matthew lived miles away, and Hugh's home was on a main road, at the top of a steep hill. Her job was to question John, not to prove he couldn't be the killer, but excluding him could save them a great deal of time. "You told us before you don't drive. Is that because you can't or by choice?"

"By choice. I have a licence," John mumbled into his chest, barely keeping his eyes open.

"Do you have access to a car or truck?"

John nodded his head as he was overcome with a bout of coughing. When the bout finished, his pale skin was flushed. "My Land Rover is parked in one of the barns."

"Have you driven it recently?" Fiona asked.

"I start it up once a week to check it's still running. Occasionally, I drive it a short distance around the farm for the same reason."

Fiona made a note about checking the vehicle. She was surprised at how disappointed she felt, although discovering he had access to a vehicle did nothing to shift her gut feeling that he wasn't the killer. Maybe it was wishful thinking, and she didn't want to accept someone who looked so feeble and defenceless could be responsible for three deaths. Peter always used to tell her she needed to put her feelings of sympathy to one side and toughen up. "We have reason to believe that Alex Woodchester visited you on the evening of his death. Is that correct?"

There was a long delay, before John said, "Now why would he want to visit me?"

"Did Alex Woodchester visit you at your home on the evening he died?"

"I can't even remember when he died," John replied.

"Do you remember a police officer visiting you to tell you Alex had fallen from the roof of your barn?"

After a bout of coughing, John said, "Yes. A nice lass from the village."

"Did Alex Woodchester visit you the evening before?" Fiona asked. She regretted sounding so sharp, but she wanted the interview over as soon as possible, and John was making it a painfully slow process.

"If you say he did, he must have done."

"No," Fiona said, feeling her frustration rising. "I'm asking you. Did you receive a visit from Alex that evening?"

John started to clear his throat to reply but was overcome with another bout of coughing. The spasms started to become more violent, and he wrapped his arms around his chest to relieve the pain as he gasped for air. The uncontrolled coughs continued to rack his body, and he started slipping to one side of his chair.

"I'm suspending the interview now. Get the nurse in here!" Fiona shouted. The constable stood by the door shot from the room. Fiona moved around the table to stop John from falling from the chair and noticed he was coughing up blood. "We need medical assistance, now!"

"I'll go," Humphries said, but before he could move, the station nurse rushed in. After a quick assessment, she called for an ambulance.

Fiona looked on as Humphries helped the nurse lower John to the floor and move him into a recovery position. Moments later, the paramedics arrived and took over. Sykes, the custody sergeant, appeared in the doorway, and Fiona gestured for Humphries to leave the room with her. They discussed what had happened in the hallway and arranged for the constable to travel in the ambulance and stay with John. When the paramedics wheeled the stretcher towards the waiting ambulance, they were joined by Linda and the custody nurse.

Linda shook Fiona's hand and said she would be in touch before following the paramedics out of the door.

"I shouldn't have started the interview," Fiona said. "He was clearly unwell."

"He didn't look great, but he was deemed fit and wanted to continue. At least it's all on tape," Humphries said.

"I thoroughly checked him over," the nurse said. "He wasn't a well man, but he wasn't in that state when I saw him."

"Write up a full report," Sykes said. "When I booked him in, there was nothing to suggest the pressure of questioning would cause him to collapse. It was unfortunate, but nothing we could have foreseen."

"Did he contact his daughter to say where he was?" Fiona asked.

"If her name is Chloe, then yes," Sykes replied.

"I'll let her know that her father has been taken to hospital," Fiona said.

CHAPTER THIRTY-FIVE

Chloe didn't take the news about her father well. She accused the police of callously and unfairly harassing her father to the point of making him seriously ill and possibly killing him. She threatened to speak to the media and said she was going to sue the police before hanging up.

Fiona had expected Chloe to be upset, but something about the call unsettled her. It wasn't what she said but how she said it that set her on edge. Although Chloe's comments were verging on the hysterical, her voice had been controlled and measured. She sounded more vindictive than upset and angry at the news about her father. Calculated, even. Almost as if she saw an opportunity to make something more of her father's collapse, rather than feeling genuinely concerned and upset.

Fiona recalled how Chloe had told them she had two influencers interested in her clothing and wondered if her name was going to be shared far and wide on social media. It didn't worry her. She was more concerned about John's health, but Dewhurst's reaction wouldn't be pretty.

"Fiona," Rachael said, appearing in front of her desk. "We've had a confirmed sighting of Paula and the children. They travelled south on the train and got off at Exeter."

"Oh, okay," Fiona said, pushing her concerns about John and Chloe to one side. "Any idea where she was heading from there?"

"No, we're trying to discover if she has family or friends in the area," Rachael said. "Andrew spoke to Jamie. She called Paula after her neighbour, Caron, called her to say she was meeting you and going to tell you everything she knew."

"We need to find her as quickly as possible," Fiona said. She still wasn't sure whether Paula should be considered a suspect because she feared the repercussions of the truth coming out, or like Jamie, was petrified that she could be the next victim. Her gut feeling was that it was the latter. She had lied to them about the events surrounding Jenny's death, but Jamie hadn't suggested she played an active role in it.

But was the omission because they were friends? Jamie had said that Paula had put herself in the centre of things when Alex told them that he was going to confess all. On the face of it, Paula had less than the others to lose if the truth about Jenny's death came out. It would be in the news for a few days that ten years ago, she had lied about being with a friend who died accidentally. Was that worth killing three people? For a professional person with a reputation to protect, maybe. Paula worked part-time in a shop when her children were at school. But she was going through a divorce. Maybe there were custody issues still to be resolved, and she feared her ex-husband would use the situation against her.

Fiona imagined herself in Paula's position. As a mother, wanting to protect her children was natural. They needed to know more about her ex-husband and the terms of their divorce agreement, but that didn't explain why she had run. Was it because she was guilty or because she thought John would try to kill her, and did she know the identity of the adult?

Alarm bells had rung in Fiona's head the second Jamie mentioned the involvement of an adult. Wouldn't the unknown adult, who had advised them to say nothing, be the most concerned about his involvement becoming known? Frightened teenagers suffering from shock and grief had contacted the person for advice as a responsible adult, and they had calmly instructed them to keep quiet. If it were someone in a position of authority, they wouldn't want that poor advice to be public knowledge.

Andrew called across the room, "Paula's best friend at work recently separated from her husband and moved to Exeter to be closer to her parents."

"Get an address and follow up on that," Fiona said. "Also, can you see what you can find about her divorce and custody of the children?"

Humphries walked over carrying two coffees. "You looked like you needed it after your call with Chloe."

"Thanks. Have you arranged for someone to check John's car?"

"They're bringing it in now," Humphries replied. "I'm about to run a check to see if the registration plate has been picked up by any of the local cameras."

"Good. We have a possible location for Paula. I'm waiting for confirmation."

"Are we still considering her as a possible suspect?"

"She's not been ruled out, but I'm struggling to see a strong enough motive for killing her old classmates."

"She probably has the least to lose from Alex telling the truth."

"Unless there's an ongoing custody battle for the children. I've asked Andrew to check," Fiona said. "Problem is, I'm yet to be convinced John was responsible either, which leaves the adult."

"Any updates from the hospital?"

"Not yet."

Andrew stood to stretch his back and walked over to join them. "Hugh's telephone records have come in at last, and they show that Paula called him several times in the days before his death. Before you ask, I'm still waiting to receive the divorce details."

"Paula rang Matthew a couple of times as well," Humphries said.

"We also know from Jamie that it was Paula who kept him updated," Fiona said. "It could mean she was more unsettled than the others or simply that she had more time on her hands. Either way, we need to find her."

"Somebody should be on their way to the friend's address shortly," Andrew said.

"If you don't hear anything back in an hour, chase them up," Fiona said.

Andrew nodded and returned to his desk.

Humphries picked up his coffee. "I'll run the check on John's registration plate." On his way to his desk, he passed Eddie coming in. "Find anything useful?"

Eddie shook his head. "I've taken everyone's details and spoken to John's sponsor, but John has never mentioned Alex or anyone else coming to visit him recently."

Fiona joined them and asked, "Did you ask them about his general demeanour that evening and since?"

Eddie nodded. "The word that kept cropping up is despondent. John has always been a quiet group member who rarely speaks unless encouraged to. The only change they have noticed in the past few weeks is his failing health."

"Did you speak to Dan Murden?" Fiona asked. "I understand he was there."

"Briefly. I can follow up on him, but he said he barely knows John," Eddie said, stifling a yawn.

"Have you seen the time, Fiona?" Humphries asked. "I thought you wanted to leave at a reasonable time. Well, it's gone that."

Checking the time, Fiona said, "Okay, yes. You all look exhausted. Let's call it a night, get a good night's sleep and hit the ground running tomorrow morning." She walked over to Andrew, and said, "Ring Exeter station and give them my number, then finish up. If they find Paula, they can ring me at home." Fiona waited until everyone else had left before ringing Stefan. It would be after ten o'clock by the time she arrived home, but she hoped she could at least see him while he was still awake.

CHAPTER THIRTY-SIX

Fiona slipped quietly out of bed so as not to disturb Stefan. He had one, possibly two more nights before he had to leave. She crossed her fingers they might get to spend a whole evening together like a normal couple before then, but she doubted it. Downstairs, she sorted the takeaway boxes and the beer bottles from the previous night for recycling, filled a flask with coffee and headed into the station.

She was the first person in, and she finished her coffee while reading through the overnight updates. Worryingly, Paula had not been at her friend's house. Exeter had widened their search, but she still had not been found. Fiona wasn't sure if it was the quiet stillness of the office or the few snatched hours with Stefan, but she managed to speed through the remaining reports and decided to review the case file from the beginning.

She was halfway through Matthew Guppy's file before intruding thoughts about John's disastrous interview started to appear. Pushing them away, she returned to wondering who the adult could have been. Nothing in the file gave any insight into who they might have been. She closed the file and rang Matthew Guppy's wife. After some vague platitudes about how the investigation was progressing, she asked, "Did Matthew have an older mentor? Someone he turned to for advice?"

Ann Guppy gave a hollow laugh. "I was asked this yesterday. One thing Matthew wasn't good at was taking advice. Or asking for help."

"So, he didn't have an older friend? Someone from his past that he looked up to?"

"No, I can't think of anyone like that," Ann said. "Is it

important?"

"It could be. If someone comes to mind later, can you ring me?"

Wondering if Matthew's reluctance to seek advice stemmed back to his schooldays, Fiona returned to his file. She tried to stop worrying about John and concentrate, but after flicking through it, she gave up. She stretched her back. She couldn't settle until she heard whether John was going to be okay and whether Paula had been found. She wandered around the office to stretch her legs in the hope it would help her focus.

Walking over to the window, she turned to see Abbie arrive. As she was having problems concentrating on the murders, it would be a good time to ask for an update on the burglaries. Switching cases for half an hour might help settle her mind, so long as she avoided her unresolved issues with Abbie. She forced a friendly smile and asked whether Ken Marsh had admitted to his involvement in the burglaries.

"Nope," Abbie said. "Despite all the evidence, he is still completely denying everything. His denials are starting to become annoying. He seems to think if he keeps saying black is white, we'll finally believe him."

"Does he admit to giving several victims lifts in the past?"

"Yes. He can't remember any dates, but he often offered to pick people up and drop them home. We've another victim who remembers having a long chat with him only days before her house was broken into." Rolling her eyes, Abbie added, "She thought he was a lovely man. So kind and considerate."

"Interesting he admits to some things, but not others," Fiona said. "Have you questioned Ian again?"

"He was cautioned for lying to us when we first asked about his father and the car but not charged," Abbie said.

"So, he's been released?" Fiona asked, working hard to keep the flutter of irritation from her voice. "You've decided he's not directly involved?"

"His mother was making a fuss and we had nothing to hold him on," Abbie said. "We've been concentrating on tying all the break-ins to Ken."

"Any luck with finding any more of the stolen items?" Fiona asked.

"We're still pressing him on that. I think he has them safely stashed away somewhere away from the house."

"Can you put his son's file on my desk? I want to take a closer look at Ian."

"Why?" Abbie asked, before thinking better of it, and saying, "I'll grab it now for you."

While other officers drifted into the station, Fiona blocked out the noise to read through Ian's file. She stopped when she came to the report on the search of the house he shared with his mother and sister. In his bedroom, they found two expensive guitars, a Taylor and a Fender hybrid. She was reaching for her phone to call his mother when the hospital rang. She ended the call, grabbed the file and walked over to speak to Abbie. She dropped the file on her desk, and said, "I'll be gone for a few hours. While I'm gone, can you call Ian's mother and ask her about her son's guitars? Where he got them, where he learned to play and whether he has ever worked for Dan Murden."

"The entertainment guy? I thought he was out of the picture."

"There were two guitars hanging on Ian's bedroom wall. If he ever played for Murden, that could be how he knew his father was in the area. Check it out for me. And ask if he ever played in a band with anyone else," Fiona said. "Make sure you ask his mother, not him."

She headed straight for Humphries without waiting for a reply. He jumped when she tapped him on the shoulder. "Sorry. What were you so engrossed in?"

"Mesmerised, more like. Searching through grainy camera footage for John's car."

"I can save you from all that. Temporarily, anyway," Fiona said. "I've spoken to the constable who accompanied John to the hospital. The doctors have confirmed it was a panic attack."

"That was some panic attack," Humphries said. "I thought he was going to die on us."

"I know, but right now, he is sat up in his hospital bed and keen to speak to us. I admit that after the last time, I would prefer to question him while he's still surrounded by medical experts. The constable is going to arrange a suitable room. I'll see if I can get hold of Linda, and then we'll head out there."

When Humphries and Fiona arrived on the hospital ward, the curtains were pulled around John's bed, and the constable stood guard a short distance away. "What's going on in there?" Fiona asked, indicating the curtains.

"His solicitor arrived a few moments ago and asked to have a word with her client in private."

A few moments later, Linda emerged from behind the curtains and spoke to Fiona and Humphries. "At least he's got a bit more colour in his cheeks. He won't tell me what he wants to say, but he wants a taped interview. I have advised him against it without discussing it with me first, but he wants to go ahead anyway. Is there a room available?"

The constable stepped forward. "We have the use of the relatives' room for an hour. He's still only wearing a gown, and they insisted he be taken there in a wheelchair. Should I tell them you're ready now?"

"Yes, please," Fiona said, following the constable for a few steps. "I expected his daughter to be here. Has she visited?"

"She hung around last night wanting to speak to him but was sent home. She popped in earlier this morning, stayed for about twenty minutes, and left shortly after I called you."

"How did she seem?"

The constable blew out his cheeks and scratched the side of his face. "Hard to tell. She swooped in and insisted on pulling the curtains around the bed while she spoke to her father."

"If you had to say, would you say upset, angry? What?"

After some thought, he said, "Agitated. Impatient. Should I go and get the nurse now?"

"Yes, please. Thank you," Fiona said before rejoining the others who were in a huddle a short distance away from the bed.

"Let's hope it goes better than last time," Linda said. "Regardless of what he says, I will step in and stop the interview at the first sign of any distress."

"I don't want a repeat of what happened earlier any more than you do," Fiona said. "But we are dealing with a triple murder and the possibility there may be more victims."

Linda pulled an overly expressive, surprised face. "I don't think my client will be going anywhere for a few days, let alone a murder spree."

They fell silent when the constable returned with a nurse. When the curtains were finally pulled, John was sitting in a wheelchair with a blanket tucked around his legs. He raised a hand in greeting as the nurse pushed the chair away from the bed. Fiona, Humphries and Linda followed the chair into a room at the end of the ward while the constable collected a chair to sit outside the room. The nurse fussed over checking John's blanket before silently leaving.

Fiona didn't think John looked much better than when he had been in the station and was pleased to see there was an emergency call button on the arm of the wheelchair. Humphries placed a tape recorder on a low coffee table, ran through John's rights and introduced everyone in the room.

Perching on the edge of a chair that threatened to swallow her whole if she sat back, Fiona said, "We understand you want to talk to us."

John ran a hand over his face. "Yes. I want to confess to the murder of Alex Woodchester and the other two."

Linda sat forward. "I would like a word with my client in private."

John waved her away. "Sit down. My mind is made up." He turned his lifeless eyes to Fiona. "Do you want to hear it or not?"

Equally caught off guard, Fiona said, "Umm, yes. Please continue."

"Alex came to see me earlier in the afternoon that day when Chloe was at work. He told me about the party on the roof and pushing Jenny over the edge. I was in shock, barely taking any of it in, but I wanted him gone before Chloe arrived home. I asked him to come back later in the evening after Chloe had gone to bed." John stopped to catch his breath. His voice became huskier and more strained the longer he talked.

"Would you like me to get you a glass of water?" Fiona asked.

When John nodded, she walked to the door to ask the constable to find some water. Returning to her seat, she asked, "Are you okay to continue?"

John nodded but started to cough when he spoke.

Linda said, "I think it's best we wait for the water to arrive." While they waited, she tried unsuccessfully to persuade John to delay the rest of the interview until they had spoken.

Once John had drunk half of the bottled water, he said, "That night, after Chloe went up to bed, I waited by the window for Alex to arrive. I met him outside before he had the time to knock and told him I wanted to talk outside so we wouldn't disturb her."

"She hadn't heard his car arrive?" Fiona asked.

"She sleeps at the back of the house with her window closed."

Fiona wasn't convinced and thought it likely the dogs barking at an approaching stranger would have woken Chloe even if the car hadn't, but she wanted to hear the rest of his story, so she remained quiet.

"I walked him towards the barn where I had hidden my shotgun earlier. I pointed it at him and made him climb up to the roof and jump."

Fiona's head spun around, and she mouthed at Humphries, "Shotgun?"

Humphries shook his head. "We completed a check some time ago. There are no firearms registered in your name."

"It was my father's. It's never been registered," John replied.

"Where is it now?" Fiona asked.

"Safely locked away where I always keep it, on the top floor."

The involvement of the shotgun had surprised Fiona, but she was highly sceptical of John's account. Everything, from Chloe not hearing a car arrive to John being able to walk the distance to the barn, seemed suspect. Possibly, the gun was a lie as well, but she wanted the interview wound up quickly so they could check.

"Let's move on to Matthew Guppy. What happened there?"

"The same. I said I would shoot him if he didn't shoot himself."

"How did you find his address?"

John coughed into his elbow a few times before saying, "I made Alex tell me."

"How did you get there?"

"I drove my truck."

"And Hugh Dolan?"

"I overpowered him and tied him to the ceiling."

"And where was this?"

John suffered another bout of coughing and drank the rest of the water. When he put down the empty bottle, he was flushed and sweating profusely. "In his kitchen."

"How did you overpower him?" Fiona asked. "Like the others, he was a fit young man?"

After a further bout of coughing, John spluttered, "I caught him by surprise and hit him across the back of the head with my shotgun. He was dazed and confused." John was racked by another spasm of coughing. "I would like to go back to my bed and lie down now. I'm not feeling too good. You have my confession."

"I think this is a good time to stop," Linda said.

"Okay," Fiona said. "Just one more question. Where exactly will we find your shotgun?"

"With my grandfather's pistol on the top floor in the back bedroom at the end of the corridor," John said. "They're in a locked cabinet at the back of the old wardrobe in there."

"Where will we find the key?" Fiona asked.

John rubbed his head. "I don't feel great. I think I'm going to be sick."

"The key?"

"I don't know. Try the kitchen drawer," John said before vomiting.

Fiona stood. "Interview terminated. The constable will organise getting you back to bed." She nodded to Humphries to come with her and hurried from the room.

CHAPTER THIRTY-SEVEN

After saying goodbye to Linda, Humphries sprinted along the hospital corridor to catch up with Fiona. He was only narrowly closing the gap when she stopped at the door to the stairwell. He caught up with her and, out of breath said, "That was a bit abrupt. You didn't believe a word of that, did you?"

"No. John didn't kill anyone. Chloe did. She's the only person he would lie for like that," Fiona said, before opening the door and running down the flight of steps.

Panting to keep up with her, Humphries said, "Where are we going? Shouldn't we be putting a call out for her to be arrested?"

"You can do that in the car. First, we're going to the farm to secure that shotgun," Fiona said, reaching the bottom of the stairs.

"You think that part was true?"

"I'm concerned by the possibility it exists," Fiona said, opening the main exit door. "He's not stupid and probably knew that we would check,"

They sprinted side by side across the car park to Fiona's car. Between gasps, Humphries said, "You've kept up with your running, then."

"I have the feeling you haven't," Fiona replied, pressing her key fob to open the car.

Jumping into the passenger seat, Humphries said, "I'll get straight back to it after the wedding," as he picked up his tablet to look for the registration number of Chloe's car. Finding it, he put an all units call for her to be stopped before calling Rachael.

Waiting for the call to be answered, he asked, "Do we want back up to meet us at the farm?"

"Let's see if she's there first." Swerving out past an oncoming ambulance, Fiona said, "I think Alex did go to visit John, but Chloe intercepted him as she tried to with us, and he told her everything. She probably sat there smiling and encouraging him while she plotted her revenge. Alex possibly felt relieved that he wouldn't have to confess directly to John." Wheels skidding, she pulled out in front of a stream of traffic, forcing Humphries to hang onto the door handle while continuing his conversation with Rachael.

Looking over his shoulder at the car driver blasting his horn in annoyance, Humphries said, "Your driving hasn't improved."

"Whatever," Fiona said, still pressing the accelerator. "Is Jamie still at the station, and have they found Paula? We don't know if Chloe is running or trying to get to the others before she's caught."

"Yes to Jamie. They're still looking for Paula," Humphries said. "Do you want a couple of cars stationed outside their homes in case she turns up?"

"Go ahead and organise it but tell them to assume she's possibly armed with a pistol and a shotgun."

By the time Humphries had made passed the instructions to Rachael, Fiona was screeching to a halt outside Little Tilbrook Farm. He looked across at Fiona slipping off her seatbelt. "If you think she might be armed, are we calling the armed response team?"

"Do you see Chloe's car?" Fiona asked, before jumping out of the car. "At least we can check whether she has her father's guns with her."

Hurrying towards the front door, Humphries asked, "Accepting it was Chloe and not John, do you think he gave us anywhere near an accurate description of events?"

Knocking on the door, Fiona thought for a while. "Possibly not. She wouldn't be able to overpower the men any more than her father, but we know she's creative." Receiving no reply other than from the barking dogs, she turned the handle and found that it was unlocked. Fiona pushed the door open, and they were mobbed by the dogs wagging their tails and jostling for attention. "We had better find them some food and water before we leave." Surrounded by the dogs, Fiona moved to the kitchen and started to pull out the kitchen drawers and rifle through them, looking for the key.

"I'll check the other downstairs rooms while you're searching in here," Humphries said, before heading deeper into the house. He returned a short while later. "Find anything?"

Fiona poked her head out of the pantry that was to the side of the main kitchen and held up a bunch of keys. "Just these so far. They look like car and tractor keys, and possibly one to the house." She threw them to Humphries. "See if the Yale key fits the front door."

Humphries tried it in the lock, and shouted, "A perfect fit," before returning to the kitchen. "One of the downstairs rooms looks like John's bedroom. And why would he sleep downstairs?"

"To avoid struggling up and down the stairs," Fiona replied. "He's probably not been to the top floor for years. Let's check up there now. See if we can at least find the gun cabinet. We'll force the lock if needs be."

The staircase to the first floor led straight up, but the steps to the second floor were steep and wound in a circle. The temperature dropped as they neared the top of the flight of stairs, and there was a lingering smell of dampness and decay. As Fiona anticipated on their first visit, the upper floor was covered in cobwebs and in places the plaster had cracked and fallen away from the walls, which were stained with mildew. A strand of ivy had forced itself through a gap in a rotted window frame and was growing along the wall. What concerned Fiona the most was the myriad of footprints that disturbed the dusty floor leading to the last room at the end of the corridor.

Inside the room was a collection of broken bed frames and heavily stained mattresses. Over the years, water had seeped through a cracked windowpane soaking the windowsill, which had bowed into a deformed shape. On the floor, beneath the window was a black bin liner. Humphries opened the bag and looked inside. He pulled out a handful of framed photographs before diving back in and pulling out a tangled mess of necklaces and bracelets. Studying one of the photographs, he said, "I think these are the items stolen from the elderly in the area."

"The pair of them have been working together," Fiona said, as everything started to fall into place in a rush. "Chloe seeking revenge for her sister's death and Ian punishing his father for abandoning him as a child. They've been in this together from the start. Why didn't we think of it sooner?"

"Because up until now, there has been nothing to connect the two," Humphries said.

"Yes, there was," Fiona said. "The guitars in his bedroom. And they attended the same school."

"Hardly a direct link," Humphries said, dropping everything back into the bin bag. "Between his pub shifts and his mother, didn't Ian have alibis for the break-ins?"

"It explains why none of it has turned up for sale and why they weren't interested in taking anything of value. They just wanted to frame his father, and they thought it would never be found if they dumped it all here. They might not have monetary value, but they were special to the owners," Fiona said, opening the wardrobe door. She pushed some moth-eaten, ancient fur coats to one side and turned to face Humphries. "Let everyone know they are armed with two guns."

CHAPTER THIRTY-EIGHT

While they searched the room for clues as to where Chloe was heading, Humphries received a call from Rachael. He shouted across the room to Fiona, "There have been no sightings of them yet."

"I'm not sure if that's a good or a bad thing," Fiona replied. "I would prefer to think they've gone into hiding rather than seeking out the others Chloe holds responsible for her sister's death, but I have a nasty feeling they think they have unfinished business. Otherwise, why take the two guns?"

"Protection?" Humphries half-heartily suggested. "They've got cars outside Jamie's and Paula's homes and have found where Paula is staying. She's in a caravan rental, and she told the officers no one knew she was planning to make the trip, which was a spur-of-the-moment decision."

"It would have been helpful if she had been truthful with us from the start, but at least she is somewhere safe," Fiona said. "Do we have a contact number for her?"

Humphries nodded. "Rachael wants to know if she should let her know what is going on. The Exeter police were only asked to check her whereabouts."

"Tell her to keep it vague but enough to ensure she keeps herself and her children out of harm's way."

After completing his call, Humphries helped Fiona to check the other rooms on the top floor. It didn't take them long. Most of them were empty of everything except undisturbed dust, and they headed down to find Chloe's bedroom.

The first room was empty. The second room they entered appeared to be the room John had shared with his wife. Bottles of long-gone-off perfume were lined up on the dressing table, and a few dated dresses and blouses hung in the wardrobe. A thick layer of dust covered all the surfaces, including the bedspread and curtains. It looked like John had picked up his clothes and shut the door of his marital bedroom after his wife left and had never re-entered it.

The third room was dark, courtesy of the ivy that had grown over the window, shutting out the daylight. The untamed ivy would eventually do the same on the top floor if not cut back. Humphries flicked on the light switch, and the naked light bulb lit the sad emptiness of the room. The room contained an empty wardrobe with a broken door hanging open at an angle, a stripped bed and a couple of boxes containing books and old correspondence.

Fiona rummaged through the boxes to see if there were any personal letters amongst the household bills but came away empty-handed. "I'm guessing this was John's room before he moved downstairs." After Humphries checked under the bed, Fiona switched off the overbright light, and they returned to the corridor.

The fourth room was a teenager's bedroom. Shoes and trainers littered the floor alongside a discarded sweatshirt, and school textbooks were piled on a desk by the window. The wardrobe was bursting with clothes, and a hockey stick stood in the corner of the room. The vivid colours of the bedspread were faded by the sunlight streaming in from the window and a thick covering of dust. Fiona flicked open the top textbook to see the name Jenny Trace neatly written inside. She checked around for any disturbance in the room and concluded no one had entered the room for nearly ten years. It was exactly as Jenny had left it that summer evening to party with her friends.

Humphries crossed the room to the window. It looked out across green fields to the front of the house, and the barn roof could just be seen in the distance. He shrugged off the room's eerie sadness, and brightly said, "The next room must be Chloe's."

Chloe's room was sparsely decorated, regimented and spotlessly clean and tidy. Her single bed was made, and all her clothes were neatly folded away in drawers or hanging in a small wardrobe. On a small desk were two folders, one full of clothing designs and the other musical scores. Humphries checked all the drawers, but they contained nothing except pens and stationery while Fiona worked her way through the neatly folded clothes. Admitting defeat, they headed out to the car.

"Where are we going?" Humphries asked.

"Back to the hospital. I want to know what else Chloe told her father. He might know where she's heading."

"Do you think he'll tell us?"

"I'll try to convince him it's in her best interests that we find her quickly," Fiona replied. "I'm worried that she has the guns and, if she has discovered the adult's identity, she's going to want to confront them before giving herself up. I'm hoping she told her father who it is."

CHAPTER THIRTY-NINE

Walking towards the hospital's main entrance, they spotted John with a group of patients either smoking or vaping. The constable stood to one side, looking sheepish. John tried to slip away as soon as he spotted them, but Fiona and Humphries quickly caught up with him. Breathing heavily, John leaned on the wall, and said, "Back so soon? Are you here to arrest me for murder?"

"You know we're not," Fiona said. "Where's Chloe?"

"I've no idea," John said. "Visiting hours aren't until later."

"Wrong answer," Humphries said abruptly.

Fiona shot Humphries a warning look. They needed information fast but wouldn't get it if John had another panic attack. Much as she wanted to shake some sense into John, they needed to take a gentler approach. "We know it was Chloe," Fiona said. "Alex came to see you but didn't get past her. Why don't we find somewhere to sit down to talk about it?"

"I don't know what you're talking about," John blustered.

"Please, John. Alex told her everything about that night up on the roof, and she's out for revenge. She told you all this earlier this morning, which is why you tried to confess to the murders," Fiona said. "I know how much you care about her. We want to find her before she gets into any more trouble. Because she will, John, unless we catch up with her first."

"No, I told you, Alex appeared when Chloe was out. I spoke to him. It was me," John forced out between gritted teeth.

"We know that's nonsense," Fiona said. "We need to find your daughter. You can't protect her anymore."

John doubled over as he endured a violent coughing fit. He slowly straightened himself, and said, "And I've said I don't know where she is."

Fiona would have preferred him to be sitting closer to the medical staff when she told him about the missing guns, but the clock was ticking, and they weren't getting anywhere. Although John didn't look great, it was probably the best she had seen him. "Both of your guns are missing," Fiona said. "She has taken them with her friend, Ian. We need to find a quiet place to sit down so you can tell us what they are planning?"

John paled and fumbled in his pocket for his tobacco tin. "I don't know anyone called Ian."

"Please," Fiona said. "It's in Chloe's best interests we find her before she does anything stupid. Let's find somewhere inside to sit down."

John nodded towards a nearby bench on the edge of the car park. "There will do." They walked at a frustratingly slow pace to the bench, with the constable following a short distance behind. John held onto the bench to balance himself as he carefully lowered himself to the seat.

Fiona sat down next to John, Humphries remained standing, and the constable walked to another bench a short distance away. Once John was settled, Fiona asked, "Where is she, John?"

"I don't know."

The urge to shake him reappeared, but Fiona calmly said, "You need to tell us what you know. Things can only get a lot worse for her. She can't escape from what she's already done, but we can prevent further bloodshed. Blood that might include hers, as she'll be considered armed and dangerous. You don't want that, do you?"

John opened his tobacco tin but didn't take a cigarette out. "She'll get away and start a new life."

"No, she won't," Humphries said, throwing his arms up in frustration. He walked a small circle before standing directly in front of John. "We will find her sooner or later. She can't run forever. When she runs out of cash, she'll be stuck. She won't be able to access a bank account or seek legal employment as we'll be on to her straight away. She's an intelligent girl, so she'll know that. And pretty. She'll have only one thing worth selling."

"Shut up," John said, gasping for breath.

Fiona shot Humphries another sharp look before gently saying, "Sadly, he's right. It won't be safe for her out there. What sort of a life will she have? Constantly on the run and looking over her shoulder, living in the shadows."

John handed his tobacco tin to Fiona. "Can you roll me one?"

Having never smoked, Fiona passed the tin to Humphries without looking at it. While he rolled the cigarette, she asked, "Where is she?"

"I don't know, but she didn't kill those men. She's been strong and brave. You have to believe that," John said, before succumbing to a coughing fit. When he recovered, he continued, "You're correct about Alex's visit. He came to see me to confess, but I was at my AA meeting, so he spoke to Chloe instead. He told her all about the party and who else was up on the roof. His guilt was too heavy a burden, and he wanted it to end. Chloe didn't understand what he meant. He asked her to sit with him on the barn roof. She wasn't expecting him to jump. She liked Alex."

Fiona doubted it was the truth but didn't question John on the explanation Chloe had given him. At least he was talking, which was progress. Instead, she asked, "And the other two? Matthew and Hugh?"

John took a lit cigarette from Humphries and put it to his lips. He coughed and spluttered after inhaling. "After Alex had done what he did, Chloe tracked them down and confronted them. They were equally to blame for Jenny's death. She thought they were cowards for hiding behind their lies, and she also blamed them for Alex taking his own life in desperation. He always wanted to confess, but they worked together to prevent him."

John suffered another coughing fit, which seemed to carry on for ages. He accepted he couldn't smoke and talk, so he threw his cigarette on the ground.

"What happened next?" Fiona asked,

Breathing heavily through gritted teeth, John said, "She told them she was going to tell the truth and show them up for the lying cowards that they were. She hoped it would destroy their reputations and make their lives difficult for a while, but she didn't expect them to take the easy way out and kill themselves."

Fiona questioned whether, deep down, John believed his daughter's version of events. It dawned on her that it might not even be her version. He could be making it up as he went along to convince them of his daughter's innocence. Otherwise, why did he mention the shotgun in his initial confession? She saw the benefit of pretending she believed his new story. "If what you say is correct, Chloe hasn't seriously broken the law yet. That could change unless we get to her fast. We know that after Jenny's death, Matthew approached an adult for their advice. Did Chloe say who it was?"

"She did mention someone but didn't give a name," John said. "One of the boys had tried to lay all the blame on him. Matthew, I think."

"Him?" Fiona asked. "Are you sure Chloe referred to the person as a him?"

John furrowed his forehead in thought. "Yes, it was definitely a man."

Fiona turned to Humphries. "Call Mathew's wife and ask her again if her husband had an older male friend of any description. When Humphries stepped away, she asked John, "Are you sure you have no idea where Chloe might be? A special place you've visited together, maybe."

John stared at the floor a long time before wheezing, "I think you're right. She will want to confront the grown-up before giving herself up. And before you ask again, I have no idea who it might be."

"Okay." While Humphries was still on the phone, Fiona beckoned the constable over. To John, she said, "You're free to leave the hospital, but don't leave the area. I expect your dogs will be pleased to see you. The constable will make the arrangements to take you home."

"I can't leave. The doctors found something on a routine blood test. Something to do with white blood cells. I'll be here a while. The way they look at me, I'll probably be leaving in a box. Make sure you get my Chloe back before then, will you?"

Despite his lies to protect his daughter, Fiona thought John was a good man who had been dealt a bad hand, and a lump rose in her throat at the look of defeat in his eyes. She assumed it was cancer, and by the look of him, he didn't have long. Seeing Humphries had ended the call, she said, "I'll do my best. Good luck with the doctors."

CHAPTER FORTY

Walking to the car, Humphries said, "You do realise he was lying?"

"Of course, but we weren't going to get anything more out of him," Fiona said, unlocking the car doors. "Give the bloke a break. He's dying."

"He's still a liar," Humphries muttered. "And guilty of wasting our time."

Fiona telephoned the station for an update. There had been no sightings of Chloe or Ian, but both of their cars had been found. Chloe's car had been left in the university car park, and Ian's had been abandoned a short distance from Birstall bus station. Officers stationed outside Jamie's and Paula's homes hadn't seen anything. As soon as Ken had been updated and released, he had insisted on leaving the station and collecting his wife from the nursing home she had been placed in. They were currently on their way home with a police escort.

Rachael and Andrew were doing a great job coordinating, so Fiona saw little point in returning to the station. An idea was forming in her mind as she drove out of the hospital and turned in the opposite direction to the station.

"Where are we heading?" Humphries asked.

"It's a long shot, but we're going to Berkhampstead School. As Matthew wasn't close to his parents and didn't have doting uncles to confide in, the only adults we know he was in regular contact with were his teachers. He was a keen rugby player, and sports coaches are often viewed differently from academic teachers by students."

"Patrick Burke, the current head, was his rugby coach. He also taught geography and denied even remembering the boys well," Humphries said.

"We also know he is a liar," Fiona said. "I thought it strange at the time that the school would deny anything significant happened the year the boys graduated, when they were fully aware one of their pupils had died."

"I assumed it was to do with protecting the school's reputation and not wanting to scare away prospective parents," Humphries said.

"So did I at the time," Fiona admitted. "But if he was the adult Matthew went to for advice, he was lying to save his personal reputation, and that's a whole different matter. The truth coming out about his part in the cover-up of how Jenny died would ruin his career."

"He is the type who would put personal survival over the good of the school if it came to it," Humphries said.

"If I'm correct, he could have made the wrong choice, then," Fiona said. "When they decided to keep quiet about the party at the barn, Alex and the others were teenagers. Their panicked reaction is more forgivable than the considered advice of an adult. Imagine how Chloe felt when she heard about his involvement. I think she knows it's only a matter of time before we catch up with her, and she'll be determined to get to him first."

"Let's hope you're correct about it being him, then," Humphries said. "And she's not on her way elsewhere to confront someone else."

"Do you have any better ideas about who it might be?"

"Nope. I think you could be right, but I'm also worried that you're not."

"That makes two of us, but I can't think who else Matthew might have turned to," Fiona said.

"His wife said he had a real problem with asking for advice and authority figures generally," Humphries said. "I wonder if that could be a throwback to him feeling let down by the advice he was given back then."

"Possibly," Fiona said. "But I'm more interested in Chloe's state of mind right now."

They drove through the school gates in silence, both hoping and dreading Fiona's hunch was correct. As soon as they rounded the corner and the school came into sight, Fiona said, "Call it in and get armed support here, now," before bringing the car to a screeching halt outside the front entrance. She shouted out the car window at one of the students streaming past, "What's happened?"

"There's two shooters in there," the boy shouted back before scurrying away with his classmates.

Humphries and Fiona leapt from the car, and Humphries started running toward the school entrance, pushing against the flow of students. Fiona called after him, "Get back here and put on a jacket." She opened the car boot and pulled out two stab jackets. "Better than nothing."

Humphries returned and put his on before grabbing the elbow of a fleeing teacher. He pulled him to one side. "Did you see the intruders? Where are they heading?"

"No. I didn't actually see them. I was told there were two people carrying guns on the premises and started to evacuate my class."

"Do you know who did see them?"

"Sorry, no. We're just trying to get all the students out as quickly as possible."

"Make sure they're moved well away from the school buildings," Humphries said.

"We were going to assemble on the tennis courts like a fire drill and do a register check."

"You need to get everyone completely off the school premises. An armed response team will be here soon. We don't want any of you on the grounds. Make sure your colleagues do the same," Humphries said, hurrying after Fiona.

Fiona was just inside the school entrance, talking to a teacher who was trying to calm the students, so they left safely rather than in a stampede. Seeing Humphries, she said, "They were seen going up to the second floor. No shots have been fired yet. This gentleman saw them and confirmed only Chloe was carrying a gun, but we can't assume Ian is unarmed. We need the armed response team here now. Did they say when they would get here?"

Humphries shook his head and pulled out his phone. "I'll see if I can hurry them along." Ending the call, he took Fiona to one side and said, "There have been several other calls, and it could be anything up to half an hour."

"What? That's not good enough," Fiona said. "By then, it could be too late."

"From the sounds of it, they are heading to Burke's office, which is about halfway along the corridor on the second floor." Seeing the number of students thinning, Humphries said, "It looks like most of the students and staff are out. Just the last few stragglers now."

"It looks that way, but I've been told two classes at the end of the corridor have barricaded themselves in," Fiona said, watching the dwindling numbers descending the stairs. "There could be other pockets of students hiding, rather than making a run for it."

"Are we going to evacuate that room?"

"If we can do so safely, yes. Are you happy to go up before the armed response team arrives?"

"Of course," Humphries said. "I don't think we can wait half an hour. If we do, Burke will die, and we'll still have the problem of trying to contain Chloe and Ian in the building until they arrive."

"A negotiated settlement by the experts would be the best outcome," Fiona said, biting her lip.

"Then, what are we waiting for?" Humphries said, starting to hurry towards the staircase.

"Wait! Are you sure about this?" Fiona asked.

"If we can resolve the situation and avoid more deaths, then yes," Humphries said. Patting his bulky vest, he added sarcastically, "I've got this to protect me."

They made their way up the stairs as the last of the students were coming down. A hushed silence greeted them at the top of the stairs. Fiona whispered, "Which way to Burke's office?"

Humphries pointed to the right. "I guess the barricaded classroom is along there at the end."

They crept quietly along the corridor until Humphries stopped and pointed to the nameplate on the door. "That's where we spoke to him."

They listened at the door but couldn't hear anything through the solid wood.

"How many students are in the end classroom?" Humphries quietly asked.

"I was told two classes, so anywhere between thirty to sixty-plus, I guess," Fiona replied, looking along the narrow corridor. "I'm not happy about leading that many students out past here. Especially as I don't think Chloe has any interest in harming them unless they get in her way. Quickly go down there, explain what's going on, and tell them to keep the door barricaded until we give them the all-clear."

Fiona pressed her ear against the headmaster's door while she waited for Humphries to return. She thought she could hear a low murmur of voices and possibly furniture being dragged across the floor, but she couldn't be sure she wasn't imagining it. She stepped back when she heard Humphries returning.

"Do we have a plan?" Humphries asked.

"I'm going to knock on the door and take it from there," Fiona said.

"That leaves a lot of room for improvisation."

Fiona took a deep breath and knocked on the door. "Chloe, it's DI Fiona Williams and DS Humphries. We spoke to you out at the farm. Can we come in?" Receiving no response, she slowly turned the handle, opened the door partway and repeated herself. She ignored the expected rebuff and stepped inside the room, trying to steady her breathing. There was nothing she could do about the trickle of sweat she felt run down her side. She doubted the effectiveness of the uncomfortable stab vest in close-range gunfire and knew that Humphries did, too. Sensing him behind her, she took another step into the room while he closed the door behind them.

"What the hell? Get out!" Chloe said, erratically waving the pistol at them before training it back on Burke.

Fiona took in the scene, noting the lack of the shotgun. A noose had been hung from the ceiling, and Ian held a knife to Burke's throat as they both stood on the desk. Burke appeared to be frozen to the spot with his hands tied behind his back. Only his frightened eyes moved as he tracked where Chloe pointed her gun. Chloe had moved closer to the open window so she could keep everyone in her sightline. Fiona found herself hoping the armed response team hadn't yet arrived. They would have a clear shot of Chloe from outside, and she wanted to avoid any bloodshed.

Waving the gun between the three of them in turn, Chloe said, "Get his head in the noose, now. Do it!"

Fiona saw the hesitation and doubt on Ian's face. "No, wait a minute," she said, holding eye contact with Ian as long as possible. "You don't want to do this."

"Yes, he does!" Chloe shouted, pointing the gun at Fiona. "Do it!"

"Stop a moment and think about what you're doing," Fiona said to Ian, before turning her attention to Chloe. "Do you think your sister would have wanted this?"

"You're claiming to know what my dead sister would have wanted. I expect she wanted to be alive," Chloe said. "This isn't only about my sister. It's about what a bunch of cowardly liars did to my family. And this is the monster who encouraged it. Thinking Jenny had taken her own life destroyed my father. If he had known she was pushed from the roof, it would have made all the difference. My mother would have stayed, and they would have had someone else to blame other than themselves, and me."

"I'm sure they never blamed you. Why should they?"

"Oh, do shut up! You don't know anything."

"What do you think this will do to your father?" Fiona asked.

"You won't be able to escape."

"My father is dying because of this cowardly freak." Chloe turned toward Ian, and shrieked, "Do it!"

Ian reached forward to place the noose around Burke's neck. Burke made a pathetic attempt at resistance, but Ian had a firm hold of the back of his jacket, and with his hands tied behind his back, all Burke managed to do was shuffle his feet.

Fiona shouted, "No!" again, and Chloe swung the gun back in her direction.

"What about your fashion business? Your plans for the future?" Fiona desperately asked, aware she was losing the argument.

With Chloe's attention swapping between Burke and Fiona, Humphries had quietly edged out of the line of fire and closer to Chloe.

"Now!" Chloe shouted.

Ian pushed Burke over the edge of the table, and Chloe's attention swung away from Fiona. Humphries seized the opportunity to launch himself across the room and bring Chloe down. In the scuffle, the gun went off before he was able to grab it out of Chloe's hand and send it skidding across the floor to Fiona's feet.

Fiona scooped up the gun, threw it to the far side of the room and dashed towards Burke. She leapt onto the desk and pulled him back towards her until his feet made contact with the desktop. As soon as she pulled the noose from around his neck, he slumped to his knees. She jumped down from the table and looked up just in time to see Ian run out of the room. She shouted after him to stop as she cursed to herself.

She sensed movement from behind and turned, expecting to see Humphries. It was Chloe holding an ornate candle holder over her head. Fiona jerked to the side just in time to avoid the blow. She grabbed hold of Chloe's shirt and sent her spinning into the desk. "You're going nowhere, young lady," she said, as she pinned her against the desk, kicking her legs from under her so she fell to the floor. Fiona quickly flipped Chloe over so she was face down and pulled her arms behind her back.

Heavily winded from colliding with the desk, Chloe managed to sneer through gritted teeth, "Aren't you going to see to your partner?"

Fiona pulled Chloe's arms tighter and placed her knee in her back, not daring to look around. It was bad enough that she had let Ian escape, and all she could hope was that he wouldn't get far. She was going to keep a tight hold on Chloe. She looked up to Burke for help, but he was curled up in a ball on the desk, sobbing to himself. She checked the gun was still in the corner of the room out of reach, and said, "There's no point trying to escape. Where will you go? The second you try to use your bank account, we'll pick you up, so you might as well stay here."

She risked a look behind to see Humphries lying face down, a short distance behind her. A small pool of blood was forming around him and the bottom of his shirt was soaked in blood, but he was still breathing. With a firm hold on Chloe, she started to rise to her feet and dragged Chloe a short distance towards Humphries so she could reach him. She lifted his shirt and realised she had to do something to stem the bleeding.

"You're not going to let him die, are you?" Chloe jeered.

CHAPTER FORTY-ONE

Fiona didn't have three hands. She would have to let go of Chloe to stem the bleeding and call for assistance. As long as Chloe was unarmed, it was a simple decision. Humphries was worth a million Chloes. She might even be quick enough to grab the gun, use it to prevent Chloe from leaving, and save Humphries. She gave Chloe a hefty shove downwards and shot across the room to pick up the gun. She grabbed it and spun around, aiming it at Chloe, daring her to move. Chloe pulled herself upright, shrugged and sped across the room to the door.

Watching her leave, Fiona pulled out her phone. "An officer has been shot. Urgent assistance required." She hurried back to Humphries, found the wound and applied pressure to it. "Both suspects have escaped. I think the girl is unarmed. The boy has a knife, but I can't say whether he has any other weapons."

Fiona dropped the phone and turned her attention to Humphries, praying Ian and Chloe had bolted down the stairs for the exit and run straight into the arriving armed response team. Only she hadn't heard any approaching vehicles. As blood seeped through her fingers, she strained to listen. She couldn't hear anything except her own breathing. She prayed that Ian and Chloe hadn't gone back along the corridor and found the students trapped in the end room while she tried to stem the bleeding. Humphries was losing far too much blood. When she applied more pressure to his wound, his eyes flickered open, and he gave her a lopsided grin. "Tina is going to be mad at you if you ruin her big day."

"I won't let that happen," Fiona replied. "I'll make sure you walk up that aisle."

"Promise?"

"Promise," Fiona replied firmly, swallowing hard on the lump in her throat. "I've bought a new dress and matching shoes, especially for the occasion."

"That's nice," Humphries said, before closing his eyes.

"Humphries! Don't leave me now," Fiona said. "Stay with me. The medics will be here any minute." She looked to the window at the sound of approaching sirens. "Here they are now." She checked for a pulse. It was weak, but there was one. She pulled out her phone again. "I need the paramedics here, now. Second floor, about halfway down the corridor." She looked over at Patrick Burke, still sobbing in a ball, and felt a surge of anger. If he had told the truth when Humphries had first visited, none of this would be happening. At that moment, she understood Chloe's urge for revenge, and she could have happily killed him herself. His bad advice, presumably to protect the school's reputation, and his later decision to preserve his standing had destroyed numerous lives.

The sirens stopped, but Fiona could still see the reflections of the flashing lights. She continued to check Humphries was breathing as she sat in silence in the bleak room as more blood seeped through her fingers. What was taking them so long? Humphries needed help now. She was about to call again when two paramedics, followed by armed police, came crashing through the door. "Please help him. He's lost so much blood," she pleaded.

She didn't feel the paramedics gently move her to one side. She sat in a dazed state until one of them asked her if she was hurt. She looked down at her blood-covered clothes and realised she was crying as a teardrop fell from her face. "No, it's all his. He saved us, and I lied to him. I said I had already bought a dress, and I haven't. But I will." The paramedic returned his attention to Humphries, and Fiona snapped out of herself. Scrambling to her feet, she addressed the two officers. "There's a group of students trapped in the classroom at the end of the corridor."

One of them put a restraining arm on her. "Okay. We're dealing with it. Let's get you out of here."

"I need to go in the ambulance with him," Fiona said.

"I'll organise someone to drive you to the hospital. You should get yourself checked over while you're there."

"Has someone called Tina?" Fiona asked, punching numbers into her phone. "I'll ring her now."

CHAPTER FORTY-TWO

Fiona sat in the hospital waiting room, oscillating between feeling numb and oversensitive to every noise out in the corridor. She jumped from her seat, sending it crashing backwards into the wall when the door opened. "Tina, I'm so sorry," she said, stepping forward and hesitating. She blamed herself for what had happened and didn't know Tina well enough to know how she would react to her.

Clutching a haversack to her chest, Tina asked, "Is Phil …?"

"I don't know. They haven't told me anything."

"Is that …?" Tina asked, looking horrified at Fiona's blood-soaked shirt.

Fiona tried to cover the stains with her arms. "I did everything I could," she said, wondering if that was true. Should she have let Chloe go as soon as she realised Humphries was down? Should they have gone in at all?

Tina balanced the haversack on her knee and pulled out a faded sweatshirt. "Here, take this. I brought some things in for Phil. I don't suppose he'll be needing them for a while, but I didn't know what else to do."

"Thanks," Fiona said, taking the sweatshirt. It smelt of Humphries. She pulled it on and felt instantly warm and safe, as if Humphries was giving her a great bear hug.

"What happened?"

"Come and sit down, and I'll tell you," Fiona said, leading Tina to the chairs. "We confronted a young girl with a gun. Humphries … She was distracted, and Humph … Phil saw an opportunity to overpower her. He took a risk and successfully disarmed her. But before he did, the gun went off in the struggle. You should be proud of him. He acted with great bravery."

"Or stupidity," Tina said, trying to force a smile. "But he's my idiot," she added with a fresh wave of tears welling in her eyes.

Fiona reached for her hand. "Mine too."

They locked eyes before Tina nodded and broke down in tears. Fiona held her in a tight hug, struggling to contain her own emotions and fears. She knew how much blood he had lost. The doctors would do their best, but it was touch and go whether he would come through. She took a deep breath. He had to come through. The paramedic said at the scene that the vest had saved his life. He couldn't die now.

The door opened, and Tina's mum walked in and held open her arms. Tina disentangled herself from Fiona and ran into them. Fiona stood and looked on, feeling awkward. The two women separated, and Tina's mum said, "His parents are on their way. How is he?"

"They haven't said anything yet," Fiona said, resuming her seat. "We're waiting to hear."

Tina pulled her mother over to the chairs and sat. "He'll be okay. I know he will. He wouldn't leave me. Not now."

Her mother patted her on the knee, understanding what she meant even if Fiona didn't. She didn't ask, and the three fell silent until the door opened again.

Fiona jumped up from her chair. "Stefan! What are you doing here?"

"I heard what happened and drove back. Are you okay?"

"I'm fine. It's Humphries," Fiona said, as his parents walked in behind Stefan, worry etched on their faces.

Realising they were one chair short, Fiona offered her chair. "Please, sit down. It could be a long wait."

"Perhaps we should leave?" Stefan suggested, looking around the crowded room.

"I should be here," Fiona said. "I need to know."

"You look exhausted," Stefan said. "His family are here for him."

Fiona started to object. He was her police family, but Tina said, "It's okay, you go. We're all here for him. I will call you as soon as we hear anything."

Sensing her reluctance to leave, Stefan said in the corridor, "It was crowded in there. I know you wanted to stay, but it's more important his family stay close."

"I know," Fiona said, leaning into Stefan as they walked. She was strong enough to stand on her own two feet. She'd always been before. But it was comforting to feel Stefan's strength beside her. "He's also part of my police family. We're a team."

"I know, but it's in the doctors' hands now. There's nothing more you can do," Stefan said. "Have you eaten today?"

"If I'm not staying here, I should go into the station. I don't even know if they have Chloe and Ian in custody."

"I spoke to Rachael earlier. Chloe was arrested as soon as she ran out of the school. Ian slipped through the net, but he won't get far. They have it all in hand, so why don't you let them get on with it?" Stefan asked. "I'm sure you'll be there bright and early tomorrow morning for the initial interviews."

Fiona felt her resolve to go straight back to work weaken. She'd never had anyone care for her quite the way Stefan did. Before Stefan, she didn't have much of a life outside the police, if she was honest. If one of her team came in after having been through a similar ordeal, she would send them home, telling them they were next to useless in their current state. Maybe she should take her own advice for once. "I'll ring them from the car, so they know to contact me if there are any developments."

When they reached his car, Stefan offered Fiona his phone. "I thought you might want to leave yours free in case there's an update on Humphries."

Andrew answered the phone and immediately asked about Humphries. Fiona told him the little she knew, and promised that as soon as she heard something, she would pass it on. Andrew confirmed Chloe was safely in a cell and everything possible was being done to track down Ian. Assured there was nothing more she could do if she did go in, Fiona agreed she would go home for the evening.

Taking back his phone, Stefan asked, "What do you want to

eat?"

"Anything, as long as it's takeout."

Fiona's phone rang as they pulled up outside a pizza shop. She shrugged when the call ended and told Stefan, "He's come through surgery and is doing as well as can be expected, whatever that means. Tina and her mum are staying overnight at the hospital and will let me know if anything changes. His parents are going home for the night."

CHAPTER FORTY-THREE

The station felt eerily empty without Humphries. Fiona found herself looking over at his desk. Everyone was subdued and quiet. Two people blamed Fiona for Humphries not being there, herself and Abbie. She had repeatedly gone over the events in her head. If they hadn't gone in there, chances are that Burke would be dead, but Humphries would be with them in the station today. She knew which outcome she preferred, but hindsight was a wonderful thing. Humphries could have disarmed Chloe without being shot. There again, Chloe could have killed all of them. Right now, she would be happier if she had been the one who was shot. She felt she deserved it.

She had a preliminary meeting tomorrow morning to discuss what had gone wrong, and there was a good chance she would be disciplined. No punishment could make her feel any worse than she already did. Several people had hinted that a forced leave of absence, while she underwent some training was the likely outcome. She had told Stefan last night that she might choose to voluntarily leave the police. She knew now how Peter had felt when Nick Tattner was killed during a house raid, and she cringed when she thought how she had added to his distress by attacking him. Now, she faced the same self-incriminations and regrets. She jumped when she felt a tap on her shoulder.

"Fiona? Ah, you are with us," Andrew said. "Chloe is ready to be interviewed."

"Okay, thanks," Fiona said, picking up the file she had been staring at without the words going in for the last half hour. "If you're ready, let's go."

Chloe appeared pale and drawn under the harsh lights of the interview room, but the look she gave Fiona was one of defiance. Fiona and Andrew nodded a greeting to Chloe's legal representative and sat. As soon as the formalities for the tape were completed, Chloe asked, "Are you done with all your mumble jumbo?"

Fiona nodded, searching for some softness in Chloe's expression. Finding none, she said, "We're ready to begin. We have a number of questions for you."

"I'm going to save you the trouble of all that palaver," Chloe said. "I killed Alex, Matthew and Hugh and tried to kill Patrick Burke for what they put my family through. I will answer your questions as honestly as I can. I also admit to coercing Ian to help me. Will that do for you?"

"Admitting your guilt will speed things up and benefit you in the long run," Fiona replied, although she wondered what Chloe's game plan was. She was highly intelligent and had shown herself to be manipulative. Fiona would doubly make sure all the correct procedures were followed. She wouldn't be able to live with herself if she made a mistake, which Chloe later used to derail the case. The cold stare Chloe gave her chilled her to the bone. The shy but friendly young woman, proud of her clothes designs, was nowhere to be seen.

"Can I add killing a policeman to my list of achievements?" Chloe asked. "I hear that doesn't go down well with you lot."

Fiona fought hard not to express the anger and repulsion she felt. Determined to give nothing away, she kept her tone even as she replied, "Let's start with Alex Woodchester. When did he visit you?"

"Eight o'clock on that Thursday evening. He wanted to see my father, but I had just returned from dropping him at his AA meeting. Instead, he confessed everything to me. How they partied on the barn roof. Would you believe he was plucking up the courage that night to ask my sister out? He was so desperate, he plied her with alcohol and cannabis in the hope it would blur her good sense. She turned him down, of course. In annoyance, when he could see she was tipsy and losing her balance, he pushed her to her death."

"Did he admit to pushing your sister on purpose?" Fiona asked.

Chloe laughed. "I'm the only one who will ever know. I could say anything I like." She turned serious and added, "But I said I would be honest. He admitted to pushing her, but he was so drunk he couldn't remember if it was by accident." Chloe slammed her hands on the desk. "I would have still blamed him, but if he had said that at the time, he would probably have gotten away with it, anyway. Instead, he conspired to lie. They all did, and it destroyed my family. That is why they were all guilty and had to pay."

"Where did this conversation take place?"

"At home, in the kitchen. It amused me to think that you and your colleague sat in the same place as we did," Chloe said. "By the way, I was serious about wanting to use you as a model. It would be a hoot. Being a locked-up damsel designing exquisite clothes will give me an edge. I'll go viral and make a fortune, ready for my release. My fans will clamour for my sentence to be reduced. Just you wait and see. You can do anything if you're famous enough on social media."

"We're talking about the murder of Alex Woodchester," Fiona said dryly. "How did you persuade him to climb up onto the barn roof?"

"Easy-peasy," Chloe replied. "At first, I didn't have a plan. I was sat there in the kitchen, seething with hatred inside, while making him cups of tea and telling him not to be so hard on himself. That we all make mistakes, they were young, and a trusted adult had told them they were doing the right thing. Can you imagine?"

"What happened next?" Fiona asked, avoiding being drawn into a conversation.

"Underage students from Berkhampstead School drinking. Heavens forbid. He was so grateful. He thought I was absolving him of all blame. Can you believe it?"

"How did you get him from the kitchen to the barn roof?" Fiona firmly asked.

"I reminded him the ten-year anniversary was approaching, and I would like us to sit up on the roof with a drink in remembrance. I had a few errands to run first, so I asked him to meet me out at the barn at midnight. It almost sounds romantic, don't you think?"

"Did he agree straight away?"

"Of course. The arrogant fool believed every word I said. I could have been an actress," Chloe boasted. "Just being in the same room with him made my skin crawl. I collected Dad from his AA meeting and saw him off to bed. I waited in my room, and as midnight approached, I grabbed a bottle of whisky I had hidden from Dad months ago and walked out to the barn. Alex was already there, waiting for me. I had the sneaky impression he fancied me. Or maybe it was just that I reminded him of Jenny. The girl that was always going to be out of his league. What sort of couple do you think we would have made?"

"Can you continue with what happened that night?"

We sat there together, drinking and laughing. Remembering all the fun things Jenny had done in her short life. I learned more about who she really was in that hour than I've ever known. She had always been described to me as angelic and flawless. Everything I could never be. I could never be good enough. How do you compete with perfection?"

Fiona shrugged and indicated Chloe should continue with the events of that night.

"He had a little cry on my shoulder as I encouraged him to drink the pain away. He mumbled something about being a father. That's when I knew for sure what I would do. Jenny would have been a fantastic mother, but she never had the chance because of him. We smoked a little weed, and he was wobbly when he stood to leave. It only took a little push, and that was that. I climbed down, walked back to the farm, and went to bed," Chloe said. "And I slept like a baby. No regrets."

Fiona flicked back through her notes. "Only Alex's fingerprints were on the whisky bottle. How do you explain that?"

Chloe pulled the sleeves of her sweatshirt over her hands. "I made sure my skin never touched it. I worried for days you would carry out tests on whether anyone else had drunk from the bottle, but of course, you didn't. It was a straightforward suicide. No further questions necessary. Just like with Jenny. That's why I didn't mind shooting your colleague. I would have shot you as well if I had the chance."

Fiona paused to make a note while she controlled her feelings. "Moving along to Matthew Guppy. Can you explain what happened there?"

"His family should know what a pathetic, weak excuse of a man he was. They've had a lucky escape if you ask me. He tried to blame everything on Patrick Burke. He kept repeating they were teenagers following his advice. He went on about how devastated they were, trying to make it all about him. Like he suffered more than we did. I only half believed Alex when he told me that Matthew had consulted with an adult, and then Matthew gave me his name. If I'm honest, I only totally believed a teacher *did* advise them to lie when Burke confirmed it himself."

"How did you persuade Matthew to shoot himself?"

"He nearly didn't," Chloe said. "That's why I made Ian come along for the ride to deal with Hugh and Patrick. Good job I did, as I didn't have the right kind of leverage for them. If being self-absorbed was a crime, they would have already been serving life sentences. They didn't care about anything as much as themselves. Sad, sad, sad."

"That doesn't answer my question about Matthew," Fiona said. "How did you persuade him to pull the trigger?"

"Boring, really. I showed him all the photographs of his kids playing with my fabrics and pointed Dad's shotgun at him. Either he shot himself, or I would shoot him and his children. Simple choice. He made the correct one. I would have felt bad harming his children. I might have gone after his wife instead."

"Moving on to Hugh. What happened there?"

"Like Patrick, he didn't care about anyone except himself. He didn't notice when he showed me in that I had pushed in the catch on the door so it wouldn't automatically lock when he closed it. Ian strolled in unnoticed, and when Hugh became difficult, he hit him a blinder across the back of his head. I told him off for hitting him too hard. Anyway, Hugh was so dazed we had him strung up before he knew what was happening," Chloe said. "I'm getting bored with this. You know what happened with Patrick because you were there. I guess you didn't like your colleague much, as you thought saving that whimpering slimeball was more important." Chloe said, pushing herself away from the desk. "That's it? I've told you everything."

Her legal representative, who had sat by helplessly as Chloe had demanded, weakly said, "As my client has cooperated fully, I trust it will be reflected in your handling of the case."

"Oh, shut up," Chloe snapped. "I'm no hypocrite. I'm not like them. I'll fully accept whatever punishment I'm given. It was worth it. I just wish I had found out sooner that they had killed my sister and conspired to lie about it."

"The interview is finished for now while we make some more enquiries," Fiona said. "But we will be going over the events in more detail during the coming days."

"Whatever," Chloe said, slumping back in her chair.

Walking back to the incident room, Andrew asked, "Are you okay? There were a few times back there I wanted to slap her."

"I shared your sentiments, but it wouldn't get us very far."

They were intercepted by Eddie as they entered the room. "We've just received some good news."

"Humphries?" Fiona asked, her heart skipping a beat.

"No, sorry. We haven't heard anything yet," Eddie said. "Ian has walked into his local police station with his mother to give himself up. Do you want to interview him there or arrange for him to be transferred here?"

"Arrange the transfer," Fiona said wearily. "Abbie can interview him first about the burglaries."

"More bedwetting about how his father let him down, I expect,"

Abbie said, joining them. "How either of them thought it justified harming innocent people is beyond me."

Fiona dug deep past her already frayed nerves. The last thing she wanted to deal with was Abbie and her opinions. "I don't want you going into an interview with that attitude. Understood? These two are clever and we can't afford the slightest slip-up."

Abbie opened her mouth to object but, under Fiona's glare, sensibly decided to leave it for another time.

Fiona turned to Andrew. "I need some fresh air. I'm going for a short walk. Can you cover for me for half an hour? And call the lab to check whether they still have the whiskey bottle retrieved from the scene of Alex's suicide."

"Will do," Andrew replied. "If you're sure you don't want some company?"

"Thanks, but no. I need to walk out my urgent desire to slap someone. I won't be long."

◆ ◆ ◆

Fiona walked the length of the high street and turned right towards the river. She leaned against the railings, watching the water flow by beneath her, never taking a pause on its journey to the sea. In winter it often became a raging torrent and had flooded the surrounding roads the previous year after a heavy rainfall. Now, it was calm and soothing as it bubbled its way along politely between the grassy banks. The sun was warm on her skin, and there was a gentle breeze. It was a perfect British summers morning, positioned between the harsh chill of winter and the fierce, piercing heat of a heatwave. A day too perfect to contemplate losing a colleague and friend.

She turned to walk back towards the station. There was work still to do. She wondered what Humphries would have made of Chloe in the interview. Her coldness today, was jarring when compared to her generosity in showing him how to play chords on her guitar and rolling her father's cigarettes every evening.

Which was the real Chloe? Was she acting then or now? Or was she like the river? Her moods driven by events outside of her control?

Fiona stopped to buy the team some decent coffee. Carrying the tray into the station, she saw Ian being brought in. Unlike Chloe, he seemed embarrassed and looked away when he saw her. Fiona looked straight ahead as she walked by.

"I'm sorry about your colleague," Ian said as she passed. "Is he going to be okay?"

Fiona glanced up at him, not trusting herself to speak. He looked and sounded genuinely sorry. There again, along with the burglaries, he was going to be charged with being an accessory to murder and attempted murder, so he should be feeling sorry for himself.

"I should have said no, but I love her," Ian blurted out. "I would do anything for her, and she knows it."

Fiona reminded herself that the burglaries in the area started before Alex's death, and she had no doubt that Chloe was his accomplice. Their distorted love wasn't an excuse for their revengeful actions. She curtly replied, "Save it for the formal interviews," and walked on.

CHAPTER FORTY-FOUR

"There's a car space over there," Fiona said, pointing. "In behind Peter's car."

"I'm flattered by your faith in my parallel parking skills, but it would take a shoehorn to get us in there," Stefan replied, driving further along the lane. After checking he wouldn't be overhanging a resident's driveway, he pulled in at the end of a long stream of parked cars. "Sorry, it's going to be quite a trek back to the church."

"It's okay, we've plenty of time," Fiona said, squeezing herself between the open car door and a garden wall. At the rear of the car, she smoothed down her dress and took a deep breath.

"Ready?" Stefan said, reaching for her hand.

Walking hand in hand along the narrow lane towards the church, Fiona recognised several of the cars. She was pleased to see most of the team would be there. Abbie and Rachael were working but hoped to come along a little later. Typical, she thought as the church gates came into view. Dewhurst's new BMW was badly parked at an angle, jutting out into the road and partially blocking the church entrance. Abandoned would be a more accurate description than parked. He had probably arrived shortly before them and parked in the space which clearly should have been reserved. She hoped she was in earshot when he was asked to move it out of the way.

Fiona and Stefan passed through the lynch gate and started to walk up the curved pathway through the gravestones. Some shiny with bright bouquets of flowers, some ancient and moss-covered, long forgotten by any living descendants. Up ahead, she saw Dewhurst talking to the vicar. Knowing Stefan would make a beeline for him, she let go of his hand. "I want a quick word with Peter before the service."

She walked across to where Peter stood in a huddle with Eddie, Andrew and his daughter, Amelia. Amelia spotted her first and raised a hand in welcome. As usual, Fiona was struck by what an elegant and attractive woman she had grown into, bursting with confidence. No traces remained of the troubled teenager with anorexia that Fiona had first met. They shared a brief hug before tuning into the general conversation.

"We had better get inside now we're all here," Peter said. "I don't know about you lot, but I never feel comfortable around gravestones."

Andrew took a last puff on his vape, sending out a cloud of cherry-flavoured vapour before slipping it into his pocket. "Best go and see the old chap off."

"Is Stefan joining us?" Amelia asked.

"I'll try to drag him away from Dewhurst on our way past," Fiona said. To her dismay when she collected Stefan, Dewhurst followed. He fell in alongside Fiona, and said, "It was a bit messy at the end, but good work on sorting the Alex Woodchester matter for me. You saw what other officers missed and ran with it."

Fighting the urge to give her senior officer a resounding slap across the face in public, Fiona said, "I think it's DS Humphries who should take all the credit for that," and quickly walked on ahead of him. The priest had moved to the church doors, where he greeted everyone as they entered. Fiona squeezed Stefan's hand, and they shared a brief smile as they walked through the church entrance. They followed the others through the packed church to a wooden pew about halfway down. Fiona scanned the altar area with a lump in her throat. Sat on the end of the front pew was Humphries, with his best man standing next to him. The honeymoon had been postponed until he fully recovered, but nothing was going to stop Tina from having her big day as planned. Before she turned into the pew, Humphries looked around and gave her the biggest cheesy grin. She smiled back and gave him a double thumbs up. He was an annoying idiot at times, but he was her annoying idiot. She shuffled along in the pew next to Stefan and picked up the order of service.

BOOKS IN THIS SERIES

A DI Fiona Williams Mystery

A Fiery End

Time to discover a brilliantly twisty mystery series.

A tradesman is set alight in his vehicle on an isolated road. His daughter is missing. And time is running out.

"I was on the edge of my seat and couldn't read fast enough."
"Totally riveting."
"Superb murder mystery and police procedural."

DI Fiona Williams is a driven detective who cares deeply about getting justice for victims and their families.
Driving home late at night, she comes across a vehicle engulfed in flames. The driver is at the wheel, oblivious to the inferno surrounding him. There is no explanation for why the vehicle was on the road or why the quiet tradesman was murdered in such a macabre way. The only witness to the fire, claims she saw nothing. Whatever she did see goes to the grave with her when she is brutally strangled. Frustration grows when the driver's daughter disappears. With time running out to find the daughter alive, Fiona is drawn into a web of powerful men determined to keep their deadly games secret. Juggling a family crisis and a growing suspicion her boss is corrupt, her judgement is hampered by her attraction to the man central to everything.

A Mother's Ruin

A single mother is brutally murdered in her garden.

DI Fiona Williams interprets the crime scene differently from her colleagues but fears her history of failed relationships taints her judgment. The wrong decision will change the lives of three children forever.

In a male-dominated department, with mounting evidence pointing in the other direction, will she find the courage to trust her instincts and narrow the investigation?

An intriguing mystery that blurs the distinction between the villain and the victim.

A Relative Death

An eye for an eye. A death for a death.
Some people will do anything for revenge.
And one detective will do anything to stop them.
DI Fiona Williams returns from a short break to a station stretched by the antics of a gang of youths, staff absences and three murders in quick succession. With unconnected victims and widely different murder methods, the only link is they seem motiveless. Forced to work in small groups rather than as a team, frustrations and jealousies flare-up between the officers creating a minefield of tension and a headache for Fiona.
As the most experienced officer, she is pulled from the initial case of a poisoned pensioner to investigate the shooting of a wealthy landowner's wife. She is annoyed the murder of a defenceless war veteran is given lower priority and thoughts of the pensioner's last moments are never far away.
The two victims have never met, and the only similarity is their murderer was someone who knew them well. The chances of it

being the same person are remote.
When a breakthrough comes in the investigation, it seems Fiona's nagging thought that the cases are connected may be correct. To fit the missing pieces together she will have to risk her life for an enemy she has worked hard to condemn.

An Educated Death

The best-kept secrets are the deadliest.
When a private boarding school pupil drowns in a lake on the grounds, DI Fiona Williams is called in to investigate. Security around the school grounds is tight, making it a closed community.
Fiona thinks the death was due to a secret society initiation rite that went wrong, but the school denies the societies exist, and her investigation hits a wall of silence.
A second pupil dies, but the silence continues.
The school is concerned with its reputation and upholding traditions, the influential parents care only about protecting their children, and the pupils have secrets of their own.
Nobody wants Fiona to expose the whole truth.

A Deadly Drop

New truths to uncover and a killer to catch.

With a family crisis looming, Detective Inspector Fiona Williams is hoping to take a break when she is called to a suspicious death in an isolated barn conversion, home to a quiet middle-aged couple.

Duncan returned home from the pub to discover his wife dead at the foot of their cellar steps. There are no signs of a forced entry or robbery, but the evidence says Pat's death was no accident. His reaction is strange, but he has a solid alibi for the time of death.

Fiona will have to dig deep into the victim's past to uncover the shocking truth. Pat's anti-blood sports stance had split the close-knit local community and created a rift with her sister. Could her sister or another hunt member be responsible?

Printed in Great Britain
by Amazon